# When Dignity Came to Harlan

Rebecca Duvall Scott

25  24  23  22  21  20        8  7  6  5  4  3  2  1

Published by:
Emerge Publishing, LLC
9521B Riverside Parkway, Suite 243 Tulsa, Oklahoma 74137
Phone: 888.407.4447   www.EmergePublishing.com

Library of Congress Cataloging-in-Publication Data:
ISBN: 978-1-949758-95-5 Perfect Bound

*They left their*
*homes and*
*loved ones*
*in search of*
*a new life.*
*They came*
*in ships, by train,*
*in wagons, on foot.*
*Their journey*
*was long, and they*
*did not know*
*the way. They cried;*
*they laughed;*
*they loved,*
*they died.*
*They are my*
*forebears,*
*Their story is sacred.*

*~unknown~*

*The novel I was born to write,* When Dignity Came to Harlan, *is dedicated to my daughter, Annabelle, who was thrilled to discover I had named the main character Anna Beth long before I had a brave, beautiful, and dignified Anna of my own! She was also the first one who laid eyes on the completed manuscript and will forever be my favorite constructive critic.*

*This book also belongs to my grandmother, Lois Elliott Duvall, and her mother, my great-grandmother, May Wood Elliott Kerr, on whose childhood this story is based. My grandmother told me many stories about May, her hardships, and her triumphs saying, "My mother's story deserves to be told. It shows the full range of human experience and will touch the lives of many — if they only knew what she suffered and how she persevered." I am proud to publish this book in my forebears' memories. Their story is sacred.*

# Part 1

## Leaving Home

*1*

"I reckon the lead's 'bout tapped out," Daddy sighed, motioning to the bowl in the middle of the table. Momma handed him the last pone of cornbread. *The last one.* Daddy never took the last piece of anything, even when the first helping of beans and bread didn't stick to his bones. I watched him tear the buttery morsel in two and pop the left hunk into his mouth. He looked around at all of us – but not quite eye to eye.

My stomach twisted into a knot and pulled itself tight. I lowered my fork, swallowing a mouthful of hot spit that had puddled under my tongue. If I'm being downright honest, I must admit I have an embarrassing tendency to get sick whenever I feel nervous. Maybe it was the heat making me nauseous… the air in the house was thick in the summertime, and it didn't help that we had eight people sandwiched shoulder to shoulder around a kitchen table built for four. But again, just being honest, I knew deep down the knot in my belly was due to my Daddy taking the last piece of cornbread instead of leaving it for one of his girls. That's what made my stomach lurch threateningly.

Jonathan, seated to Daddy's left, cleared his throat. "Y'reckon work in the mines'll pick up, Mr. Atwood?" My brother-in-law was eighteen years old and intent on proving himself worthy of the recent union to my oldest sister, Martha, who turned sixteen last month. I noticed the newlyweds holding hands under the table, him rubbing her knuckles with his thumb, and when he glanced at me, I made a kissy face just to see his ears flame up red. Even with my stomach aching so, I didn't dare miss an opportunity to tease Jonathan! He narrowed his eyes at me and let go of Martha's hand, crossing his arms instead – like a man, like my Daddy sitting next to him.

"Work's been dyin' down fo' some time now," Daddy mumbled. He sat the other half of his cornbread on the edge of his plate and stared at it. Maybe his stomach was clenched up, too. "Tappin' lead jus' ain't what it used t'be... n'minin' sure don't pay like it used't, neither – not 'round these parts anyways." He took a drink of water and swished it around in his mouth before swallowing. "I think it's 'bout time this fam'ly finds another way t'make ends meet."

Jonathan ran his hand through his sawdust colored hair, mussing it up a bit. "I didn't know it was gettin' that bad." Worry tinged his voice.

My younger sisters, Janie and Emily, glanced at each other and continued to shovel beans into their mouths. Those two were the troublemakers of the family. Well, at least Janie was. Emily was sweet as the day is long but was generally deemed guilty by association. Momma had already warned us to only open our mouths to eat dinner tonight, because Daddy had something to tell the lot of us and we best sit and listen quietly. That was a tall order for those two.

I felt a tug on my blouse and looked over at my baby sister, Olivia. A sigh escaped my throat as she had her finger up her nose *again*. I swatted her hand away, and she giggled loudly. Suddenly Momma's fork clattered to her plate and all us girls jumped in our seats. When Momma gets mad you best duck and cover.

"Ben, if y'don't tell 'em then I'm a gonna, n'let me remind ya, the news'll sound better comin' from their Daddy than their Momma," she spit the words at my father.

Daddy stared at Momma and took another swig of water, swishing it around in his mouth for a good *long* time. The night's tension was beginning to swell up inside me like a toad frog down at the pond – swelling until the croak just had to come out or the poor toad burst, one or the other.

"Daddy, what's goin' on?" The words burst out of my mouth before I could bite my cheek quiet. I quickly slipped my hands under my thighs, partly to anchor myself and partly to protect my behind from a switching. You don't just interrupt adult conversation at the dinner table. The sticky sweat under my legs dampened my fingers and felt good, and bless her heart, Momma wasn't even paying attention to me.

"Ben, if y'don't get *on with it*... I swear," Momma warned. She reached up to secure the bobby pins that held her long, chestnut hair in a tight bun, and Janie flinched away from her sudden movement. She was seated dangerously close to Momma, and she, by far, was the usual recipient of Momma's frustration.

"*Darn it*, Laura!" Daddy slammed his own fork down now, shaking the table. "I'd tell 'em if you'd jus' let me get my words out!"

Momma crossed her arms and sucked in her bottom lip. I could see her teeth biting down on the edge of it, turning the pink part white. Janie, Emily and I stole glances at each other and collectively slunk down in our chairs a few inches. No one wanted to be Momma's target tonight, not with her strung up tight and ready to pop like a fiddle string.

Daddy roughly wiped his mouth and hands with a napkin and sat his clenched fist alongside his plate, the napkin still sticking out between his fingers. "Now this ain't gonna affect Martha n'Jonathan, but it will the rest of us. Girls, we've decided t'throw the towel in on Leadwood n'we're gonna move." It was his turn to spit the words out, like they tasted bad in his mouth.

"*Move?*" Janie and Emily echoed in unison, forgetting themselves and sitting up straight again. I, however, stayed slouched down, still watching Momma for signs she was going to pop.

"Closer t'church, Daddy?" Janie ventured. Church was the next town over and just about the most important thing in my family, so it made sense we'd move closer. We walked an hour to get there in the warm months and drove the wagon in the cold ones... neither of which were particularly enjoyable, but you'd *never* catch us kids complaining about the distance to get to the Lord's house on the Sabbath.

Momma sighed over the beans left on our plates and excused herself from the table, mumbling something about waste not, want not.

She reached over our heads and gathered the dishes, carrying them in a heap to the wash bin on the counter. With the news of moving, I had nearly forgotten that my stomach had clinched up so... but Momma busying herself behind me yanked at that knot until I grimaced in pain and shifted uncomfortably. I had the ominous feeling life as I knew it was about to change.

Jonathan was next to speak. "Where're y'thinkin' is better than Leadwood, Mr. Atwood?"

"*Momma*," Martha cut in. "What is all this talk? Y'all've never lived anywhere but Missouri. Besides, what'd Jonathan n'I do without y'n'Daddy jus' down the road?" Momma kept her back to us and kept scrubbing the fire out of dinner plate after dinner plate.

"Martha," Daddy said gently, reaching to pat his eldest daughter's hand while conscious of my mother's every move and sound. "Y'n'Jonathan're makin' it jus' fine. He's got a good job down at the mercantile, n'those kinds o'jobs never go bad... people *always* need t'buy goods. But y'Momma n'me, the rest of us... our luck is run out in Leadwood." He looked around at us kids, defeat tugging downward at the corners of his mouth.

"Girls, I'm sorry t'shock y'with this 'cause I know y'don't understand, but there's no more money in the lead mines. We have t'go somewheres money can be made. I'll die 'fore I let y'go hungry, or without a roof over y'heads... n'we're nearin' that point."

"But where'll we go, Daddy?" I whispered what everyone was thinking. I looked around at my family, my eyes wandering to the knotty pine walls of our little two-room log house.

Momma gave birth to all five of us girls in this very house. I had learned to cook in this here kitchen, and by the fireplace in the next room, Momma had taught all of us who were old enough to hold a needle how to cross-stitch and crochet. I couldn't imagine living anywhere else but in Leadwood, Missouri. *I don't want to leave home.* The feeling welled up inside me like I was going to drown in it.

"We'll head t'ward Harlan County, Kentucky," Daddy said. "It's as good a place as any. We'll be leavin' nex' Saturday... ain't no time t'waste."

"Nex' Saturday?" Janie looked at Emily with excited eyes. She might be a troublemaker, but she was also adventurous... which is probably why she got herself in so much mischief to start with.

"Harlan," Jonathan pointing his finger at Daddy. "Ain't that coal country? I think old man Daniels was talkin' 'bout it in the store the other day... he said several families from these parts were plannin' t'head east soon. I'd never've guessed y'n'Mrs. Atwood were one of 'em, though."

"We've been discussin' this fo' a while now," Daddy said. "There's s'posed t'be tons o'coal buried up in them Kentucky mountains. Ev'ryone's talkin' 'bout how good coal minin' jobs're paying. I even heard some businessmen, all dressed up in suits n'ties, over at the restaurant the other day. They were from the east n'paid with a hundred-dollar bill. They said we didn't know what we were missin'... stayin' 'round these parts while all the jobs dry up n'leave us fo' dead."

Momma turned around and leaned against the counter, sliding her hands in her skirt pockets. She had played her cards right; she knew we'd follow our Daddy anywhere.

"Daddy, cain't y'jus' work harder n'get that hundred-dollar bill here?" Emily asked.

"Emily Lou-Ann Atwood!" Momma exclaimed, her hands flying out of her pockets as she rushed toward the table and a wide-eyed Emily. "Y'watch y'mouth 'fore I scrub it out with soap!" Emily and Janie both sank back down in their chairs, poor Emily in tears. We all knew she hadn't meant anything by it, but Momma was looking for a reason to explode.

"Y'Daddy works hard t'put food in y'mouths, clothes on y'backs n'a roof over y'heads... n'here y'sit complainin'," Momma scowled. She was closest to my chair and was gripping the back of it now. I sat still as a bird in a bush with a roving cat just feet away.

"*Work harder, Daddy*," Momma mumbled under her breath. "Y'should be ashamed o'y'self, n'if you're not, I'll shame y'right here in front o'ev'rybody."

"Laura, don't be harsh with 'er," Daddy said softly, winking at Emily who looked utterly terrified. He leaned on the table with his elbows, stretching out his lower back that always ached in the evenings. Daddy had been a miner since he was fourteen – after Grandaddy got sick and he had to leave school to make a paycheck for his Momma, younger brother, and sisters.

"This is a big change fo' us, the biggest of our lives." Daddy looked around at all us girls, and Jonathan and forced a smile. "Truth be told, we prob'ly should've made this move a long time ago. If we stay in Missouri, I'll be out o'work in 'bout two weeks' time... and we'll starve 'fore winter." He took a drink, swished and swallowed slowly, and let the words sink in. He gathered his next words carefully. "Harlan'll be a good experience fo' us, y'jus' wait n'see."

Momma went back to the dishes while Jonathan tried to lighten the conversation, but our minds were thoroughly fixed on the move and edgy with the unknown. Even happy little Olivia was beginning to whine and squirm in her highchair after an extra long dinner.

Martha graciously announced she and Jonathan best be on their way home, and that gave us all reason to stand up and stretch our legs. My thighs made a squelching noise when they pulled apart from the chair, and my sisters giggled. Daddy winked at me with a slight grin and invited Jonathan to have a tobacco pipe with him by the fireplace.

"It's gettin' late, Daddy," Martha said, walking over to give Momma a hug. "We bes' get t'bed."

Jonathan's ears lit up tomato red and Janie pointed with a snicker, which got Emily and me giggling also. Newlyweds were so easily embarrassed, and uncontrollable giggles at the most inopportune time was a good way to blow off some steam.

"*Chores come early,*" Martha hissed at the three of us. She fancied herself grown up now she was married, but it didn't take much for her to stoop to our level like a kid again.

Janie and Emily covered their mouths with their hands and turned their backs to each other, trying to squelch their laughter before Momma stepped in to do it for them. I turned my attention back to Olivia and bit the inside of my mouth to stop my own urge to chuckle. She had stuck a bean up her nose and was fussing, so I dug it out with my pinkie finger and heaved her out of her highchair and onto my hip.

Everyone said goodnight to each other, and Daddy shut the door after Jonathan and Martha. He rubbed his lower back with both hands and said, "Girls, y'can be excused from cleanin' up t'night. I'll help y'mother."

Janie and Emily gave a collective whoop of joy and ran helter skelter for the back door. The unexpected gift of outside playtime before bed was something to be seized immediately and savored. I, however, wiped off Olivia's hands and carried her to the next room... hoping to quietly stick around and listen to my parents' conversation.

I sat my baby sister down in front of the fireplace on the big oval rug Momma had crocheted and handed her the little cornhusk doll from our bed. Livie had taken to me as a baby and never let go, so I took care of her like a mother hen would a prized chick. Momma said our bond was because we were both born on the same day, the 26th of February, ten years apart, but sometimes I thought it was because Livie's the fifth child. Momma was so busy with the rest of us I paid Olivia the most attention. I didn't mind one way or another – she was the silver lining to any grey day, even when she stuck beans up her nose.

Once she was settled and playing, I tiptoed ever so quietly back over to Momma and Daddy's bed, which shared a thin pine wall with the kitchen. I slowly lowered myself onto their mattress, careful not to make it squeak, and strained to hear what they were saying after they thought us kids all scattered.

"It's the bes' thin' fo' the fam'ly," Momma was saying under the clatter of dishes. "It'll be hard jus' fo' the firs' little while, but we knew that 'fore we told 'em."

"Hard fo' the *firs' while*," Daddy scoffed. He lowered his voice to a forced whisper. "Laura, I tried to be positive like y'wanted me to, but we don't even have money t'get started on. What're we s'posed t'live on 'til I get a job in Harlan? *Where*'ll we live? No one'll take in a couple with fo' girls in tow. It's not like Leadwood where we have fam'ly n'friends... we'll be strangers there, completely on our own."

"We'll get t'know people, Ben, n'we'll find our feet again. We've worked through hard times 'fore – this won't be any diff'rent. We've enough food t'las' us a couple o'months, and then we'll figure somethin' out 'til we get y'on at the coal mines." Momma spoke nonchalantly, like she had thought this whole thing through several times over.

I shifted my weight unconsciously and the mattress creaked. My breath caught in my throat as I squeezed my eyes shut, listening hard and praying to remain undiscovered. I could hear my sisters playing tag in the front yard and Olivia babbling to her doll on the floor, but my parents' voices had fallen silent. I leaned closer to the wall, figuring they were talking softer, and then Daddy leaned around the corner and cleared his throat. I opened one squinty eye at him.

"Anna Beth, honey, can y'take Olivia *outside*?" he said, kindlier than I deserved for eavesdropping. "We'll call y'when it's time fo' bed." I apologized immediately, *my* face now flaming red like Jonathan's ears, and obediently walked to the hearth, scooped up Olivia, and out we went.

I paused on our little front porch, a swing on one end and two handmade chairs on the other and looked out across the Missouri horizon. The warm, golden, and pink colors swirled around in the sky and drained behind the trees like going down a funnel, and fireflies sprinkled the groves and bushes, flashing their lights in a silent song only they knew. It was beautiful as always, but I had trouble finding my usual joy in it when I knew I may never see it again. *Who knew what sunsets looked like in Kentucky coal country?*

"Anna Beth!" Janie panted. She stopped running. "What're they sayin' in there?" she asked, hands on hips, still breathing heavily. Emily stopped chasing her to listen, too.

I put Olivia down and held her hand as she toddled down the porch steps. "Nothin'," I shrugged my shoulders.

"Oh, c'mon," the girls whined.

"Y'heard Daddy," I snapped. "We're movin', n'that's all there is to it." I couldn't bring myself to tell my sisters about the rest of the problems... how Daddy was worried about finding a job and a house, and how we wouldn't have any friends to lean on if we needed them. They were too young to be worried with such things, evident by how they went right back to their rousing game of tag without pressing for more details. *Who am I kidding?* I was nearly too young to understand the gravity of our situation at twelve years old myself... but that's something else I would never admit to *them*, or anyone for that matter.

I made up my mind right then and there that I would just have to wade into this move like wading into a pond or lake I'd never seen before – slow and steady, feeling around for my footing and trying to avoid the sharp edges at the bottom that you never see coming.

*2*

Daddy sold the belongings we couldn't take with us to neighbors for keeps and the mercantile for resell, and Momma set her mind to packing up what she called the essentials. Each day we girls came in from playing, the house was emptier and emptier, and finally bare as a cornfield plowed over for planting. My stomach kept knotting itself up as I saw each piece of furniture, trinket and memento go out the door.

I begged Momma to consider Mimi and Pop's writing desk essential... it had *always* sat in the corner by the fireplace, and Daddy had told us all the stories of his parents, the grandparents I never knew. Pop had written love letters to Mimi from that desk when they were courting, Mimi had written to Pop when they were newly married and he was away at war, and finally they both wrote to my parents when we moved to Leadwood. The desk was small and worn around the edges with years of use and love, and I doubted it would take up much room in the wagon. I also figured we could carry on its tradition and write letters to Martha from it when we got where we were going. Momma shot the idea right down, though. She said I was being foolish, that a desk couldn't feed or shelter us, and she insisted Daddy sell it to the mercantile in exchange for money we could live on. I cried when I saw it carried off.

"I guess we're really gonna do it, Anna," Janie leaned over and whispered in my ear during dinner that last night at home. We usually sat across from each other at the table – but Daddy had sold it the day before, and we were sitting on the floor in all the wrong order… a family truly out of joint.

I ignored Janie and helped Olivia scoop some beans onto her spoon. Moving made me powerfully sad, and the excitement Janie and Emily had mustered up burned like salt in a wound.

"I think y'all'll really enjoy Harlan," Daddy said for the millionth time. He had taken to reassuring us any time it got too quiet, waving Harlan in our faces like those fancy men had waved their hundred-dollar bill in his.

I kept my eyes on Olivia, who was dumping the beans off her spoon and poking them between the wooden planks of the floor. I was sick of *Harlan, Kentucky*… and we hadn't even set foot there yet.

"I've heard it's got beau'ful rollin' hills like Missouri, but with a lot more trees n'green. When we get a house our own, maybe we can plant another garden, too. We can grow big tomaters, red ones like Jonny's ears… n'we'll call 'em *Jonnymaters*! What d'y'all think o'that?" he continued. "We could even set up a sign outside n'sell 'em big, red suckers."

Janie and Emily giggled, but I wasn't even in the mood for a Jonny joke. I put my spoon on my plate, afraid if I took another bite that I would toss everything I had forced down.

"Now, y'kids need t'know it won't be all fun n'games," Momma interjected, giving Daddy the *eye*. She didn't like us teasing Jonathan and Martha, so she certainly disapproved of him doing it. "It won't be easy at firs'." She kept pressing that thought into us like you'd press your finger into someone's arm until it bruised. "We have t'get money n'find a place t'live 'fore we can plant *anythin'* in a garden our own."

"We'll help out, Momma," I finally spoke up, fully aware that I would be the oldest now that we'd be leaving Martha behind. The respect and independence of the oldest were my only silver linings. "Won't we, girls?" I looked at Janie and Emily expectantly; it fell to me to rally my sisters like troops. They just rolled their eyes at each other and continued to eat their beans without answering… boy did that boil my blood.

After dinner Momma settled us girls down on blankets where our bed used to be, Janie and Emily under the window by the front door and me and Olivia across from them along the wall. Daddy wanted to be pulling onto the main road out of town at six o'clock sharp, and she said our sleepy heads weren't going to hold up the family. We laid quietly for the better part of an hour, and when Daddy finally settled down next to Momma on their pallet by the kitchen, he started in about Harlan instead of telling us a bedtime story.

I quickly lost interest and rolled over to face the wall. I felt all loose inside, yet jerky at the same time, like a kite way up in the air with too much string being tugged on and buffeted this way and that by the wind. The hard floor pressed up through the threadbare quilts, the knots in the pine planks poking my ribs. I tried to get comfortable to no avail. *Would my bed in Harlan be as soft as the one Daddy sold in the mercantile?*

With a sigh I rolled onto my back again and stared at the ceiling. Olivia, groggy with sleep now, crawled on top of me and nuzzled her head into my chest. We had shared a bed since Momma weaned her from the breast, and I often fell asleep with a face full of her curly blonde hair tickling my nose. Her locks always smelled of thick honeysuckle, though, so I didn't mind. It was my very favorite thing about my baby birthday sister. I felt her body relax into mine and her breathing deepen and become rhythmic. My jittery nerves and stomachache started to calm as if someone was reeling in my wandering kite and I, too, took a deep breath in and let it out slow and steady.

I glanced across the room at my sisters. They were snugged up like two snoring pigs in a blanket. My eyes wandered to Daddy and Momma lying on their pallet by the kitchen, their bodies spooned together, and Daddy's arm draped over Momma's waist. It comforted me in a deep way to know how fiercely he loved her, even though she was headstrong and difficult to get along with sometimes. I just wished *one* of them could have come up with a better plan than this move East. Before I even realized what was happening, a hot tear leaked onto my cheek and I sniffled, wiping it away with the back of my hand as more pressed on the back of my eyes. I didn't fancy crying much, especially when I was just settling down! I guess sometimes the big emotions bubble up and there's nothing you can do to stop it.

Momma's eyelids fluttered open, and our gazes tangled in the darkness. My heart started pleading, *Don't you know we don't want to go? Surely there's another way*, as stillness pressed in on us both. The air was too thick to breathe it in slowly, and I was afraid if I gasped to fill my lungs that the worries buried deep inside me would spill out on the floor between us. Momma didn't take to crying much, either... except on the rare occasion at church when something really touched her.

I forced myself to look away, rolling back to face the wall again. I was determined *not* to make a sound – not while my mother was awake to hear – and eventually my body exhausted itself, and I was able to breathe through barely audible little snatches, regaining my composure a bit at a time. I must have drifted off to sleep at some point because the next thing I realized Daddy was shaking me awake.

A bit of sunlight was creeping in through the window above me and I rubbed my eyes open. They felt heavy and swollen from holding in the tears. I instinctively reached to pat Olivia, but Daddy caught my hand and rubbed his thumb across my knuckles in a calming sort of way.

"Don't wake Livie jus' yet," he whispered. "Let's get the wagon packed firs', then we'll gather y'sisters." I nodded and stifled a yawn, watching Daddy creep outside, carefully closing the front screen in its jam so it didn't slam.

I sat up and stretched, pulling the cover up to Olivia's shoulders again, then tangled my light brown hair into a French-braid and dressed. Quiet as a mouse, I tiptoed past Janie and Emily's pallet and snuck out onto the front porch to find my parents. The morning air was already sticky with heat; it hit my face and clung to my cheeks and brow. I ran my hand over my braid a second time. *Here we go*, I thought with a sigh. *Moving day whether I like it or not.*

My parents were at the wagon, the back of which was already half full of barrels of meal and water. I walked up and gripped the wagon wheel that was just about as tall as me and felt the coarse wood under my fingers. This wagon would be our home for at least a month's journey.

Momma finished securing a few hairpins in her bun and asked, "How'd y'sleep?" Her forehead glistened with sweat and her long dress stuck to the curves of her bosom and hips.

"Okay, I guess," I fibbed. I had barely felt like I closed my eyes.

"There's some boxes in the kitchen that need t'be loaded." She wasted no time with the instructions. "Y'father n'I'll get the heavy ones, but y'can pack the small ones. Try not t'wake y'sisters goin' in n'out – we can move faster without 'em underfoot."

I went on about my business and the three of us made short work of packing the rest of the wagon. About a half hour later I climbed in the back and looked around, hands on hips. It was an awful small space for four girls to ride. We would have to squeeze in around the boxes, but with a few blankets for padding I imagined it may be tolerable enough. Not that we had a choice. Daddy climbed up on the bench in front, and I poked my head through the canvas opening. He was sitting there holding the reigns, staring down the road in front of us. Momma had gone back inside to rouse the girls, and I seized the opportunity to talk to just him.

"How long'll it take us t'get t'Harlan, Daddy?" I knew the answer but wanted to hear the strong, calm voice that always had a way of making me feel safe say it.

"If God be supplyin' good weather, it should take 'bout a month, honey," he said, stepping down from the wagon to double check the yoke on our oxen, Bessie and Dessie. He had also tied our mare, Ginger, and cow, Charlie, to the wagon and packed up the chickens, who were clucking madly from their wire cage by my feet. We planned to drop Charlie and the chickens off at Jonathan and Martha's house before heading out of town. Daddy and Jonathan had agreed that Jonathan would sell our milk cow, keep a dollar for his trouble, and forward the remainder to Daddy in a money order to Harlan's local post office. Momma had insisted they keep the chickens for themselves, though, as a parting gift from us to them.

"Will we have enough food?" I asked as he climbed back up in the front of the wagon. "I mean, without Charlie's milk n'the chicken eggs?" I glanced at the boxes of bread and beans in the back corner of the wagon, and my stomach gnawed on my backbone. They were stacked near the barrels of meal and water... and all together it still didn't look like a month's worth of food for six people.

"Yes, Anna Beth – even if we run out o'what we packed; I can hunt fo' game. All *you* need t'worry 'bout is bein' strong n'keepin' y'spirits up so y'sisters won't be sad or worrisome themselves. Big sisters're influential that way, y'know." He looked at me over his shoulder with those big blue eyes and winked a *you're special* wink at me. "Can y'do that fo' y'Daddy?"

A smile broke out across my face. I knew he did that wink for all us kids from time to time, but it really did make each one of us feel like we were his favorite. "No one can hold it t'gether better than *me*, Daddy," I said.

He smiled and patted my arm. "That's m'girl."

The screen door slammed shut; Momma and the girls traipsed down the porch steps and into the glow of the early morning. We had left our house for good and not one of us would set foot there again. Daddy had arranged for Jonathan to sell our homestead and forward that money as well.

I went to the back of the wagon and Momma lifted Olivia into my arms, then Janie and Emily climbed up and over the hatch. We sat down quietly in the back, my sisters' eyes sticky with sleep. Momma climbed up front next to Daddy, who cracked the reins, and we lurched forward. Daddy looked back only once and Momma not at all, but I fixed my eyes on that two-room log cabin. We were leaving our old life behind, heading toward a new life with an untold story of our family. The unknown had a way of making me feel sad, mad, scared, curious, and hopeful all at the same time. I blinked back the tears before my sisters could see them. *Daddy expects me to set the example and that's what I'm going to do*, I thought as I roughly wiped my nose on my sleeve.

Martha and Jonathan just lived a few minutes up the road, and Daddy tipped his hat to them when we pulled the wagon into their yard. They came down from the front porch as we piled out of the wagon. Daddy walked around to Momma's side and offered her his hand as Jonathan came around the back to us girls.

He lifted Janie and Emily to the ground, and they both ran to hug Martha. My oldest sister's splotchy face revealed she had probably been crying for hours, even though she wore a smile now. I handed Olivia to my brother-in-law, and he sat her feet on the ground. She toddled right after our sisters. Jonathan turned and reached his hands out for me next.

"I can do it m'self," I said, a bit of my Momma's grit seeping out suddenly and making me coarse. I pulled my dress up to my knees, straddled the back of the hatch and jumped to the ground. I stumbled when my feet hit the grass, though; my long skirt tangling around one ankle. I recovered quickly and smoothed my skirt straight, my face reddening.

"Let me guess," Jonathan mused. "You're the oldes' now, eh? Don't need help from nobody?" He gave me a wink of understanding instead of the usual wisecrack and my confidence swelled.

"Well, I am *twelve*," I said.

Daddy came around the back of the wagon, untied Charlie, our cow, and handed her rope to Jonathan. The cow mooed loudly in protest and shook her head, causing the old cowbell to jangle back and forth. I was going to miss that sound and wondered if we'd get a new cow in Harlan.

"Take good care o' her," Daddy told Jonathan. "She should bring in a decent dollar... don't take less than nine, okay?" Jonathan nodded and started toward the barn, pulling the stubborn cow behind him.

Emily ran up and tugged on Daddy's sleeve. "*Daddy*, why cain't Charlie jus' go with us?" she whined, staring after Jonathan. She loved that cow more than any of us, probably because she was the best milker and we bragged on her for it.

Daddy squatted down in front of her, eye to eye. "We don't have a way t'feed Charlie on this big o'trip, honey, or a way t'save 'er milk from spoilin'. It would be wasteful fo' us n'difficult fo' 'er. Besides, who knows how long it'll take us t'get settled in Harlan? She'll be much happier stayin' here," he said gently.

"But how will we get *milk*?" Janie said, walking up to Emily and Daddy with her arms crossed.

"We're gonna drink water," Momma answered from a few feet away, "n'that's the end of it." Janie and Emily knew better than to say another word, opting instead to slink back into the wagon.

"Do y'all have enough food?" Martha asked, untwining Olivia's little fingers from her cross necklace and kissing her hand. "Y'need anythin'?"

"We'll be fine," Daddy hugged his oldest daughter. "If we run out o'bread n'beans, we have a barrel o'meal t'get us through. We can live on fritters well into a second month, easy."

"And you'll send a telegram when y'get there, Mr. Atwood?" Jonathan asked. "So, we know y'made it safe n'all." Daddy nodded and clasped Jonathan's hand, their fists gripped tight and shaking slightly – a feeling only they knew passing between them.

It made me think of church, how after preaching, God's people would gather in the altar and fellowship one with another. They cried alongside suffering brothers and sisters in Christ and laughed during seasons of re-joicing. On occasion I'd seen my Daddy get so happy that he'd shout for joy, his hands raised high enough to touch Heaven... if it would just drop a *little* lower. He had told me after that he had been feeling God's spirit, the Holy Ghost he called it, and I would understand better when I was older. I never forgot it, neither.

Daddy squinted up at the rising sun and said, "We bes' be goin'." He let go of Jonathan's hand and patted him on the shoulder. "Take care o'm'girl, y'hear?" Jonathan nodded and dutifully wrapped an arm around Martha.

Momma kissed Martha on the cheek, then peeled Olivia from her arms. "Y'all stay well," Momma told her and Jonathan. "We'll write as soon as we get settled."

Tears suddenly spilled over Martha's cheeks, like a dam broke inside her. "Oh, Momma," she choked out after a sharp inhale. "*Please* be careful. Watch fo' wolves n'coyotes... they're bad this time o'year, 'specially 'cross the prairies!" Momma nodded, gave her a quick hug, and then climbed up front with Olivia in her lap.

I kicked the dust up and walked to Martha, tears still streaming down her cheeks. When I couldn't think of anything clever to say, I just wiped my nose with the back of my sleeve again and wrapped my arms around her waist. I wanted to get a good grip and never let go... even though we sometimes fought like cats and dogs. Martha ran her fingers over my braid and kissed my hair, resting her cheek against the top of my head.

I turned my face to the side, pressing into her like a child searching for comfort, and stared at her and Jonathan's house. It was even smaller than ours, but the windows were propped open across the front and there were two old wooden chairs on the porch, a half-drank glass of water by the leg of one. It was a good starter home. I could even smell fresh-cooked bacon wafting from the kitchen.

Momma had told me once that if you looked at something long enough it would sear the picture right into your memory, like branding a cow with a hot iron. That's how she remembered her own parents and hometown when she married Daddy at fifteen and moved away. I wanted to brand myself with Leadwood, Missouri. If where I came from ever slipped from my memory, then the puzzle pieces that fit me together as Anna Beth Atwood would be lost. *Who would I become if I forgot my roots?* It hurt my head to think of such deep things.

Martha took my face in her hands, tilting it up so our eyes met. She smiled, her tears drying up some. "I'm dependin' on y't'write, Anna Beth. Write n'tell me how ev'ryone's doin'... 'specially Momma," she said quietly. I noted how her skin smelled like bacon and honey biscuits and let the warmth of her hands melt away my worries momentarily. I took a deep breath. I wanted to sear that smell and touch into my memory, too.

"C'mon, Anna," Daddy called from the front of the wagon. "It's time." I knew my sisters were watching me from the back, and I determined to let go and walk away... but I just *couldn't* bring myself to do it.

That's why Martha finally pushed me away with a quick nod. "Jus' write, okay? You're gonna be fine," she said, crossing her arms. "You're all gonna be fine, and we will, too." There was the old rough-around-the-edges

Martha I was used to, the tender moment passed. I took a few steps backward and swallowed hard.

"I'll write y'back," Martha promised. "Ev'ry time y'write me, I'll write ya. Now get goin' 'fore Daddy gets down after ya."

I turned and ran to the wagon, glancing back at her and Jonathan one last time before climbing into the back with my sisters. Daddy cracked the reins over the oxen and the wagon pulled forward, knocking me to the floor next to Janie.

"I'll send money fo' the cow," Jonathan called as we pulled onto the dirt road in front of their house. He waved as Martha blew a few kisses. She was crying again; I knew by the way she kept wiping her eyes.

"We'll send word when we get there," Daddy called back, holding up his hand in a final farewell.

The girls and I waved long as we could, the wind tunneling through the wagon's canvas top whipping loose strands of hair into my face and stinging my eyes. I wouldn't dare blink, though. Then we went around a bend, and Martha and Jonathan slipped out of sight. The breath caught in my throat, and my heart grew heavy with regret. *I should've let Jonathan help me out of the wagon. I should've run back and hugged Martha just one more time. I may never see them again.*

I closed my eyes as that thought sunk deep in my belly, trying to distract myself by recalling the bacon and honey scent on my sister's hands. I fought the wild, panicky urge to beg Daddy to let us stay in Missouri because I knew such a thing would only make leaving harder for all of us. *Parents know best.* Martha had beat that into me over the years when I didn't agree with this or that, and now came the time to accept it and teach it to my sisters. *Parents know best.*

I settled next to Emily, choking back tears of my own, and Olivia climbed into my lap like a warm cat. I wrapped my arms around her. She held up her little cornhusk doll and said, "Kiss, Annabeph!" My sisters and I had made it for her before she was born, and she never went anywhere without it.

I kissed the doll's straw head, and Olivia giggled like a ray of sunshine in the darkness of my feelings. I squeezed her tighter and inhaled the honeysuckle scent of her hair. I might not be able to retain the smell of Martha's bacon, but I could take the honey with me.

*3*

A month passed like an inchworm creeping across a long tree branch in spring. The good Lord had *not* provided favorable weather for our travels… we had suffered several summer thunderstorms, which soaked our food, clothes, and wagon cover, and in the last week alone, Daddy had stopped to patch two broken axels! The rain had made the wood weak and the road muddy, and he figured we still lacked at least two hundred miles from reaching Harlan, Kentucky.

The camp morale was already waning when one of our oxen, Dessie, keeled over dead while topping a hill in Illinois. Using her for meat was not an option because there was no way to salt and dry it while on the road, so our frustrated and exhausted father said he was going to leave her for the buzzards. Janie and Emily cried something awful, though… so, Daddy ate his words and took the better half of a day to bury Dessie proper-like while the girls gathered flowers for the funeral.

We were all in pretty ornery spirits by then, especially Ginger, our horse, who had to be hitched up to our last ox to pull the wagon in Dessie's place. She bucked and whinnied something awful, and we barely picked up a trot for two whole days as they learned to pull together. At one point she nearly broke the wooden hitch kicking with her rear hooves, and that would not have been easy to fix while traveling across the prairie. Daddy got *so* angry he whipped Ginger good with the reins… and when Janie and Emily started boo-hooing in sympathy, he threatened to whip them, too.

The worst part, however, was that we only had the barrel of water and meal left from our provisions. The rest of the food had either been eaten or ruined by the rain. We begrudgingly threw out what had molded about a week before. Daddy assured us that Momma was good at food rationing and we wouldn't starve – in other words, we best quit our bellyaching. We took the hint.

Once Ginger and Bessie started working like a team, Daddy drove the wagon hard. My sisters and I fell asleep to the steady grind of the road and woke up to it in the morning. All four of us girls were sore and bruised from sleeping in that jolting wagon bed. Even when we had to do our business, Daddy would only *slow* the wagon down. We would jump off the back, run to some brush by the side of the road to relieve ourselves, and then run and catch back up. Stopping for dinner was the only reprieve, and we relished the time to get out and stretch.

Momma called for dinner every night when the sun first drooped in the sky, and Daddy would obediently pull the wagon off the dirt road. He'd gather some brush to start a small fire, and Momma would wield the trusty cast iron pan and fry us one fritter each. Sitting together on a blanket in the grass by the wagon wheels and eating our coveted fried meal was the highlight of each day. Daddy kept his gun handy, too, just in case we saw wolves and coyotes.

Most of the time we'd just sit a spell and dream aloud about our new lives in Harlan. Daddy wanted to find a good job, of course, so he could build Momma a four-room house instead of the two-room we had back home. Momma wanted to buy new fabric and make us girls matching dresses for the new church we would attend. I mustered hope that Harlan would have a wonderful schoolhouse and teacher, but Janie and Emily confessed they wanted to throw the towel in and go back home... they were plum tired of this adventure.

Nearing our sixth week, we came upon another wagon heading in the opposite direction. The sun was boiling high in the afternoon sky, and the wagon coming toward us looked like a watery mirage. My sisters and I crowded in behind our parents at the front of the wagon. I could make out a man and woman on the bench... we hadn't seen another living person besides each other in forever it seemed! Daddy told us to sit back down before the wagons got too close, though, and with a few moans and groans we did as we were told.

As the wagons neared each other, Daddy pulled back on the reins and slowed Ginger and Bessie to a stop. "Howdy, folks," Daddy said, tipping his hat.

"How d'ya do?" the man's voice answered.

Daddy rested the reins on his knee, and Momma leaned around him to smile at the strangers. "Doin' fine," Daddy said. "Might I ask where you're headed?"

"Who is it?" Janie whispered loudly in the back. She started to crawl on her hands and knees to get a peek, but I pulled her backwards by the hem of her dress. She fell sideways, crushing Emily's hand with her knee, and Emily yelped in pain. They both stuck their tongues out at me in retaliation.

"They're *strangers*," I hissed at Janie. "Sit still n'hush up like y'were told; it's grown up business – not fo' y'kids."

"You're *one o'the kids*, Miss High n'Mighty," Janie retorted.

I shushed her quiet. Olivia put her finger over her mouth and shushed Janie, too. Emily slapped at Olivia. I shoved her back into Janie, then held my fist up and narrowed my eyes at all three of them.

"If y'all don't b'have, I'm gonna give y'a reason t'mind." I bit my lip like Momma, so they could see the edge of my teeth, and it worked. They fell still and quiet – and we all strained our ears to hear the conversation up front.

"So, you're comin' from Kentucky?" Daddy was saying. "That's where we're headed."

"Yeah... I tried t'get a minin' job in Edmonson County, but they're few n'far b'tween," the man sighed. "We want t'start a fam'ly n'need a decent wage, so we're movin' on t'the nex' place t'try our luck."

Daddy nodded. "I know what y'mean. We married one daughter off n'got fo' more in the raisin'." He lifted his hat from his forehead and wiped the sweat away with a handkerchief. "I'm lookin' t'find work in Harlan County," he continued. "Do y'know anythin' 'bout them parts?"

"We didn't pass through Harlan, no," the man said, drawing a deep breath. "But if it's anythin' like Edmonson County, you'll be turnin' back soon enough. I think everyone heard Kentucky's air is filled with gold dus' or somethin'... there're too many men n'not enough jobs. Seems like hard times ev'rywhere y'go these days."

Daddy nodded as Ginger stamped a hoof and shook her mane. "Well, thanks fo' the news. God speed fo' y'road ahead." They exchanged good-byes and Daddy snapped the reins, moving us forward again.

Janie and Emily peered out the back, trying to get a glimpse of the couple as their wagon pulled past and disappeared over the hill, but I watched my parents. Momma leaned over to whisper something in Daddy's ear. She patted his sweaty back and stared into his face for an answer, but he just looked straight ahead like she wasn't even there. Momma finally pushed the hair from her exasperated face, tucked the loose strands behind her ears, and stared off toward the mountains. I don't know what she had said, but long as I watched them, they never did look back at each other.

Dinner was so quiet that night we could hear the wind whistling through the trees in the distance. When we got back on the road, Janie scooted close to me. "Anna, why did that man say we might be turnin' 'round soon?" she whispered, stealing a glance at Momma up front. We were supposed to be settling down to sleep.

"Jus' that there might not be a job left fo' Daddy," I whispered back. "Lots o'people're travelin' all over looking fo' work. I reckon most of 'em had the same idea 'bout the coal mines." Olivia had already fallen asleep in my lap, so Emily crawled to the other side of me and scooped her fingers into Olivia's curly hair.

"Is the air in Harlan *really* filled with gold dus'?" Emily asked. "We'll be rich, if 'tis."

"I don't know," I shrugged my shoulders. "I've never been near a coal mine. Maybe."

Janie wrapped her arms around her knees and buried her face, peeking at me out of the corner of her eye. She had a hard time being serious about anything, and I could see the struggle. "What will we do if there *ain't* a job left fo' Daddy?" she asked quietly.

"Will we turn 'round n'go home?" Emily hoped. Olivia stirred and slipped her thumb into her mouth, sucking hard a couple of times and then letting it hang on her bottom lip.

"Anna, *tell us*. Will we go back home?" Janie pressed.

"If Daddy cain't find a job in them Harlan mines, we'll jus' head on somewheres else," I snapped, suddenly irritated and quite tired of the conversation. "Daddy told us that the lead mines in Leadwood were dried up, so stop thinkin' we'll ever go back... we have t'find a *new* home where he can make money. Money buys food n'a roof, 'member?" Janie buried her face more firmly in her knees, and Emily slumped against the wagon, crossing her arms.

"We don't need fancy food or anythin'," Emily said. "We could eat grass like Ginger n'Bessie n'be vegenarians." I rolled my eyes. There was woman in Leadwood that only ate vegetables, and that fascinated Emily.

"It's *vegetarians*," I corrected, "n'people cain't live on grass like animals." We all fell quiet, listening to the pad of Ginger's hooves on the dirt road beneath us. My sisters bedded down shortly after, the lull of the wagon rocking them to sleep against their will.

I was content, however, to just sit and think in the quiet darkness. I could see the sliver of moon out the back of the wagon and pulled the blankets up on Janie and Emily so they wouldn't get a chill. I felt a tad sorry for being short with them – I knew they didn't understand the situation we were in. I took a deep breath of Olivia's hair and let my heart hope hard. We'd be pulling into Harlan any day now, and I prayed our plans would fall into place. My parents knew more than some strangers on the road that hadn't even been through Harlan. They just had to. *Parents know best.*

*4*

"Anna Beth," Momma whispered, reaching back from the front bench to shake my shoulder. "We're here." I stirred awake, feeling my body swim upward out of a heavy sleep. The day was just dawning, the sun barely a wedge of orange in the sky. Then her words registered: *We're here*! The wagon slowed to a stop and Ginger whinnied. "Get up n'sift the meal, but don't wake y'sisters," Momma said.

I quietly scooted myself upright and surveyed the pile of us. We were packed together like sardines in the narrow width of the wagon bed. Janie's bottom arched into my thigh, her bare feet sprawled across my knees. Emily's head was resting in the dip of Janie's side; one of her hands slipped under Olivia, who was still in my lap. *Being the oldest has its downside*, I thought wearily. *Like getting up first all the time.* How was I supposed to untangle myself from this heap without waking my sisters?

I gingerly wriggled out from the jumbled mass of bodies and limbs, and my sisters spilled into the empty hole I left behind like quicksand. With a yawn I stepped around them to the meal barrel in the corner, carefully leaning the lid against the wall of the wagon so it didn't make a sound.

I glanced outside for the first time... Kentucky *was* greener than Missouri, with stair step hills that built into mountains in the distance. The air felt moist from the glittering morning dew, and I took a deep breath. Daddy had said them mountains were the Cumberland Mountains. He told us the peaks reached into the sky like giant upside-down ice cream cones, and mountain climbers said the snow on top tasted like *vanilla*. What a delicious thought... my stomach growled for the cold treat but would have to settle for a hot morning fritter instead.

"What's the verdict?" Momma peered in the back of the wagon. I ran my hand through the grain, my fingertips scraping the bottom. There wasn't enough left to get us through the whole day, maybe one more meal like the widow woman and her son in the Bible. What was left had weevils wiggling around in it, too.

"It'll las' through breakfas'," I sighed.

It was aggravating how we had stored the food well, but more bugs found their way into it the longer we traveled. That's how I became the morning meal-sifter. I would throw any beetles and mealworms I could find out the back of the wagon, and we would use what was left. Daddy teased and said any bugs that *did* sneak into our fritters were just added protein. He got a kick out of making us girls gag.

Daddy came around and helped me and Momma lower the barrels of meal and water to the ground, then he mumbled something about brush and fire and headed towards some nearby bushes and trees. He kicked a rock along the road with the toe of his boot. I stole a quick glimpse at Momma. Her arms were crossed over her chest as she stared after Daddy. She looked like she had barely slept. Dirt smudged her cheek and her bun was loose, too. It made me nervous to see her so untidy.

Momma glanced my way and I quickly averted my eyes. Once she and Daddy had thought us all asleep last night, they had started arguing. It had something to do with the couple we met on the road, and their tones and body language told me it was one of those "none of your business" fights only a husband and wife can have. I wanted to ask her what was wrong, partly because I was nosy and partly because I truly cared, but when Momma's mad she's like a mule that bucks without warning... so I bit my tongue rather than receive a swift kick in the behind.

"Wake up y'sisters, Anna," Momma ordered. She looked after Daddy one more time and started toting the barrels to a nearby tree to start breakfast.

I ducked back inside the wagon and nudged Janie's foot with mine. "Wake up, girls," I said. "We're here." I leaned down and gave them a shake. "C'mon, get up now." Janie and Emily shrugged away from my hands with a moan and groan and hid their eyes in the crooks of their arms.

"Why've we stopped?" Janie mumbled.

"T'eat breakfas'. We're in Kentucky – almos' t'Harlan now," I said, leaning down to scoop up Olivia. I caressed her cheek with my thumb. "Wake up, Livie," I cooed, swaying gently back and forth. Olivia's face crinkled in the brightening sunlight, and her eyes slowly fluttered open. She gave me a big toothy smile and stuck a finger in her mouth. I couldn't help but smile back. I kissed her curly top head and took a second to inhale the honeysuckle that reminded me so much of home. *I can't wait to have a home again!*

Momma came back to the wagon and I handed her Olivia, who buried her face in Momma's neck with a sleepy yawn. I could smell fritters frying in the skillet, and my mouth began to water.

"Anna, I told y't'get 'em up," she scolded. "We've got a lot t'do t'day, n'only so much daylight t'do it in."

She walked away and I sighed at my sisters, hands on hips – then kicked them a little. When they started moaning and groaning again, I leaned down and growled real low, "If y'two don't get up right *now*, I'm gonna give y'a reason t'grumble."

Janie cracked open one eye and looked at me with a pouty frown. "*Gee,* Anna, we're jus' *jokin'* 'round," she said. "We're awake." She elbowed Emily and those two opossums sat up.

"Why do y'have t'be so mean t'us?" Emily asked, rubbing her nose on her arm.

"I'm mean 'cause y'all have no respect fo' the eldes', which I am now whether y'like it or not," I said. "Now get up, 'fore Momma comes back, n'we *all* get in trouble." Then I climbed down from the wagon and left them to get moving before they could think of a retort.

Momma, Daddy, and Olivia were under a giant oak tree a few yards from the wagon, Daddy smothering the fire out with a blanket and Momma and Olivia sitting on a fallen trunk. I pulled up the hem of my dress and jogged to them, breathing the fresh air in deeply. Our journey was just about over, and it felt great to move my body and know I was moving toward a different kind of day.

"Y'sisters up?" Momma asked when I reached them. She handed me a small cornmeal cake that I could probably pop whole into my mouth, but I wouldn't. Since I didn't know where our next meal was coming from, I'd take little nibbles and make it last as long as I could.

"Yes, ma'am," I nodded. Olivia nodded, too, her mouth crammed full of fritter. She grinned up at me from Momma's lap and bits of fried meal fell out the corners. I laughed and shook my head at her. She giggled and shook her head at me, shaking loose more crumbs.

Daddy dragged the blanket over and sat down about the same time Janie and Emily walked up. Momma handed them their little fritters and they settled on the log next to me.

"So, *this* is Harlan?" Janie finally asked, looking around at the trees thickly sprinkled throughout the green fields. Her eyes settled on the tall mountains in the distance. They *did* look to touch the blue sky. "I guess it's kind o'pretty," she admitted. "Lots more hills n'valleys than flat land, though."

Daddy took a drink from the water dipper and swished it around for a long while, and I remembered that night at dinner when he told us we were moving. After a hard swallow he took another bite of his fritter and chewed the heck out of it. He usually always had something to say to build up Harlan in our minds. Him sitting quietly on the day of our arrival, not making eye contact, made my stomach squirm uncomfortably.

"Where're we gonna live now that we're here?" Emily asked.

"Do we still have t'sleep in the wagon?" Janie grimaced.

"Or can we get a house t'day?" Emily hoped.

Neither of my parents spoke, so I piped up. "Momma n'Daddy don't have money fo' a house *yet*. Daddy's gotta find work firs', *'member*?"

"Then *where're* we gonna live, Anna?" Emily asked.

"And *what're* we gonna eat?" Janie had stuffed the rest of the fritter into her mouth and was trying to talk around it. She put her hands on her hips and raised her eyebrows, making a striking resemblance to a little banty rooster, feathers all ruffled and posed for a fight.

"I don't really want t'eat grass," Emily said, thinking back on our conversation the night before. "I was kiddin' 'bout that... Oh! n'we need another milkin' cow! I want some milk somethin' fierce," she muttered excitedly through her own mushy fritter. A piece fell out of her mouth onto her lap and she stuffed it back in and kept chewing.

"That's enough, girls," Momma finally spoke. "Y'Daddy n'I need t'talk t'ya 'bout more pressin' matters."

Daddy stood up suddenly and a look I had never seen before passed between him and Momma, then he looked down at his muddy, broken-down boots. "Laura, let's not do it this way," he said quietly. My heart started to thump in my chest, and my stomach twisted up tighter. *What curve ball were they going to throw at us now?*

"We discussed this, Ben... y'*know* it's the only way," Momma said. "We'll be t'town soon; we have t'tell 'em the plan."

Daddy took a deep breath and exhaled slowly, looking back toward the wagon. "Then y'tell 'em by y'self. I'll hitch the wagon up. We need t'be back on the road 'fore the sun gets too high if we're gonna make it there by noon."

We all turned and stared after Daddy as he walked away, hitting his hat against his trousers with every step. He and Momma had spats like any married folk, but he had *never* left her to tell us something that concerned the whole family by herself.

I was the first to look back at Momma. She was staring at the smoldering embers of the dying fire with saddened eyes, her arms tight around her youngest daughter. Olivia squirmed in her grasp and reached for me, but Momma wrestled her still and shushed her quiet. She swallowed and raised her eyes to survey us girls sitting there on the log like little ducks – one, two, three.

"Well," she steadied her voice, "y'all know that y'Daddy n'I love y'all very much." Her eyes floated from Janie to Emily to me, but it was like we were made of glass and she was looking right through us. "Y'know we want t'make a better life fo' y'all, n'that's why we've come t'Harlan. Y'all understand that, right?" We nodded in unison.

Momma cleared her throat. "I'm sure y'all realize that times have already gotten hard fo' us on this journey, but they're gonna get harder fo' jus' a little while longer... then it'll get better again." She paused to rub her temple, struggling to find the next words. "These're *poor* times, girls; it'll be tough fo' Daddy t'find work. He's gonna look ev'rywhere n'do all he can, but we don't know how long that's gonna take. It could be a couple o'weeks, or a couple o'months."

Janie and Emily looked at me, utterly confused. I swallowed, mustering up a little courage to raise my chin to meet my mother's. "Momma, we *know* it's gonna be tough t'get settled, but we'll get through it," I said. "Daddy'll find a job, n'we'll be fine. God *always* provides."

"That's right, Anna. When Daddy finds a job, we *will* be fine... but it's up t'that time we mus' be smart 'bout," Momma nodded. Her voice turned quite tender. "The truth is we don't have much money left, girls. We don't have a place t'live, n'we're out o'food. So, Daddy n'I've decided that once we get into town, it'll be bes' t'find some good folks t'take y'all in fo' a bit. Then, when we get work n'a place to live set up, we'll come back n'get y'all."

I stared at my mother, not sure I heard her right. "You're gonna do *what* with us?" I questioned. *Were they giving us to strangers because they can't care for us anymore?* My cheeks flushed hot with a rush of sudden fear, my mind racing a mile a minute trying to figure this out before I had to explain it to my sisters.

Momma slowed her speech and softened her words with as much control as I'd ever seen. "When we get t'town, we're gonna see if there're folks that'll take y'all in – jus' fo' a while. Maybe y'all can work... do dishes, laundry, cookin', whatever, in exchange fo' room n'board. She paused a moment before going on. "I know this comes as a shock, but this is what y'father n'I feel'll be bes' fo' ev'ryone. When Daddy makes enough money n'we find a place t'live, we *will* come back n'gather ev'ryone home again. It'll jus' be a short time apart n'then t'gether fo'ever."

"You're givin' us away t'*strangers*?" Janie whispered, the words sounding sticky in the back of her throat.

Emily was chewing her bottom lip so hard she was making it bleed. I crossed my arms over my stomach... no matter how tasty the fritter was going down, I knew it was going to burn coming back up. Momma rubbed her hands across her face, and Olivia took the opportunity to escape her grasp and run to me. I pulled her into my lap; she wrapped her arms around my neck and hid her eyes from our mother.

"We're not *givin'* y'all t'anyone," Momma finally said, her hands open and pleading. "You're jus' gonna have t'stay with new neighbors fo' a little while, work fo' y'keep if necessary, n'then we'll be back fo' y'all as soon as we can manage. I *know* it's hard t'understand these grown up thin's when you're young, but if there was any other way, we'd do it. We jus' don't have the means t'take care o'y'all until we make some money fo' shelter n'food... so it's not fair t'ya, y'see? We don't want y'all sleepin' in the wagon n'beggin' fo' scraps from people passin' by. This is bes'. I promise it'll be okay."

Emily dug her toe in the dirt. "It sounds like you're gettin' rid of us," she mumbled. "Like we did Charlie n'the chickens... except we gave 'em t'fam'ly. You're givin' us t'*strangers*."

Momma stood up, her patience about spent. "Sometimes thin's feel bad n'the moment, girls, but y'all have t'remember that as soon as we find work n'have a place t'live, *we'll be back t'get y'all*. It's jus' temp'rary."

Janie had been thrusting her hand back and forth over the log's rough bark and suddenly stopped. "But we can help y'n'Daddy," she said earnestly. "It's not like y'have t'do it all alone. We're big like Anna. We can pitch in n'make money, too, n'I don't care t'sleep in the wagon. I liked it...." She kicked dirt at the dying fire. "I'll work harder than anyone." When Momma didn't say anything she started pleading, "I'll do *anythin'* y'tell me to, jus' let us stay t'gether! Emily n'I won't even fight with Anna anymore. *We'll be good*, Momma! You'll see!"

Momma nodded and reached for Janie, but my sister jerked backward like Momma was going to hit her. "I'll go ask Daddy," Janie yelled and took off running toward the wagon. Momma looked back at Emily and me with pleading eyes.

"Emily," she said gently, waving her hand forward. "Come here t'me, baby."

Emily shook her head and took off after Janie. "I'm gonna ask Daddy, too!" she called over her shoulder.

Momma squinted up at the sun and blinked back tears. She was the tough but dependable one, and it tore me up to see her aching so. Momma looked down at Olivia, who was still nestled in my lap, and wiped her eyes with the back of her sleeve. I stood up and hoisted Olivia onto my hip. Livie locked her legs around my waist and scooped her fingers into my braided hair, afraid I would hand her back to Momma.

"It's 'cause we *love* y'all," Momma said quietly. "This ain't 'bout y'all bein' good or bad, or even pitchin' in t'do y'part," Momma said to me. "*You* know that, right?" I could see in her eyes she needed someone to agree with her or she was going to fall apart at the seams.

Janie and Emily screeched in the distance, and I turned around in time to see Janie kick the wagon wheel and both girls run away from Daddy, who was down on one knee with his head in his hands. Ginger whinnied and bucked at the wagon hitch sympathetically; she would have gladly run away with the girls any day.

"We're goin' back t'Martha n'Jonathan's!" Janie yelled hatefully as she headed off down the road. "Y'should've jus' given us t'*them*, like Charlie n'the chickens!"

Daddy didn't chase after them, either. Instead he glanced toward us, his eyes locking with Momma's for a moment as something passed between them that was nearly tangible – and it stung. This decision was breaking us apart individually and collectively.

"We jus' cain't make it work any other way!" Momma threw her hands up in sudden exasperation. Olivia tensed in my arms. "*Neither* of us want t'resort t'this, but we have t'do what's bes' fo' y'kids. We have t'make sure y'all have food n'shelter, then we can fix life back the way it's s'pposed t'be...." She looked at me with such pain in her eyes. "When you're older you'll understand why this is bes'."

She opened her arms and took a few steps toward me and Livie. I guiltily untangled my sister who began to fuss and cry and shoved her into Momma's arms, stumbling backward myself and almost tripping over the fallen log. I didn't want Momma to touch me, and I felt both justified and ashamed of it. Then I started to feel lightheaded.

"It'll only be fo' a little while, Anna, I *promise*," Momma's voice snuck in through the thick haze of thoughts swirling in my mind. "We'll come back fo' y'all as soon as we can get ev'rythin' in order. Y'understand that, don't ya? You're the oldes' now. We at leas' need *you* t'understand."

My throat tightened and my saliva ran hot. My fritter was creeping up my throat again but I swallowed it back down. It scratched and burned like wildfire as it slid back to my stomach with a somersault. I looked at the wagon just in time to see Janie and Emily slinking over the hatch. They must have realized there was nowhere to run to and had come back, for better or worse.

"I *promise* we'll come back," Momma kept insisting.

"I know, Momma," I forced the words out like a man spitting tobacco. "I b'lieve y'n'Daddy know what's bes'." *Parents know best. Parents know best. Parents know best.* My stomach was really churning now, and I took note of a grove of trees clumped together just up the road. I longed to be hidden in the brush of it just for a few precious minutes by myself. I just needed to gather my thoughts and think through this new twist.

"Anna, are y'okay?" Momma asked, concerned. She had stepped close enough to lay a hand on my shoulder without me realizing it, and my stomach flipped violently under her hot touch.

"I'm fine, Momma... I jus' have t'relieve m'self. I'm gonna go over there." I nodded to the grove and took off walking at a brisk pace. I glanced back over my shoulder. "I'll come t'the wagon in a minute, okay?"

"Take y'time," she called after me, wringing her hands together at first and then smoothing her skirt down. "I have t'clean up breakfas', n'then we'll be ready."

I quickened my walk to a jog and then gave into a full out run. I ran as hard as I could, pushing my legs to go faster and faster even though they burned. I probably hadn't eaten enough lately to exert such energy. By the time I reached the grove and hid behind a thick tree trunk my cheeks were on fire. I tried to catch my breath and calm myself down, but I was shaking too hard and then I started heaving... I doubled over and fritter exploded *everywhere.* Just when I thought I had nothing left in my whole body, another swell would come. By the fifth heave, I felt weak and chilled – but thankfully, empty. I shook spitty strings from my mouth and nose, gasping to get air back into my burning lungs. Once my belly settled, I wiped my face with some leaves and straightened my back, hands on my hips, taking slow and steadying breaths with my eyes shut tight.

"I *hate* bein' the oldes'!" I suddenly cried out loud. I covered my face and felt it contort under my hands. *Why did I have to be the strong one? Why did I have to set the example?* I swiped furiously at my wet eyes and crossed my arms, rubbing my elbows, trying somehow to get a grip on a life that had just spun out of control... again.

A rock lay near my foot and I kicked it into the shadowy underbrush, causing a squirrel to sprint up a nearby tree. I followed the little creature with my angry eyes. When it had settled deep in the top branches, I jumped up and hit at the lower leaves. Animals scattered from their hiding places, and birds flew into the sky, squawking at me indignantly.

"Go 'head! Fly 'way!" I yelled at them. "At leas' y'can come back home! I won't *ever* see m'home again! I don't even *have* a home!" I looked up at the bits of white, fluffy cloud drifting through the sky. It deceptively appeared to be a perfect day. *Why did life have to be of few days and full of sorrow?*

I remembered the preacher taking that scripture as his text one time. I thought of how Daddy had started work in the mines at fourteen, and Momma, married at fifteen, worked hard to run the household and raise the family. When we were not at school, my sisters and I helped make ends meet; at twelve years old I could cook full meals, without burning myself or the food. I could also sew, cross-stitch, crochet, and work the garden. *But why is whatever we do never enough?* Surely, we could just work harder and stay together!

This living with strangers for a while idea seemed like the *easy* way out to me. I crossed my arms. *That was it.* Daddy and Momma were taking the easy way out for once in their lives. They were tired of taking care of us, so they were giving us away. I shook my head and tried to force the ornery thought from my mind. That could *not* be the reason... I knew it in my heart, I *knew* they loved us – but that was of little consolation when I was feeling so betrayed and bitter.

I crumpled in the grass where I stood, my legs totally exhausted. A nearby sticker bush ripped the edge of my dress, and I didn't even care that I had put a hole in one of the two changes of clothing to my name. It was reassuring to have the firm earth rise to meet me, cradling me in its soft dip, to stop the feeling of falling. I took a deep breath and squeezed my knees against my chest, resting my cheek against them as I peered through the trees. I could see Momma walking across the field to the wagon with the last barrel. Daddy was hitching up the horse and ox. I knew my time to be selfish, to stay hidden in the trees like it froze time, was dwindling. I was going to have to leave the rest of my family like I had left Missouri and Martha and Jonathan.

Another scripture came to mind. *The prayers of a righteous man availeth much.* I decided that instead of a good school and teacher in Harlan, I would now hope I had found enough grace in His sight that the good Lord would hear the prayers of this little girl from Leadwood – so far from home.

A little further up the road a creek came into view and Momma told Daddy to pull over. She then made every one of us take a bath in the cool, clear water. The current ebbed and swirled around a few good-sized rocks, and if you watched close enough, you'd see a trout swim past or a crawdad scuttle around your toes. It had been at least three weeks since we washed *that* good, and while my sisters relished the opportunity to swim in between Momma's scrubbing behind our ears and under the arms – I couldn't get the stranger arrangement off my mind.

After washing ourselves, we scrubbed our travel clothes and hung them on the wagon to dry, then donned our Sunday best in their place. I figured either Momma didn't want anyone to know we were poor at first glance, or she wanted people to take a liking to us, so they'd take us in. Maybe it was a bit of both. Daddy looked nice in his church overalls with a clean long-sleeved shirt underneath, and mine and my sisters' dresses were the same floral pattern, each with a thin layer of itchy lace around the hem, neckline, and sleeves. Janie was already tugging at her dress and grumbling.

*We need to look our best*, Momma had said. *We must make a good first impression.* Momma's Sunday best wasn't that much better than her work clothes, however. She was clean and neat, but still plain. I knew it was because she spent her extra money on fabric for us girls every Christmas, never on herself, and the thought of us in our nice flowered dresses while she wore plain blue made the guilt bubble up. Momma and Daddy didn't want to give us away because it was the easy choice; they had always sacrificed to provide for their children.

"What's gonna happen now, Anna?" Emily whispered. We had all piled back in the covered wagon, and it was bumping along the dirt road toward Harlan, a town nestled between the two biggest coal mountains I had ever seen. Olivia had fallen asleep in my arms for an early afternoon nap, and our parents sat up front, still not talking unless they had to.

"We're gonna do whatever Momma tells us t'do," I said, the words tasting sharp like a broken tooth in my mouth. I tucked the hair that escaped my braid behind my ear.

"I don't *want* t'live with strangers, though," Janie said quietly, her first words since she ran away screaming from Daddy.

"None of us *want* to," I said, "but we *have* t'be brave. Y'all should try."

"I don't know how t'be brave," Emily whimpered. She wrapped her arms around her knees and stared out the back of the wagon. "What if they don't like us? What if they're mean t'us?"

"Momma n'Daddy would never leave us with mean folk, Emily. B'sides, Momma said we won't have t'stay very long." I twirled my fingers through Olivia's soft curls. "It should be easy fo' Daddy t'find a job," I added. I was pep-talking myself as much as them. "He works hard; people'd be foolish not t'want 'im in their mine. When they get enough money, they'll come get us. Then it'll be like it used t'be in Missouri." I fought to hold my voice steady. Assuring them was part of being the oldest now and being the one my sisters could lean on. Deep down, however, I'd give up the respect and independence to answer to Martha again.

"But what if they *never* come back?" Janie dared to ask.

"What an awful thin' t'say!" I snapped. I quickly gathered that frantic feeling that had wondered the same thing back in. "Momma *promised*," I softened my words, "n'she might be tough, but she's *never* broke a promise – y'know it."

"Well, there's a firs' time fo' ev'rythin'," Janie mumbled, stubbing up. "I wished I'd've stayed home with Martha n'Jonathan."

Emily's eyes filled with tears at the thought. "I don't *want* t'live with strangers, Anna!"

I sighed and wrapped an arm around Emily, still holding limp Olivia with the other. "Y'*know* Momma n'Daddy'll come back fo' us," I said as tenderly as I could. "They love us too much t'leave us somewheres fo'ever. It's jus' until they get a place our own n'can buy food fo' the whole lot of us."

I looked at Janie, who was opening her mouth with a retort. "N'I don't want t'hear *one* more word 'bout it," I said sternly. She shut her mouth with a humph and looked out the back of the wagon, arms crossed.

We rode quietly for a while, but when we began seeing buildings our curiosity got piqued. Janie and Emily peered out the back. I carefully laid Olivia on some blankets and joined them. Shops were dotting each side of the dusty street now, most of them built with wooden planks and shingled roofs. They were all about the same size, except for two brick buildings that stood out. Their signs read *Harlan County Bank* and *The Michaels' Hotel*. The hotel was taller because it had an upstairs. There wasn't anything that fancy in Leadwood! Behind the buildings lay rolling hills sprinkled with wooded areas here and there, and far beyond that were the twin mountains topped with vanilla ice cream, one on each side like we were the cherry in the middle.

The wagon slowed to a stop, and we rushed to the front and crowded behind our parents to see some town folk walk across the street, kicking a cloud of dust up with their feet as they traipsed by. A little boy waved at us, clinging to his mother's dress as they hurried past. Janie waved back and he stuck his tongue out at her, then hid behind his mother's skirt.

"Well, I never..." Janie breathed. "That's what I get fo'' bein' brave!"

We settled in the back again, and Emily, who couldn't read well yet, asked me to read her all the different signs. I pointed to the right, to a dimly lit building with a low sloping roof. "That one says *Saloon*, n'that one nex' t'it says *Michael James, M.D.*," I said. I motioned to a small building on the left. "That there's the barber shop." Daddy parked the wagon and I leaned out the back, staring at the big yellow sign with bold black letters high above us. "*The Corrigan Mercantile*," I read to the girls.

The wagon tilted to one side as Daddy climbed down from the front bench. He tied the reins down on the brake and patted Ginger. "Good girl," he sighed. "We *finally* made it t'Harlan County." Then he motioned to me.

"C'mon with us, Anna; Janie, y'stay here n'watch y'sisters," he said. The girls whined, but he pointed his finger at them. "Do *not* get out o'the wagon, y'hear?"

"Yes, sir," they grumbled.

I climbed down from the back of the wagon and shot my sisters a proud look. I bet we were going to buy a bit of late lunch and supplies before looking for friendly neighbor folk, and *I* was going to help. The oldest did have its perks *sometimes*. Janie and Emily stuck their tongues out at me in retaliation, and Olivia, who had woken up a few minutes before, giggled at us and stuck her tongue out, too. I *had* to stick mine out then, just to please my baby sister, but I quickly smoothed my dress and walked up the steps to the covered porch with my parents.

Daddy opened the door and tipped his hat to a woman leaving the mercantile, then held it open so Momma and me could walk inside. A tiny bell above the entrance rang our arrival, and the few people inside turned to look at us.

It took my eyes a bit to adjust to the dim interior, which was the only light coming from the windows at the storefront. Fresh goods, mostly fruits and vegetables, were piled in huge wooden bins under the front windows, and shelving stuffed full of canned goods, tools, and trinkets lined the long, narrow aisles. The air smelled like the penny peppermints we'd buy in Jonathan's store back home, and I guessed a store wasn't a mercantile unless you sold penny peppermints. The smell alone reminded me so much of Leadwood that I half expected to see Jonathan push through the back curtain and toss me a piece of candy.

Instead, an older man in overalls pushed by us on his way to the door, and we all stepped sideways to let him pass. Daddy tipped his hat again in greeting.

The man nodded. "Sir, ladies. Y'all new t'these parts?" he asked kindly.

"Yes, we jus' pulled in this afternoon," Daddy smiled.

The man surveyed us, his eyes resting on me. "Pretty child," he winked. I thanked him for the compliment, then he welcomed us to town and disappeared into the bright sunshine outside.

"C'mon," Daddy said, patting me on the back. "Let's find the owner."

We walked down the center aisle, and people stopped their shopping to steal a look at us. Some of them smiled and went back to their business while others whispered behind their hands. Daddy tipped his hat to all of them and Momma smiled, holding to the crook of his arm. I stuck close behind them, keeping my eyes on the household goods, tools and trinkets going by like nobody was staring. I thought at first their interest was because we were new faces in town... but then I remembered we were wearing our Sunday best on a Tuesday afternoon. I guess that alone *would* strike anybody as odd.

At the back of the store a man emerged from behind a thick green curtain. This man was older than Jonathan and wore a long-sleeved shirt damp with sweat. He wiped his hands on a white apron tied around his wide middle and smiled as we approached the counter, his rosy cheeks lighting up his round face with a warm smile.

"Howdy, folks! Fine day, ain't it?" He stretched out a hand to Daddy.

Daddy shook it and nodded. "Very nice, n'*this* is a mighty fine store you've got here."

"Well, thank y'kindly. My grandfather opened this store many years ago when the coal mines firs' opened. He knew the mines would bring good business t'town, a businessman he was. It's been in our fam'ly ever since." The man thumbed over his shoulder at the curtain behind him. "M'wife n'I live in the back. Tom Corrigan's the name. Are y'all passin' through or stayin' in Harlan a spell?" Daddy shoved his hands in his pockets, and I heard him jangling the change in the bottom. Those were probably his last coins, like the woman's two mites in the Bible.

"We jus' pulled in t'day, sir, but I hope t'find work n'make Harlan home. I'm Ben Atwood n'this is m'wife, Laura, n'our daughter, Anna Beth."

He motioned to the front windows at the wagon parked on the street. "I have three more girls outside."

"Where might y'all be comin' from?" Mr. Corrigan asked. He fished in a nearby candy jar and offered me a red licorice. Momma refused it on my behalf and thanked him anyway; my parents never allowed us to accept what we couldn't pay for... that's why we never told her Jonathan snuck us candy all the time.

"Leadwood, Missouri," Daddy said. "The lead mines gave out, so I thought we'd give coal a try."

"Good, gracious!" Mr. Corrigan exclaimed, his eyes growing wide with surprise. "You've traveled a good piece!" He opened the curtain with one hand and hollered, "Dorothy? Come out here fo' a minute n'bring some water fo' our weary trav'lers!" He patted Daddy on the arm. "Leas' we can do is give y'a cool drink a water after such a long haul."

A plump woman with a tight bun of graying hair pushed through the curtain and joined us a few moments later. She sat a tray of glasses down on the counter and smiled. Her smile wasn't as warm as her husband's, but it was still nice when you hadn't seen anyone but your family for over a month.

"These here're the Atwoods," Mr. Corrigan told her. "They've come clear from Missouri."

"Happy t'make y'acquaintance, n'glad y'all made it safely," she said.

Mr. Corrigan handed us each a glass of water from the tray, the ice cubes clinking against the glass as he moved them. I had only gotten ice cubes in my drink one time back home, and that was when I was invited to a fancy birthday party for the richest girl in town. I glanced at Momma before accepting my glass, and she nodded her approval. I carefully picked it up with both hands and took a sip; it felt like melting snowflakes sliding down my throat, cold, smooth, and refreshing. I took a longer drink and swished it slowly like Daddy does before swallowing. I could feel the coolness go all the way down to my belly. *Oh, won't the girls be jealous when they hear this!* I mused.

"There's many men like y'headin' t'the coal mines," Mr. Corrigan was saying. "The jobs're fillin' up quickly, but I think there might be a few left. Do y'all need some groceries t'get y'selves started? There's the Michaels' Hotel jus' down the road – I'm sure they'd have a room while you're lookin' fo' somethin' more permanent – n'there're lots o'little shops n'the railroad station pas' that."

My parents glanced at each other and Daddy cleared his throat. "Well, truth be told Mr. Corrigan, groceries n'a hotel're a little above our means currently. We jus' wanted t'see if y'all needed help 'round the store while we get on our feet in this fine town."

"Oh, Mr. Atwood – I'm sorry, but I cain't take on another man," Mr. Corrigan said, his smile fading with genuine regret. He glanced at his wife. "We're barely makin' ends meet as it is. Times ain't jus' hard fo' the minin' folk, y'know."

"I didn't mean me," Daddy pulled a laugh out from somewhere inside. "I meant m'daughter." He put a strong hand on my shoulder, and I nearly choked on an ice cube.

I looked up at Momma, who nudged me forward. Everyone was looking at me and time felt sticky and slow, like someone chewing toffee and struggling to pull their teeth apart. My parents had boxed me in between them and were offering up the oldest and most able-bodied daughter first! I hated that the thought hadn't even occurred to me. I looked from my parents to the Corrigans and swallowed hard, praying they couldn't take on girls neither.

Daddy was beginning to sweat. He wiped his brow with his handkerchief. "Y'see, I need t'get a job firs', some money comin' in…" he offered his explanation.

"N'ya don't want t'drag y'children all over the county while y'do it," Mr. Corrigan finished with a sympathetic nod. "That's certainly understandable; y'all have been livin' out o'wagon fo' how long now, a month or more?"

"A little over six weeks," Daddy admitted.

"N'it's hard t'start over from scratch, 'specially with children underfoot," Mrs. Corrigan smiled at Momma.

"We 'preciate the understandin'," Daddy said, his hand still firm on my shoulder. "Anna Beth here is our oldes'. She's twelve, n'I assure ya, she's strong n'willin' t'work hard. She can earn room n'board, n'we'd be back fo' 'er as soon as we're able."

I stared up at my Daddy, his jaw clenched, every muscle in his face set, but he kept his eyes steady on the Corrigans and didn't look down at me. *They might as well have put me on a pedestal and turned me in circles.*

"I'm sure she would be a great help," Mr. Corrigan agreed, leaning his elbow on the counter with a sigh. "But m'wife n'I, we really handle the store quite well by ourselves. If we *needed* the help, we'd take 'er in a heartbeat... but we jus' *cain't*."

Daddy nodded and glanced at Momma. "We understand," he said quietly. He was a proud man, and no matter how Momma spun it about us working for our keep, I think he still saw it as asking for charity.

"Do y'all know another fam'ly who *could* use the help?" Momma interjected, seeing that Daddy was about done pressing these folks. "People you'd trust y'own with?"

The Corrigans glanced at each other. This was not a question they got asked every day. "We do have a daughter," Mr. Corrigan said, straightening up and tapping his chin, "married n'livin' in Ohio now. If we were in y'situation when she was young... goodness, I don't know *what* we'd do."

Mrs. Corrigan inhaled sharply. "Come t'think of it," she nodded to Momma, "there is a nice fam'ly on the outskirts o'town, down on the farmin' land – Jack n'Grace Grainger. They stay mostly t'themselves but're respectable young folks. We sell a lot o'their crops here in the store." She looked at her husband. "I would want Shelly t'stay there, if we needed help. Grace is such a gentle soul."

Mr. Corrigan nodded approvingly. "Jack is a strong man, too. The farmin' land is the flattest you're gonna get in Harlan, n'it's hard work since we have more mountain type soil. He n'his wife managed the farm by themselves up 'til his wife had some setbacks, n'he's done mos' o'this season's sowin' by 'imself. I bet he'd 'preciate help bringin' in the harves' 'fore winter."

"Y'reckon they'd be willin' t'take in a few o'the girls?" Momma asked hopefully. "Our nex' two oldes're accustomed t'farm chores, also."

Mr. Corrigan shrugged his shoulders. "Maybe... no harm in askin'," he smiled encouragingly.

Momma looked at Daddy. "I don't want t'split 'em up, if we can help it," she said softly.

"They might have t'be, Laura," he answered. "Y'heard the man – taking on one, let alone three or fo' mouths t'feed is a mighty big request of anyone."

"Are there any other families y'all would consider?" Momma turned her attention back to the storeowners. "Our nex' two're nine n'eight. If we could find care fo' the three oldes', we can take the two-year-old with us, if push came t'shove."

"Well, the Pracketts n'the Carters live closer t'town," Mrs. Corrigan said. "They n'the Graingers, at leas' Mrs. Grainger, go t'church on Sundays when they're not working the fields. I imagine they'd let the girls go t'school when they could spare the help, too."

Daddy got directions to the possible households and thanked the Corrigans for their hospitality. "I'm sure we'll be back in town soon t'do business," he said.

"Good luck, Mr. Atwood," Mr. Corrigan smiled as we turned to leave. "I wish we could've been more help, but I hope these other homes pan out. When y'get settled, do come back in n'get y'groceries; we do both cash n'credit." Daddy shook his hand, and Mrs. Corrigan nodded the same sentiment to Momma, who smiled her appreciation.

As we pushed through the door back out onto the porch, the sun nearly blinded me. I blinked into the bright afternoon, sniffing and swallowing back a release of tears from being so nervous my parents would leave me with those folks and just drive away. Daddy still had his hand on me, and I shrugged it off. I wanted to run down the street and hop a train clear out of town like Janie would have, but instead I ran down the porch steps and climbed into the back of the wagon with my sisters. My parents climbed up front, the wagon tilting right and then left, and Daddy snapped the reins without even a word to comfort me.

"What's wrong, Anna?" Emily asked nervously. She looked like a frightened rabbit backed into the corner of the wagon.

"What happened in the store?" Janie added, her eyes narrowing in suspicion. "They tried t'give y'away, didn't they?" I wrapped my arms around my knees and buried my face. Our parents *told* us the new plan, that it was best for everyone, but I guess deep down I didn't *really* think they could go through with it – when it came right down to it.

"Nothin' happened," I mumbled. "I jus' don't feel good. I'm hot n'hungry, that's all." Janie and Emily glanced at each other and then back out the wagon hatch at the hilly scenery crawling by. I was grateful they didn't press me further.

As the wagon neared the edge of town, the church on the ridge came into view. It was a quaint little building, its steeple stretching up toward the puffy summer clouds with a cross on top. The white paint was peeling off the front steps, but the flowers around the sides looked fresh and well-tended. It looked both loved and worn, reminding me of our little church house back home. I wondered if its parishioners believed in being saved by grace and baptized like we did. Daddy said not every church was the same.

We rounded a bend and dipped down a spell and saw the schoolhouse next. It too was a one-room building like the church but had a seesaw and tree swing out front. Past that the dirt road forked in two. Mr. Corrigan had said the right fork would take us down to the farming homes they had suggested, and the left one arched up and had a few larger homes before leading on to the next town. Our wagon pulled to the right and my stomach sank.

I stared at my three sisters, trying to brand them into my memory. Janie and Emily were talking softly to one another, and Olivia, who had been playing in the corner of the wagon with her cornhusk doll, came and nestled back into my lap like a baby bird finding its nest. If the same family didn't take us all in, who knew when I'd see them again… I had already lost

Martha. I fought with Janie and Emily often, but that didn't mean I wanted to be separated from them. Then there was little Olivia, my baby birthday sister. We were two sides of the same heart knit together in the middle. Tears welled up in my eyes, and I turned my face to the wall trying to be brave. *What would I ever do without my family?*

*6*

When the wagon slowed to a stop, I raised my head. Olivia was still snuggled in my lap, fingering her cornhusk doll and babbling happily.

"Anna, come look at *this* house!" Emily said breathlessly. "I bet there's three or fo' rooms in it!" With a sigh, I sat Olivia down and crawled to join her and Janie.

The ranch-style farming house *was* bigger than our two-room log cabin in Missouri. It was nestled in what looked to be the foot of the coal mountains on the only stretch of flat land around. A sea of cornfields stretched out beyond the house, but the house itself sat on a square piece of mowed grass with a white picket fence running along the dirt road in both directions as far as you could see. Dingy clapboard siding and a wooden porch that dipped a bit in the middle made the place look old and tired. There were farming tools scattered around the shed to the left and an oxen harness laying in the front yard, weeds growing up around it until just the top shown. Someone had planted brightly colored day lilies to border the porch, though, and that at least communicated a touch of love.

"It's not anythin' t'get so excited 'bout," I mumbled, sitting back and rubbing my upset belly. I wanted to just lie down and close my eyes. Maybe I'd open them again and this day would vanish like a terrible dream.

"She's jus' bein' a sour apple," Janie soothed our sister since Emily's face had fallen at my disinterest. "It has t'be *twice* the size o'ours back home – n'*that's* somethin'."

Daddy came to the back and motioned for us to climb out. "C'mon girls, this is the firs' stop." He helped Janie, Emily, and Olivia to the ground then he reached out his hand to me.

"I can do it m'self," I said, completely aware that I was making the same mistake with Daddy that I had Jonathan – but still not caring because I was terribly upset with him and Momma both. Small rebellions were the only way I felt I could show it.

I swung my legs over the wagon hatch, jumped down, and attempted to walk straight past my father. He reached out and grabbed my arm, and when I tried to pull it from his grasp, he just yanked me close and held me tight to his chest. He already smelled like dirt and sweat, even after the morning bath.

"*Anna*," he said quietly. "Don't make this any harder than it already is." He took hold of my elbows and leaned down in front of me. "Y'Momma n'me would *never* do this, if we didn't absolutely have to… y'*know* that," he said, shaking me slightly. I looked away, biting the inside of my cheek so I didn't cry. He gave me a good shake, and I jerked back to look him in the eye. "Anna, tell me y'know that. Tell me right now."

I gritted my teeth and nodded. *Knowing* didn't make it hurt any less.

"We *will* come back fo' y'all – as soon as we can support a fam'ly," Daddy promised. Momma had said the same thing, but this was the first time Daddy backed it up.

I glanced over at Momma and my sisters. They were standing near the peeling white gate, Momma licking her thumb and wiping dirt smudges from Janie and Emily's faces while Olivia stood and held tight to Momma's skirt. When Momma moved on to straightening their clothes and hair, they started squirming and fussing. I met Daddy's gaze again. He had dark circles underneath his eyes that made him look miserably exhausted, and my heart softened.

I swallowed hard. "How long 'til y'come back?" I whispered, afraid of the answer.

Daddy stood up and patted my back. "That depends, honey. We'll come back as soon as we can." I looked at the ranch house and crossed my arms. "Give us at leas' 'til Christmas at mos'," he offered.

"Christmas?!" I sputtered, nearly choking on the thought. "Christmas is *fo' months* away!"

"It mightn't be that long at all, Anna Beth, but there's a lot t'be done. I have t'find a job n'then save enough money t'get us a house. Give us 'til then 'fore y'start worryin' y'self 'bout it," Daddy reassured me. When he saw my eyes welling up with tears he squatted down with a sigh, so we were eye to eye again.

"Think of it this way – if y'stay *here*, you'll be fed n'have a roof over y'head, n'you'll be able t'go t'church n'school. Then one day you'll wake up n'we'll be back t'take y't'our new home. Momma'll fix us dinner, n'we'll sit 'round the table fo' hours… n'we'll tell stories of our adventures apart. We'll cry n'laugh n'hug… it'll be back t'how it's s'posed t'be." Daddy forced a smile and pulled me into another tight hug.

"Y'sisters *need* t'see that you're not afraid," he reminded me. "You've always been the stronges' o'm'children, Anna… more than Martha even. Y'*can* set the mark. Will y'do it fo' me?" I looked deep into my father's eyes. He was just short of a broken man and I knew it.

"I'll do m'bes', Daddy," I said earnestly. "But will *you* try t'be back '*fore* Christmas? Please? Fo' me?" Daddy smiled and kissed my forehead.

"Y'do y'bes', n'I'll do mine," he said, shaking my hand like we made a deal. He stood up and wrapped his arm around me, and together we joined our family at the fence line.

Olivia immediately reached her little arms up and I hoisted her onto my hip. I *wanted* to be brave, but when your heart is thumping all out of beat in your chest, like a drum searching for its rhythm, it's mighty hard to muster courage. Then a woman walked out on the porch, the screen door slamming shut behind her, and my heart whammed a loud beat against my ribcage nearly taking my breath away. Daddy tipped his hat. *Here we go*, I thought, *ready or not*… and I drew a deep, steadying breath.

The woman was tall and slender, her simple, blue dress hemmed just above the ankle. Her blonde hair was pulled into a tight bun like Momma's, a few spirals curling down the sides of her milky white face. She shielded her eyes from the late afternoon sun and squinted out at us. I figured we were a sight. Not every day a man, woman and four kids in their Sunday clothes show up in front of your house – especially a house well off the beaten path.

"Can I help y'folks?" she called as she came down the porch steps. She stopped a few feet short of the gate and stuck her hands in her apron pockets. "Do y'have business with Jack?"

"Yes, ma'am, I hope so at leas'," Daddy nodded. "I'm Ben Atwood n'this here's m'wife, Laura. These here're our children. We jus' pulled in t'Harlan County this mornin'." He reached out his hand and she stepped forward to shake it, then stepped right back again. "The Corrigans from the mercantile directed us this way," Daddy offered. "Are y'Mrs. Grainger?"

"Yes, Grace," she said. "M'husband, Jack, should be comin' in from the fields anytime now." She nodded toward the sea of corn. "He's been out there all day."

"We're from Leadwood, Missouri, ma'am," Daddy said, trying to make light conversation. "We've been travelin' fo' the las' month'n-a-half or so. I'm looking t'get a coal minin' job here in town."

She nodded and her eyes drifted to us girls. Janie was digging her toe in the dirt and then lifting it up, watching dirt sift off the sides of her shoe. Emily was fingering the lace on one of her sleeves. Grace's eyes settled on Olivia, still in my arms, and Livie laid her head on my shoulder, looking at her warily.

"It'll take us some time t'get settled," Daddy continued. "So, we're hopin' some fam'lies 'round these parts can use our children's help... jus' 'til m'wife n'I get thin's up n'runnin'." Mrs. Grainger's eyes flew back to Daddy.

"Y'want people t'take y'children in?" she asked, furrowing her eyebrows – in confusion or disapproval I could not tell.

"Not *take them in*, ma'am; we're not lookin' fo' charity," Daddy backtracked quickly. "M'girls're accustomed t'hard work; I'm sure they'll do anythin' needed t'*earn* their room n'board. It'd jus' be 'til I can find work n'get enough money t'secure us a place t'live... it's difficult fo' a fam'ly this size t'start over, y'know?"

Mrs. Grainger nodded and brushed a curl from her face. Her eyes pulled toward Olivia again, like she was a magnet. This time Livie waved a chubby little hand at her, just a little wave though.

"How long're y'thinkin'?" Mrs. Grainger asked, crossing her arms.

"Several weeks? Couple months? It depends on where n'when I can find work," Daddy said. "I hope by Christmas surely." Daddy looked my way and winked.

A man finally rustled through the tall, shadowy stalks in the distance, and Mrs. Grainger glanced over her shoulder at the soft noise. He was walking with his head down, headed toward the little shed by the chicken coop. "There's m'husband now," she said. She cupped her hands around her mouth and hollered, "Jack! We got visitors!" The man startled and looked in our direction. He paused to adjust his hat, and Mrs. Grainger waved.

He glanced back toward the shed, then stabbed the pitchfork he was carrying into a nearby mound of dirt and started toward us. As he neared the fence, he dusted his hands off on his trousers and looked at his wife expectantly. She was quiet-natured to start with, but next to her big, strong husband she now looked like a timid, little mouse.

"Jack, this here is Mr. n'Mrs. Atwood n'their fam'ly. He's come all the way from Missouri fo' a coal minin' job," she introduced us.

Jack Grainger was tall with broad shoulders, his suspenders stretched tightly over his chest. His face was pockmarked and the lines across his furrowed brow gave a permanent air of disapproval. His long-sleeved shirt had yellowed arm pits, most evident when he lifted his hand and pushed a mop of oily black hair across his forehead. He wiped his hand on his trousers again and then reached it out to Daddy. I stared at the deep grooves carved into his tanned, leathery face. His eyes were dark like his hair.

"Nice t'meet y'folks," he said. His voice was gruff, and his hand swallowed up Daddy's. "What brings y'all out our way? Excuse m'clothes," he added, looking down at himself. "It's almos' harves' time; I'm mighty busy these days."

"I understand," Daddy nodded. "I used t'tap lead in Missouri, n'mos' nights I'd come home so black m'wife'd make me take a bath 'fore she'd let me in the house fo' dinner."

Mr. Grainger glanced at Momma, and Daddy decided not to waste any more time. He cleared his throat and explained our situation again, and when he had finished, Mr. Grainger was looking down his nose at us girls. He wiped the sweat from his brow with his shirt sleeve and shot a cross look at his wife.

"How is it y'reckon they can help us, exactly? Farmin's not child's work," he said. Mrs. Grainger's eyes fell – I think she might've wanted some of us.

"It's not a *normal* child's work," Daddy took back the conversation and patted my shoulder. "Anna here's the oldes' n'stronges'; she can do farm work. She helped me a great deal 'round our garden n'yard back home." I looked up at the Graingers and forced a weak smile. I knew the part I had to play.

Mr. Grainger rubbed his stubbly chin, drinking me in with his eyes as he considered the suggestion. "All due respect, but harvestin' fields ain't anythin' like bringin' in the garden vegetables," he said. He must have thought it was funny and laughed like he had made a joke.

"I'm *sure* she'd prove a great help t'y'all – if you'd give 'er a chance," Daddy insisted. He took a deep breath and laid it out flat. "All hands on the table, sir – n'ma'am," he added with a nod to Mrs. Grainger, "we're new here, n'we don't have many places t'turn. The Corrigans thought enough of y'n'the missus t'recommend y'home with very high regards." Mr. Grainger glanced at his wife again with an unbelievable chuckle.

"I don't see why we cain't take in a couple of 'em, Jack," she said carefully. "Y'could use *any* kind o'help at this point, n'I could use some comp'ny 'round the house, too."

Mr. Grainger's jaw clenched as he ran his hand through his hair, mussing it up. The joke was over. He twisted his hat in his hands and then hit it against his leg. It made a thwack that startled Olivia, and she wrapped her arms tightly around my neck.

"All right," he sighed loudly, gesturing to me. "I'll take the oldes' one. She'd be the mos' use."

My legs suddenly felt weak, like they were going to give out any second. I looked up at Daddy, who was thanking the Graingers for their hospitality, and tried to push through the feeling and stand tall like him. I had to set the mark because I knew my sisters were watching my every move, aware that it would soon be their turn.

"I'm sure she'll prove 'er worth," Daddy said, shaking Mr. Grainger's hand a second time. "We'll be back fo' 'er as soon as we can."

Momma and Mrs. Grainger started speaking quietly with one another, discussing other town folk that might take my sisters in, and Daddy joined their conversation. Mr. Grainger seemed to be listening, too, but his eyes were still on me. I lifted my eyes to meet his stare and felt my insides start crawling all over themselves. I fought down a sudden wave of nausea and leaned into Daddy's side, praying he and Momma would change their minds and take us with them after all.

"We thank y'kindly," Daddy looked back to Mr. Grainger.

Mrs. Grainger reached out and lightly touched her husband's arm. "Jack, what d'ya think 'bout takin' the baby in, too?" she asked quietly.

Mr. Grainger laughed again, a bigger, heartier laugh than before. "Grace! A *baby* cain't help me in the fields!" He shook his head at the lot of us. "D'ya b'lieve the thin's women folk think of?" he said mostly to Daddy.

Mrs. Grainger's face flamed red like Jonathan's tomato ears, but her voice remained calm and persistent. "*I* can take care o'the little one while y'n'the girl're in the fields; I'm sure the baby'd be better off here than goin' on a job hunt with such little food n'shelter available." She smiled kindly at Momma, the color in her cheeks draining a bit as she relaxed again. "Was it y'intent t'let 'er stay somewheres, or were y'plannin' t'take 'er with ya?"

Momma glanced at Daddy, who shrugged. "It's up t'you, Laura," he said.

She looked at me next. "Well, Anna Beth actually takes care o'Olivia most the time. They're birthday sisters, both born on February 26, ten years apart. If y'all didn't count 'er as trouble, I'd let 'er stay with Anna. I 'ppreciate y'considerin' 'er well-bein', 'er not bein' able t'work fo' 'er keep n'all." I think she was hoping to stir up some sympathy with stone-faced Mr. Grainger.

Grace looked at her husband with pleading eyes.

"Aw, I don't know, Grace," he huffed, rubbing the back of his neck. "It hasn't been that long since…" his voice trailed off. He glanced at my parents like he shouldn't say anything, then shrugged his shoulders. "I married a young one, y'know, figurin' she'd be up t'child bearin'. But Grace here los' our firs' baby 'bout three months ago, n'the doc ain't sure she can even have another."

Momma looked at Grace, her face full of genuine pity. "I'm so sorry," she whispered. Grace nodded, and I couldn't tell if she was sad or embarrassed that her husband told such a personal thing to strangers.

Everyone looked back to Mr. Grainger; even Janie and Emily were standing still and listening now. He let out an exasperated breath and threw his hands up like he was done with the whole conversation and ready to move on. "Okay, okay. That's fine. We'll take the two, but no more," he said warningly to his wife. "I can barely afford t'put food in our own mouths… but y'all assure me the oldes' can earn 'er keep?" he directed his attention back to Daddy.

"Yes, sir," Daddy said. "She can work enough fo' 'er n'Olivia both. If there's a problem, y'can leave word at the mercantile. We'll try t'stop in there ever so often t'get supplies n'mail; our son-in-law back home is forwardin' our mail here t'Harlan. Hopefully, gettin' established here in town'll be easy n'we'll be back 'fore the firs' cold snap."

"We'll certainly pray fo' good luck n'y'swift return," Mr. Grainger said. I think he would have preferred us never to have darkened his doorstep than to be stuck in this forced arrangement. Perhaps it just took him time to warm up to new ideas and it would all be okay.

"I hope the other fam'lies're as kind as y'all," Daddy said. "The Corrigans told us the Pracketts n'Carters might need help. We'll see if they can take in our other two girls firs', then move on t'the suggestions y'all gave us."

Mr. Grainger looked up at the sun. It was getting late, and he hadn't put away his tools or cleaned up for dinner yet. Momma and Daddy took the hint and thanked them again, then Mr. and Mrs. Grainger excused themselves to give our family time to say good-bye. Mr. Grainger headed for the shed, jerking the pitchfork out of the ground as he passed, and after Momma gave our clean, dry work clothes to Mrs. Grainger, the blonde woman walked back inside the house, closing the screen door quietly this time.

Momma took Olivia from my arms and I turned around, instinctively wrapping my arms around Daddy's waist. Just six weeks ago I had stood with my arms locked around Martha, not knowing if I'd ever see her again. I didn't want to feel like I was losing my Daddy, too, but I *did* feel that way, and the ache of it scraped the pit of my stomach – stinging like a raw spot deep inside.

Daddy kissed my head and whispered, "Be strong, now. Y'*can* do this."

I nodded and forced my arms to let him go, moving on to hug my sisters in turn. Then I stood and looked up at Momma. "I'll be all right," I said quietly. My voice sounded like it was coming from far away. "I'll help 'em as much as I can, I'll watch over Livie, n'I'll wait ev'ry day fo' y'all t'come back." Momma leaned down and kissed my cheek, a quick, firm peck that lingered on my skin after she stood up.

"Do all that y'can t'make 'em happy, n'don't cause trouble. Make sure Olivia b'haves, too. They're doin' us a huge favor by takin' in two o'y'all." Momma couldn't help but say her piece. Then she surprised me as she pulled me into a fierce hug. She exhaled slowly. "I don't know how long you'll have t'stay, but y'sure don't want t'wear out y'welcome in the b'ginnin', y'hear?" I nodded and she let go of me. I took Olivia's hand, and we watched our family gather into the wagon without us.

"Momma? Daddy?" Livie questioned, looking up at me confused. I reached down and picked her up. She reached her hand out toward the wagon. "Janie? Emwee?"

"Hush, now, Livie – they'll be back," I said, patting her back until she dropped her hand against my chest and started fiddling with the itchy lace on my dress.

Janie and Emily peered out the back at us; they suddenly looked awfully small to me. Tears were streaming down their cheeks, and they wiped them on their sleeves, trying to wave. Daddy snapped the reins and steered Bessie and Ginger in a loop and back onto the dirt road up toward town. Olivia and I watched the wagon until it disappeared around the bend, and then I truly felt alone, even with my sister in my arms. I took a deep breath of her hair, trying to stay calm. *This is how Martha felt when we pulled away from her and Jonathan.*

When I mustered the courage to turn around and face the farm again, I saw Mrs. Grainger standing on the front porch of the house. Her hands were fidgeting with her apron, but there was a gentle smile on her face.

"Are y'all hungry?" she called, sliding her hands deep inside the apron pockets. "I got a big pot o'beef stew on the stove. Y'n'Olivia're welcome t'eat y'fill. She eats table food, right?" My stomach growled at the thought of meat; we had been living on fried meal for weeks now.

"Yes, ma'am," I said. "She's two'n-a-half. She's been eatin' whatever suits 'er fo' a while now." I said, looking down the road after my family one more time. The dust had already settled, like the wagon had never even come this way.

I shifted Olivia to my other hip and looked back at Mrs. Grainger. Going into that house would somehow make all this *real*. I didn't want to do it, but I knew I couldn't be rude after such hospitality was extended to us. Daddy's words rang in my ears. *We need you to be strong. You can do this.* Mrs. Grainger opened the screen door and stood against it patiently. Dusk was just beginning to fall, and the warm glow from inside the house was beckoning. *I can do this.* I repeated to myself. Then I took a deep breath and pushed through the white gate.

Olivia squealed at the sudden movement and kicked her legs, bouncing herself on my hip. "Go, pony, go!" she giggled. I walked up onto the porch, and Mrs. Grainger gently wrapped her arm around both of us.

"Ev'rythin'll be jus' fine," she said softly in my ear, giving my shoulders a little squeeze. I could feel her hand shaking slightly and knew I wasn't the only one nervous about all this. "I know this mus' feel *awful* right now, but you'll be happy here."

We walked inside and she pointed left toward the kitchen. The whole house smelled of hearty beef stew and my mouth started to water. Grace winked at me and pulled out my chair across from Mr. Grainger, who was already eating.

"They'll be back 'fore y'know it, child… jus' wait n'see," she smiled – and then she sat the biggest bowl of delicious stew I had ever seen in front of us.

*Part 2*

# Welcome to Harlan

Half an hour later, we were almost through our second bowl of beef stew. I carefully gave every other spoonful to Olivia, as not to spill a drop, and Mrs. Grainger generously dipped a third helping into our bowl when it neared the bottom. I thanked her, and we continued to gobble it down. It was the savoriest meat I had *ever* tasted, and the potatoes and carrots melted in my mouth! I imagined anything would taste good after a month and a half of cornmeal, but it was obvious that Grace was genuinely a good cook.

The Graingers' kitchen was long and thin, a table and four chairs at one end with a pot-bellied stove, counter, and cabinets at the other. There was a door leading to the side yard in the middle, close to the stove. The table was pushed against the wall under an open window, and yellow curtains flapped gently in the night breeze. I could see their careful, even stitches around the edges, and it reminded me of how Momma had been teaching me cross-stitch in the evenings before the move. I wondered if we'd pick the lessons back up at our new home when we all got settled.

I glanced around at the striped wallpaper and wondered if the *whole* house was papered. None of the houses in Leadwood were papered. Jonathan's store had a few assorted rolls of wallpaper for sale, but they just sat collecting dust for five dollars apiece. When the bottom was falling out of lead-tapping, which was the town's main trade, I guessed papered houses were the last thing on people's minds.

"Good grief, child," Mr. Grainger suddenly snapped. His gruff voice startled me back to the present. He was sitting across the table, next to his wife. "I thought y'daddy said y'didn't eat much." His elbows were resting on either side of his own bowl, and a bit of stew dripped down his chin. He wiped it away with the back of his sleeve, keeping his eyes on us.

"I'm sorry," I said quickly. I sat the spoon down and reached for my napkin. Olivia reached for the bowl of stew and nearly sunk her whole hand in it before I could grab her wrist.

"No, Livie," I whispered in her ear. "We're done." She whined but didn't try to reach again.

"Anna, it's okay," Mrs. Grainger interjected, glancing at her husband. "Y'all eat up. We know y'all're half-starved from the long journey... there's more than enough fo' all of us."

Mr. Grainger's lips formed a tight, straight line. "There is, huh? N'are *you* the one out there plantin' n'harvestin'? Makin' sure y'put food on this here table? How d'ya know how much food we have t'spare? Y'ain't stepped into the fields in months."

Mrs. Grainger lowered her own spoon. He had said something that stung her, but I didn't know what. I bet it had to do with that lost baby, though.

"It's okay," I said quickly. "We're gettin' kind o'full... I don't want t'overdo on empty stomachs n'all. Thank y'fo' the fine cookin', ma'am, n'thank y'sir," I nodded to Mr. Grainger, "fo' puttin' it on the table n'sharin'."

Mr. Grainger looked at me with those dark eyes, and I felt cold all over, like I had a chest full of ice. "Eat all y'all want," he finally smirked in reply.

I didn't dare pick up my spoon. Instead I thought about Daddy's eyes; they were blue, and light danced around the edges when he laughed. I missed him already, something fierce.

"I *told* y't'eat up, girl," Mr. Grainger leaned forward on his elbows and growled.

I swallowed and quickly picked up my spoon, and with a shaky hand I fed Olivia the rest of the bowl, sparing only the last few bites for myself when she got full and sleepy in my arms. I watched Mr. Grainger out of the corner of my eye the whole time, but he never looked up from his bowl again. Soon enough he stood up and disappeared into the other room, his wife reaching for the dirty dishes left behind.

*Why did we have to eat three bowls like little pigs, face first in their slop?* I chided myself. I hadn't asked for the extra bowls – Grace had offered them… but obviously Mr. Grainger thought it was taking advantage of their hospitality. Momma would have certainly been ashamed of my behavior, and that made me feel just awful.

"Let me help y'clear the table, ma'am," I offered, eager to redeem myself. I sat Olivia on the floor, handed her the cornhusk doll she had carried all the way from Missouri, then gathered the rest of the dishes. Mrs. Grainger had a full wash bin on the counter, just like Momma always did… and in an instant, like recalling my Daddy's eyes, my heart also ached for my mother.

"Tell me 'bout y'self n'Olivia," Mrs. Grainger said, handing me a drying towel with a smile. "I'll wash, y'can dry." She soaped up a dishrag with a white cake of soap and got to work. I spread the towel out in my hands and waited for the first dish.

"There's not much t'tell, ma'am," I said quietly.

"Firs' of all, call me Grace. N'there mus' be somethin' t'tell. How old're y'all? How far've y'gone in school? What faith did y'practice back home?" she peppered me with questions while rinsing a bowl in the warm water. Then she shook it and placed it in my hands.

"Well, ma'am… *Grace*, I mean… m'full name's Anna Beth Atwood. I'm twelve years old, n'Olivia turned two a few months back." I kept my eyes on my work, careful not to drop her nice dishes.

"N'school?"

"I finished the seventh grade las' year," I told her proudly. "Times got hard las' fall n'the boys that were thirteen n'older left school t'help their fathers on the farms n'in the mines. The older girls left t'help their mothers run thin's at home, too. By summertime, we were down t'only nine kids. I was one o'the oldes' at twelve… Momma could've made me leave, too – but I'm grateful she didn't."

"N'how could she spare ya, the oldes' of y'sisters?" she asked.

"Well, she still had Martha. She's actually the oldes' sister, but then she got married. If we'd o'stayed in Missouri, I wouldn't have gone back fo' eighth grade." I said. I didn't know where the dishes went after I dried them, so as I finished, I stacked them on the sideboard. I took note of where she stored each of them in the cabinets above us, though, so tomorrow I could finish the job right.

"What all've y'learned?" Mrs. Grainger asked. "Seventh grade's quite the accomplishment."

"I can read n'write, if that's what y'mean," I said. "N'I can do some maths... but I'm not the bes' at it. We learned hist'ry n'science, too... a little bit o'ev'rythin', I s'pose."

"You're an hones' little thin', ain't ya?" She smiled as she closed the last cabinet and wiped her hands on her apron.

I put the towel on the counter and nodded. "Yes, ma'am. Daddy always told us *honesty's the bes' pol'cy*. People notice when others tell the truth, n'they don't right forget it. He said y'never know when their confidence might come in handy down the road."

Mrs. Grainger nodded, "Y'father gives sound advice, Miss Anna Beth. Don't forget what you've learned from y'parents; they sound like very good people. I admire 'em wantin' t'do what's bes' fo' y'kids, even though it's hard."

Olivia wandered over to me and reached up her arms. "*Up*, Anna," she whined. I gathered her into my arms and kissed her cheek. She nuzzled her head into the nape of my neck in return and stared warily at Grace again. "Where Momma?" she whispered.

Mr. Grainger coughed somewhere in the back of the house, and the sudden noise startled Grace. She looked in his general direction with a jerk, then back at me. "D'ya want t'go outside fo' a bit, Anna? Can I call y'jus' Anna? We can sit on the porch, n'Olivia can play in the yard 'til it gets too dark."

I shrugged my shoulders with a nod, and Grace ushered us out through the kitchen door, then around the side of the house to sit on the front porch steps. Olivia tottered out into the yard chasing after a lightening bug, and I told her to stay close. Mrs. Grainger sat down next to me, and I scooted over just a bit, wanting to give myself more space but not offend her kindness.

"Y'father, I can see by y'raisin', was probably well read in the Bible – weren't he?" she asked, crossing her arms in her lap.

"Yes, ma'am, we went t'church ev'ry time the doors were open. Daddy also gathered us 'round the fireplace fo' prayer 'fore bedtime mos' nights, n'he always turned grace 'fore meals. While we were travelin', he even turned grace over *fritters*."

That made Grace laugh, then she glanced over her shoulder toward the house, her smile faltering just slightly. "I wish m'husband could live it ev'ry day. I go t'church, but he's often too busy t'uphold his religious respons'bility," she confided. Her eyes wandered warmly to Olivia, who was standing stock still to better examine a ladybug on the fence post.

"M'father, though, *he* was like yours. He'd go down in the holler by our house ev'ry night n'call on the Lord. Sometimes, when I was s'posed t'be in bed, I'd sneak out o'the house n'follow 'im t'his favorite prayer place. I *loved* t'hear m'Pa pray. When he'd really get ahold o'the Spirit, the hills echoed with the yearnin' t'be heard... sometimes it was full o'grievin' n'sorrowful sounds, but mos'ly it was grateful fo' all His blessin's, big n'small." She sighed and leaned back on her hands. "Sometimes, in the shelter o'those great oak trees, it felt like God was right there in the midst of us." She paused, staring out toward the mountains like she was looking back in time. "He never said so, but I think he knew I was there listenin' n'feelin' it right alongside 'im."

"Does he live 'round here?" I asked, plucking up a piece of grass and twirling it between my fingers. How she talked about the Lord and *feeling* His Spirit reminded me of our church back home. My parents had told me every person in the whole world gets an opportunity to feel after the Lord and find 'im for themselves, and I was still waiting to feel something... something I had never felt before, something I was sure could only be the God of all creation Himself talking to little old me.

"No, he passed away several years back. It was the coldes' winter I can 'member. He was on his way home from a trip, n'when he didn't come home Momma went out lookin' fo' 'im. She found his body lyin' jus' off the road a couple miles away, in a fresh bank o'snow, n'she told me his hand was clasped over his heart n'his eyes cas' upward t'Heaven. He was frozen through n'through, o'course, but t'think of 'im knowin' where he was headed when his time came still makes me feel all warm inside." Mrs. Grainger glanced at me and shook her head. "I shouldn't be tellin' y'all this with y'parents jus' settin' out! Forgive me. I los' myself fo' a moment."

"It's okay." I gave her a quick smile. "I know they'll be back soon. Daddy promised. Besides, I love stories, so y'can tell me all y'want o'yours."

"Well, in that case," she continued, "I was a little older than you when m'Daddy went t'res'. I was fifteen, n'the nex' spring Momma 'ranged fo' m'marriage t'Mr. Grainger. She felt like I was old enough t'be a good wife n'mother, n'truth be told she couldn't afford t'feed all us kids without m'Pa. I was the oldes', n'my fo' younger brothers were able t'fill m'Pa's shoes n'work the farm."

"Y'must've been horribly sad," I frowned. I thought it hard to live with strangers for just a while, but my current situation paled in comparison to Grace *marrying* a stranger, especially a gruff man like Mr. Grainger! I shuddered to think of it.

"It *was* hard at firs', n'I was sad," she admitted. "Mr. Grainger was nine years older than me, n'he already had taken over his father's farm. His parents passed in an accident 'bout a year 'fore we married – I think his Pa was a mighty hard man n'a drinker to boot. Anyways, Momma said Mr. Grainger was turned diff'rent n'was an upstanding man in the community – she told me t'be proud that he accepted someone like me." Grace shook her head. I waited for her to continue.

"Sometimes I think a good name's all that matters t'folks 'round here, but then again, I *do* know the Bible says t'choose a good name over great riches," she said. I thought about Mr. Grainger and his oily hair and yellow armpits. Secretly, if that's what a good name was, I would be tempted to take the riches.

Grace shook her head again and laughed this time. "Oh, listen t'me go on n'on again! I know m'husband can seem a little rough 'round the edges, Anna, but appearance ain't ev'rythin'. If y'show 'im proper respect, he'll return it ten-fold. We have a good life together, all thin's considered."

I nodded. "I'll try m'bes' t'do that, ma'am." Lord knows I didn't want to get on Mr. Grainger's bad side.

Silence fell between us. We listened to the crickets chirping in the grass and watched Olivia, who had sat down by the porch's flowerbed to play with her doll. The sun had drooped low in the sky, the edges barely hanging on the mountaintops. After a while longer, Grace stood up and patted me on the back.

"Let's head t'bed," she suggested. "I'm sure y'all're both worn plum out."

I got up and headed for Olivia, who had sprawled on her stomach in the soft grass, looking at her doll. Her eyes were nearly closed. I scooped her up, and she curved into me, like we fit together just right. I could feel her hot breath on my neck as she succumbed to sleep. I carried her up the porch steps where Grace was holding the door open.

"I assume Mr. Grainger'll take y'into the fields at firs' light," she said. "Teach y'the ropes n'all. D'ya think Olivia'll be okay with me 'til y'get back fo' lunch?"

"I imagine so," I said, standing patiently while Grace quietly shut the door behind us. "She usually follows me 'round ev'rywhere, but if she has 'er doll t'play with it should be fine… n'a snack. She *loves* t'eat."

"Don't we all," Grace laughed. Olivia stirred at the sound, and I patted on her as Grace went to gather some blankets from another room. "Jack n'I sleep in the back room," she said when she came back. She motioned to the shut bedroom door off the fireplace room. Then she led us back to the kitchen, laying the blankets on the table.

"You're welcome t'sleep in the sittin' room, but I think the kitchen'll be more comfortable. If we leave the window open, it's the cooles' room in the house… n'if you'end up stayin' into winter, we can leave a log burnin' in the stove fo' heat."

"The kitchen's fine," I assured her. "Thank y'kindly."

"You're welcome, Anna Beth of Leadwood." She winked at me and began to spread the blankets out between the stove and table, close to the side door. By the time she was done we had a nice, soft pallet. She folded the top blanket back a bit, and I carefully shifted Olivia from my shoulder to the pillow; she was heavy like a sack of taters, her mouth sticky with beef stew.

"We've been used t'a bouncy wagon bed, so this is gonna be a nice change," I said.

Grace grinned and handed me a white piece of clothing that had been tucked under her arm. "This is one o'm'night gowns. It'll be a little big on ya, but at leas' y'won't be sleepin' in y'clothes."

I took it and rubbed the fabric between my fingers. It was *so* soft, probably silk! *This is store bought, just to sleep in*, I considered with another pang of homesickness. Store bought clothes were too expensive for my family; Momma made all our clothes. I looked down at my floral and lacey dress, remembering how Momma had saved her canning money all year to buy enough material to make each of us girls a new dress. We wore these to church last Christmas morning, matching smiles and matching dresses, just like every year before. We always got compliments, but nothing Momma made was as fancy as this silk nightgown.

"Thinkin' 'bout y'fam'ly?" Grace asked, pulling me back from Christmas time in Missouri. She was still standing near the pallet, watching me finger her silky gown.

My face burned red. "Yes, ma'am," I whispered.

"Call me *Grace*, Anna," she smiled.

"Sorry… Grace. Yes, I was thinkin' 'bout Christmas time. Ev'ry year Momma makes us a new dress." I looked down at the nightgown in my hands. "I wonder if she'll be back in time t'make us one this year."

Grace wrapped an arm around my shoulders. "We'll pray they'll be home long 'fore Christmas, but fo' right now y'bes' get some sleep. Mornin' comes early in this house, n'there's a powerful lot a work t'be done."

I nodded and we said good night. She blew out the candle on the table, and I watched her slip through the doorway, disappearing into the darkness of the house. I sat down on the pallet next to Olivia and was immediately seized by a sudden fear. The moon was casting shadows into the corners of the room; this unfamiliar house was the worst kind of stranger! The arrangement of furniture, colors and even the leftover smells of not-my-Momma's beef stew were unsettling to my senses. For a panicky moment I couldn't make sense of where I was, or why I was in this place with these people and not at home or even the wagon with my family. Mrs. Grainger was nice enough, but I didn't *know* her and her husband. They didn't know us, neither.

I laid down and closed my eyes tight, trying to remember how Martha's hands smelled like honey biscuits and bacon. I could *almost* feel the safe warmth of her hands on my cheeks, but when I opened my eyes the sensation fled into the shadows, leaving me in this strange room, ripped open and bare again. I watched dark, fuzzy shapes contort slowly across the kitchen walls. My thoughts jumped to clowns in a traveling circus.

I remembered when the circus came to a town near Leadwood; I was nine years old, and we didn't have enough money to go. Jonathan and Martha were courting, however, and he had saved his money up for the special occasion. For weeks after, Martha teased my sisters and me about how we didn't get to go see the circus... but every once in a while when she was in a particularly good mood, she would have mercy and tell us about far away creatures like tigers, elephants, and lions. I couldn't really picture a ring of fire and an animal willingly jumping through it unscathed, but it must have been a marvelous and wonderful sight!

I bit my lip and sat back up, groping in the darkness to find Grace's nightgown on the chair nearby. I undressed quietly, carefully folding up my Sunday dress and sitting it back on the chair, and then I pulled the gown over my head. It was slick against my skin, spreading an oddly warm sensation all over my body. A strange gown in a strange place went together better than an itchy old Sunday dress in a new place. I sighed and laid back down, facing my sister, trying to get comfortable.

Olivia was sleeping peacefully, her angelic features glowing in the moonlight. I loved those delicate, little blonde curls the most. They bounced around her face when she giggled. The thought brought a smile to my face as I snuggled close to her, closing my eyes. I breathed deeply, over and over. The honey scent of her hair was thick and irresistible, and I began to feel my muscles relax. I pretended we were back in Missouri, cuddled together in our bed under the window like always. The breeze from the window above helped me believe it. I could see Janie and Emily across the room on the other side of the fireplace, and Momma and Daddy by the kitchen. Daddy had his arm hanging over Momma's waist as they spooned together. Every time he snored, Momma would nudge him. I took another deep breath of honey, and *finally* drifted off into the darkness swelling around me.

*8*

The next morning a gentle and apprehensive hand shook me awake. Momma's touch was always rough and quick because she was busy with morning chores. I blinked heavily, confused as a striped kitchen came into focus. Then with a jolt I remembered where I was and what all had happened. I bolted upright in the pallet, and Olivia made a garbled noise and rolled over with a yawn, settling back into her sleep.

"It's okay, Anna," Mrs. Grainger whispered. "I don't mean t'scare ya." Her blonde curls were already pulled up in a tight bun, a few framing her face.

"No harm, ma'am," I said, rubbing my eyes open all the way. "*Grace*, I mean."

"It's early. I'm gonna take Olivia t'the back room so she can get 'er sleep out." Grace reached over me and carefully scooped my sister into her arms.

When she left the room, I pulled the silk nightgown over my head with one swoop and slid back into my comfortable brown skirt and cream-colored blouse that had been exchanged for my Sunday dress on the chair nearby. I tucked the blouse in all the way around and smoothed my skirt down with shaky hands.

Grace walked back in and nodded approvingly. "Y'dress fas'! That's good. Jack's already waitin' fo' y'by the shed." She handed me a pone of cornbread left over from dinner the night before. "Eat this on y'way out…"

she winked at me as she slipped a second square into my dress pocket, "n'*that's* fo' later. When I was with child, I used t'nearly starve in them fields. I found cornbread stuck t'm'ribs better than anythin' else on the long days."

"Thank ya, ma'am," I nodded as she opened the kitchen door, and then I walked down the steps out into the side yard.

"N'Anna, know this," she said suddenly. "I know how tirin' the fields can be, n'how cross Jack can get when he's tired. Do what he says n'ask no questions; you'll get along jus' fine." I swallowed my nervousness down with another nod and headed toward the shed and chicken coop.

The sun was just beginning to warm the morning sky with colors of pink and orange, like God had dipped his paintbrush in a rich pallet and brushed it across the sky with a few swipes. I stuffed the cornbread into my mouth, hungrily devouring it, contemplating how God could make beautiful sunrises here and in Leadwood and all over the world for that matter. He really must be big enough to hold the whole world in his hands. That was a comforting thought.

Up ahead Mr. Grainger leaned against the wooden shed, one foot resting on a chopping block with an axe splintering the top. He watched me walk up, his arms crossed over his chest. When I got close enough, he spat a black glob of tobacco at the side of the stump, some of it catching on the toe of his boot. When he stood up, he dragged his shoe sideways through the grass to clean it, then spit again. The second glob landed closer to my shoe. I took a step back and he narrowed his eyebrows. I cleared my throat, trying to force my heart back down in my chest.

"Good mornin', Mr. Grainger," I said as polite as I could. "How can I be helpin' y't'day?" He chewed the remainder of his tobacco slowly and just kept staring at me.

"You're late," he finally said.

"I come on out soon as Grace woke me, sir," I offered, squinting into the brightening sun.

"Don't argue with me, girl, n'don't make excuses." He picked up a burlap sack from the ground and shoved it into my hands, then motioned to a pair of pruning shears and a hoe lying in the grass. "Take those," he ordered, picking up his own sack and grabbing the shovel that was leaning against the shed. "We'll *see* how much help ya're n'if y'daddy was nothin' but a liar."

I gasped, taking great offense to his words, but bit my tongue so hard I tasted blood. I could not mess this up for myself and Olivia, nor did I want to disappoint my Daddy. After us eating like pigs last night, me backtalking would probably be strike two, and y'know what they say. Strike three and you're out.

Mr. Grainger chuckled as I held my tongue, then took off walking at a long stride. I grabbed the tools and hurried to catch up with him. The green stalks of corn in front of us waved gently in the breeze, clusters of yellow dotting the expanse of the field. *How will we harvest a crop this size by ourselves?* I didn't have any farming experience besides tending a small vegetable garden!

Mr. Grainger stopped at the edge of the fields and I stopped just behind him, trying to catch my breath after hurrying along with those heavy, awkward tools. He considered me for a quick moment, then launched right into explaining what was to be done.

"We're startin' here in the cornfields – I've already been workin' it. When we're done here, we'll move t'the taters, then beans after that." He paused to spit another wad of tobacco into the grass. "I aim t'be finished by mid-fall, 'fore the weather turns cold n'frosts overnight. Frost'll kill the crop n'no crop is no money... I trus' y'know what no money would mean." I nodded with a gulp. No money meant no charity cases.

"Now, I'll show y'how t'pop corn *one* time, then you're on y'own," he continued. He grabbed a nearby cornstalk, wrapped his strong hand around the green and yellow ear, and twisted it hard. "Y'grab it, green n'all, n'pull up as ya twis' 'round." The ear popped right off, and he dropped it into his sack.

I nodded my understanding, trying to show my best manners and impress him even though he had nearly called my Daddy a liar, which he *wasn't*.

He jerked the pruning shears from my hand and held them up. "If y'cain't pop one, cut it right here at the base." He pointed with the shears to the place where the ear met the stalk. Then he shoved the shears back into my hands and pointed to the hoe. "If y'see a snake, cut its head off with that."

I looked down at the rusty hoe and swallowed hard. "There's snakes?" My voice came out like a squeak. I remembered too late I wasn't supposed to ask any questions.

"Look at me when y'speak, girl," he growled. My head snapped up and our eyes met. "O'*course*, there's snakes."

"Yes, sir. I'm sorry." I kept my eyes on him until he looked away first. Daddy always told me to look people in the eye so they could see you were honest.

"Y'start in this row. I'm startin' the nex'. We'll both move wes'," he said, pointing to the left. "We'll skip ev'ry other row since we're workin' the same field. Got it?"

I adjusted the sack around my neck and spoke louder, hopefully sounding more confident than I felt. "Yes, sir."

"I cain't afford t'be slowed down by the likes o'you. If y'need help y'better holler loud. I'll probably be several rows ahead 'fore it's time t'break fo' lunch," he said, walking to the row beside mine. He looked back at me, wiped his nose on the sleeve of his shirt, and disappeared into the cornstalks like a rock thrown in a pond. The stalks around him rippled out as the field swallowed him whole, leaving me all alone on the edge.

I looked down the long row in front of me. The corn towered above my head on both sides, the tops curving inward, creating an ominous, shadowy tunnel. The cornfield across from our old school, where my sisters and I had picked the perfect ear for Olivia's doll, did not look this foreboding. Maybe because we were all in there together, and it was a happy affair.

I glanced back at the Graingers' house. *Livie's gonna be scared when she wakes up in this strange place and can't find me*, I worried. I sincerely hoped for both our sakes that she wouldn't cry the whole time I was gone. I sighed and stared at the farm tools in my hands. *Might as well get on with it*, and with a slow breath I pushed into the corn row.

I laid the hoe and shears at my feet, grabbed an ear of corn, and pulled hard. I twisted and yanked up at the same time, but it didn't pop like Mr. Grainger's had. I stood on my tiptoes and pulled harder. Nothing. I rested my hands on my hips for a moment and then reached down to pick up the pruning shears. With careful aim I squeezed them around the corn's base, and the ear fell to the ground with a thwack. I grinned. *This might not be so hard after all*, I thought smugly as I stooped to put it into my sack.

It didn't take long at all to realize, however, that this was false hope. The shears were heavy and became harder to wield as my muscles tired – and I tired quickly. Sweat soaked through my blouse, and the skin between my thumb and pointer finger started to blister after only a few rows. At one point I laid the shears on the ground and examined my hands. The painful, red bubbles were squishy under my dirty finger, and my hands ached when I closed and opened my fists. I prayed the blisters wouldn't break open. I didn't want dirt and grime getting into the open wounds to fester.

Daddy cut his hand in the lead mines one time that I could remember. His tool slipped and cut his palm wide open. Momma cleaned and wrapped it best she could, but the sore bubbled up angry, all white and bloody, and the skin around the edges turned a blackish-purple color. He finally went to the town doctor and got a salve to rub in the wound, and it did eventually heal – but it left a deep scar and a hefty bill to add to our growing debt. That was the beginning of my knowing there wasn't enough money to go around all the time even though they tried to keep it from us.

I knelt and peered into my sack. It had gotten too heavy to carry around my neck, so I had been dragging it along behind me. Bugs were crawling all over the corn frantic-like; it reminded me of sifting weevils out of the cornmeal those last weeks of our trip. As hard as the journey had been, I'd rather go back to digging for mealworms and starving with my family than harvesting corn in Mr. Grainger's field any day.

A faint ringing sound stirred me from my thoughts. I stood up and tried to determine which way to go. I thought the sound was coming from my right, but cornfields had a way of turning a person all around and up-side down.

"Anna!" Mr. Grainger bellowed, his sound much closer. I scrambled to pick up the shears and hoe and tug on the sack of corn with my free hand. I hurried as fast as I could, but by the time I stepped out of the row onto the neatly cut grass, Mr. Grainger was standing with a sack thrown over his shoulder and two more resting at his feet. The sun beat down on me like his glare, and my stomach growled loudly much to my embarrassment.

"We're gonna have t'work on y'bein' prompt," he said.

"I'm sorry, sir," I said, still a bit out of breath.

Mr. Grainger leaned around me and looked at the sack behind my legs. "Y'managed t'fill it, huh? I only gave y'one sack this mornin', but after lunch I'll be givin' y'two. Now that y'have the hang o'poppin' corn, I expect y't'work faster." I nodded as he bounced his sack higher on his shoulder and picked up the other two with his free hand. His arm muscles bulged under his sleeves. "We'll drop these off in the shed n'head t'the house fo' a quick lunch, then work 'til dusk."

He started walking, and I grabbed my bag with one hand and started to pull it across the grass, balancing the shears and hoe in the crook of my other arm. Mr. Grainger turned and looked at me.

"Why're y'draggin' y'sack, girl? Too heavy?"

"I'm gettin' a blister on m'hand, sir," I said, not wanting to confess that it was indeed too heavy. I needed to help this man, make him keeping us worth his while. Last thing I wanted was him thinking I was too weak for the job.

He dropped his sacks and grabbed my hands before I saw it coming. His sweaty, dirty hands made me cringe, and I impulsively tried to pull away. He let my good hand slip lose but tightened his grip on my blistered hand, yanking it back toward him.

"Don't be so jumpy, girl; let me take a look." He examined my fingers and pushed against the blister with his thumb. I held my breath cause it hurt like the dickens, then my stomach flipped. I breathed a sigh of relief when he let go of my hand and picked up his sacks.

"That ain't nothin'. *Carry* that sack. I won't have y'draggin' it all the way t'the shed n'rippin' the bottom out," he said. As he walked away, I looked down at my sack full of corn to the brim.

I laid my tools down and tried to pick it up. No matter how I tried, I couldn't get my arms around it. I finally managed to wrestle it over my shoulder by the strap and hoist it onto my back, my knees buckling as I leaned forward to balance the weight. I looked down at the shears and hoe. If I reached for them, I'd tip right over and spill the corn. *We're coming right back out this afternoon*, I reasoned, and decided to leave them where they lay. I took slow steps toward the shed and made it to the door just as Mr. Grainger heaved his last sack inside.

"Give me y'sack," he said, holding out his hand.

I slipped the strap off my shoulder and as it slid through my hands my blister broke open. I jerked my hand to my chest with a gasp, and my sack fell to the ground. Corn spilled out everywhere! Hot tears stung my eyes as I looked at my blurry hand; clear fluid mingled with blood oozed from the sore.

Mr. Grainger cursed, and my pain turned to sudden fear… the only time I had ever heard similar words was when a man got drunk at the saloon in Leadwood and the bartender threw him out in the street. Daddy and I were walking by, and Daddy just squeezed my shoulders and steered me on past.

"I'm terribly sorry, sir," I apologized, kneeling to gather the corn. The chickens had come running and were fighting me for it as I shooed them back.

"Move," Mr. Grainger growled. He pushed me out of the way, and I hit the grass, chickens scattering in all directions and clucking madly.

He stuffed the corn back into the bag with just a few handfuls, then tied the top and swung the bag inside the shed with the others. "Run on n'tell Grace t'bandage that hand. I don't want t'look at it while I eat m'lunch," Mr. Grainger added, his lip curling up with the words like they smelled rotten, "n'don't think it gets y'out o'afternoon work, neither."

I clambered to my feet and took off like a jackrabbit toward the house. Grace saw me coming out the window and opened the side door with a smile that quickly turned to concern. Olivia pushed past her and jumped up and down on the steps. She was wearing the little tan play dress Momma had made her, her sunny curls bouncing around her chubby, delighted face.

"*Anna!* Anna's comin'!" she pointed at me and squealed with surprise.

I reached my sister and wrapped my arms around her, being careful not to let anything rub my hurt hand. She laughed and patted my head with both hands. I squeezed her tight and just breathed. My heart was racing a mile a minute. Mr. Grainger had cursed and pushed me. *Daddy never would have done such things nor would he have allowed it.*

"I missed ya, Livie," I whispered to my sister, tears dampening my eyes again. I missed much more than her, but she was all I had left to cling to.

*I could pack up our Sunday clothes and walk to town, find Momma and Daddy,* the thought jumped into my head. Before I could wrap my mind around it, though, a second pressed in at the edges. *They'd blame me. Momma would say I messed up a good situation, and Daddy would have disappointed eyes.* I knew staying here with a roof and food was a good opportunity for us, even if I hated it.

"Miss ya," Olivia echoed, bringing me back to her and Grace, who was standing over us with eyes full of genuine worry. I swallowed my feelings, hard like a rock and rough around the edges, stood up and swung my sister onto my hip.

Olivia pointed at Mrs. Grainger. "Gace," she said.

"Yes, Livie, that's Grace," I nodded. "Did y'have fun this mornin'?"

She eagerly held up her cornhusk doll. "Daw," she grinned. "Gace. Daw. Me," she said, pointing to herself.

"She played dolls with ya?" I asked. Oliva's grin widened and she nodded. I forced a smile at Grace. "You've made a friend."

Grace's face relaxed and she winked at me. "It didn't take long. She woke up missin' y'n'not knowin' where she was, but I brought 'er out on the porch n'showed 'er all the corn n'told 'er y'were workin' out there, n'that you'd be back here soon. She stopped cryin' when I brought out the cornbread, n'then we played with 'er doll after the breakfas' dishes. She's a real good girl."

Grace opened the door and I followed her into the kitchen. She had already set the table for lunch, left over beef stew and corn bread. I lowered Olivia into one of the chairs. My stomach growled loudly. The food smelled delicious after the long morning I had.

"I take it y'had a rough start?" Grace asked, glancing at me as she gave every place setting a spoon.

I held out my hand. "I broke a blister. Mr. Grainger said y'could bandage it?"

"Oh, *Anna*." She stopped what she was doing and hurried to the wash bin to wet a rag. She came back quickly and dabbed my hand gently, shaking her head. The wet cloth stung, but I tried not to flinch. "Y'had t'use the shears," Grace observed.

"I cain't twis' the corn off like Mr. Grainger can," I admitted. "I don't think I'm tall enough or somethin'."

Grace pulled me toward the wash bin and soaped up my hand. I clenched my jaws together and bore the fiery sting, but tears pressed on the back of my eyes. I bit the inside of my cheek to keep them from watering over. I didn't want her seeing any weakness and telling her husband.

"I never could pop the corn well, n'I'm taller than ya," she confided. "Those shears n'I developed a love-hate relationship, we did. They helped me harves' the corn, but they tore up m'hands somethin' awful." I glanced at her hands and saw light tan scars.

Grace rinsed the soap out of my wound and dabbed my hand dry with a clean towel. Then she wrapped it up with several long, white slips of cloth, tying the ends in a knot. "That should keep y'hand from blisterin' further," she said. "Remind me 'fore y'go out again, n'I'll wrap y'other hand, so y'won't get any more."

"Thank ya, ma'am," I said sincerely.

"I 'preciate y'helpin' us with the harves', Anna," she added, patting me on the shoulder. "Jack cain't do it by 'imself, even though he'd kill 'imself tryin'."

Mr. Grainger came through the kitchen door and it slammed shut behind him, startling all three of us. Olivia cowered in her chair as he walked to the counter and grabbed the wet rag from the wash bin. I noted his white shirt with yellow stains, remoistened around the arms and neck, with renewed disgust. Sweat dripped from his black hair down his face, which he wiped off, then wrapped the cool, wet rag around the back of his neck.

"Why ain't y'eatin' yet?" he asked me. I looked at Grace.

"I was bandagin' 'er hand, Jack," Grace said gently. "She opened a blister this mornin'."

"That could've already been done n'her halfway through lunch by now. Y'all were standin' in here jawin'. Y'intend t'baby 'er the whole time she's here?" He spit the words at his wife as he walked to the table and sat down, reaching for a piece of cornbread. He kept his dark eyes on Grace; they were dancing like he was daring her to answer.

"I wasn't..." Grace started carefully.

"Good, 'cause she's got t'toughen up. She's here t'help *us*, not the other way 'round," he finished. "I don't take in no charity cases."

I quietly lowered myself into the chair next to my sister. "I'll eat quickly," I offered.

Grace sat down next to her grizzly bear of a husband, and we all ate in silence. Olivia stared warily at Mr. Grainger, munching on a pone of cornbread, but I didn't look at anyone. I just concentrated on alternating spoonfuls of stew between myself and Olivia as quickly as I could without spilling. For the life of me I couldn't grasp why he hated me so. I hadn't been here more than a day and had tried my best to be good, respectful help.

"How much longer 'til the harves' is in, Jack?" Grace finally spoke, cutting the air between us all like a knife.

"Y'know how much is left," he grumbled. "A month or two."

Olivia and I finished the last bit of our beef stew, and she slid out of her chair to go play with her doll on our little pallet. "This was delicious, ma'am," I thanked Grace for both of us.

"You're welcome, Anna," she smiled.

Mr. Grainger scooted his chair out and stood up with a huff. "It's yesterday's soup," he rolled his eyes. "Nothin' special. Come on, girl, back t'work." He adjusted his suspenders and walked toward the side door.

"Jack, y'all've only been here fo' twenty minutes!" Grace protested.

Mr. Grainger grabbed the door handle and wheeled around at her. "N'that's *ten* minutes too long with a field that size left t'be harvested!" he hollered. Olivia shrunk into a ball at his feet.

He pointed out the window toward the swaying corn. "*You* haven't been out there in three months, if y'member, so don't go talkin' like y'know somethin'," he growled. Grace's gaze fell to the floor, and he turned his dark eyes on me. "Let's go, I said."

"Yes, sir," I answered quickly. I followed him into the side yard with a quick glance back at Grace, who stood on the stoop, holding the door open. I nodded, trying to let her know I would be fine, but inside I was shaking like a leaf.

Olivia ran to the door and hollered after me, realizing suddenly I was leaving.

"I'll be back soon, Livie!" I called. "Be a good girl fo' Grace now."

Grace picked Olivia up, who squirmed in her arms until Grace started swaying and patting her back. Livie wiped at her eyes with the back of her hand, allowing herself to be soothed, but her pouty lips and rosy cheeks nearly broke my heart in two.

Mr. Grainger disappeared in the shed and came out with more gunnysacks. He threw two at me and took five for himself. He glanced around. "Where's y'tools?"

I gathered my wits back together and pointed toward the fields. "I left 'em at the edge o'm'corn row, sir," I remembered. "I cain't carry 'em 'long with m'sack."

"Y'stupid girl. If it rains, they'll rus'," he snapped. He picked up his own tools and took off walking, shaking his head. I followed at a sprint.

"I'm sorry, sir! I'll bring 'em back t'the shed ev'ry time from now on," I assured him.

"That's right, y'will. If y'cain't get it all in one, y'make trips. Got it?"

"Yes, sir."

We reached the fields, and Mr. Grainger pushed right into the row he had been working before lunch without another word. I looked down at the two sacks in my hands; I was several rows behind. I didn't know how I would ever work fast enough to catch up to him *or* fill double by dinner! *I'd give my left leg to be back in our bumpy wagon somewhere between Missouri and Harlan.* I sighed, found my tools, and begrudgingly let the corn swallow me whole.

*9*

My first day went downhill from lunch. My bandaged right hand caused the shears to twist and shave green slips off the stalk; I couldn't hold the blades straight enough to make a clean cut. I tried shifting the weight of the tool to my left hand and using my bandaged hand to push it closed. That yielded a little more success, but in no time at all my left hand started to burn.

I tucked the shears under my arm and examined the fresh blisters on my other palm. In my nervousness to not upset Mr. Grainger, I had forgotten to remind Grace to bandage my good hand. I took a deep breath and returned to the tedious work, every open and close of the shears sending pain through my hand and up my arm. The sun was stretching to touch the west by then, the air cooling slightly as early evening crept closer.

As I toiled down the rows, I became lost in my thoughts. I wondered mostly where Momma and Daddy had ended up. Did they sleep in the wagon somewhere in town? Did Daddy luck into a job on his first day and was he now hard at work in the coal mines making his first paycheck? I also wondered if the other families recommended by the Corrigans had taken in Janie and Emily. If so, would we go to the same school come fall? *School. Mr. Grainger probably wouldn't let me go.* I frowned while I worked on. I already missed Janie and Emily and that surprised me a bit. They were the life of the family, their mischief and laughter always making us grin, even when we didn't want to. It wasn't long before the tears came, and this time

I let them fall. They streamed down my cheeks and dripped off my chin, and no matter how much I wiped them away with my sleeves, my eyes just kept leaking.

Dusk slowly settled around me like a blanket, and it got eerily dark in the stalks. I had filled a bag and a half but wasn't going to be able to see long enough to fill the last half. I wiped the sweat from my forehead with the back of my bandaged hand and thought of a warm dinner and cool bath. Both of my hands throbbed now, along with my head, and my eyes felt swollen and heavy. At least I had gotten all my tears out when no one could see.

The bell rang in the distance, and I heard Mr. Grainger holler. He sounded equally far away. Butterflies turned my stomach inside out and I froze. I had left my full bag at the grass's edge before starting this row… *but would he get angry and curse or push me again for not filling the second sack all the way to the top?*

"Get out here, girl!" he bellowed impatiently. He was moving closer.

I picked up the hoe and shears, grabbed my half bag, and took off at a sprint – yanking loose corn from the stalks and stuffing them in the bag as I passed by. I emerged from the corn to see Mr. Grainger and his five sacks resting at his feet, all full to the brim. He looked me over; I must have been a sight. I was sweaty and dirty, and I could feel my hair slipping out of its braid and sticking to my damp, wet cheeks.

"How'd y'fair?" he asked, already taking inventory of my sacks with his greedy eyes.

"One-n'a-half, sir," I said. "Maybe three-quarters," I hoped.

He chuckled and spit some tobacco juice in the grass. "T'morrow you'll've three sacks, mornin' n'afternoon. You'll get faster ev'ry day," he said. I wasn't sure if that was encouragement or an order, but I nodded regardless.

Six bags in a day was not possible, and my mind wandered to the poor Hebrew children in the book of Exodus when Pharaoh gave them more work to do because he assumed they were being idle. I would just have to make the best of it like they did, until God sent Moses to rescue them. Maybe Daddy was already on his way back to rescue me.

"Bring y'sacks t'the shed, then y'can feed the chickens. There's plenty o'chores t'do 'round here when you're not in the fields," Mr. Grainger said, walking on toward the shed.

"Yes, sir," I sighed wearily, following after. I could already see Mr. Grainger, who didn't want us in the first place, was going to make this stay as difficult as possible… and a seed of resentment sprouted little shoots of anger and frustration within me. Daddy always said we should never *hate* people, so I tried to look for the good in Mr. Grainger before the bad took over my mind, but all I could think about was oily hair, yellow armpits and curse words.

"Hustle up, girl – Grace'll have dinner on the table soon!" Mr. Grainger barked as I lagged behind. I was bone tired but mustered a jog, making three trips to Mr. Grainger's two. At least he didn't say anything else; he just watched me scurry back and forth.

When I had hauled my last bag of corn to the shed, Mr. Grainger waved me inside. The little space was dark and dank, smelling strongly of earth. There were no windows, just glistening dust floating in the last rays of sun forced through the cracks in the planked walls. It was hot, too, and sweat began to trickle down the back of my neck and hollow between my shoulder blades. My blouse stuck to me uncomfortably as I handed the sack to Mr. Grainger.

"That ought t'do it," he said, tying up the last sack of corn and dusting his hands off. He had heaped the bags one on top of another to make the most of the space. Five of them stacked just about touched the sloping tin roof at its highest point. He motioned to a trough of loose corn to my right. "I break a few ears up each day fo' the chickens. Grace feeds 'em some handfuls in the mornin', n'I feed 'em again at dusk. You'll be takin' over those chores now," he said, "n'I'm gonna get ready fo' dinner." He pushed past me and stepped down from the shed, headed for the house.

I looked back at the trough and closed my eyes momentarily, thinking about the chickens we gave Martha and Jonathan. Those silly sisters of mine had named every one of them. My favorite was Sassafras, who tried to steal the grain from the other chickens when they were distracted. I opened my eyes, gathered the hem of my dress up, and pretended I was back in Missouri about to feed *our* chickens. That made the burden a bit lighter. I was careful to hold my dress low and lady-like, like Martha had taught me. I scooped some corn into the makeshift pocket and stepped down from the shed, slinging a handful of corn across the ground.

"Here, chick, chick, chick," I called. The chickens came running from all directions, clucking and ruffling their feathers. They started to fight over the kernels, and I grinned. There were a few Sassafrases in this group, too!

I threw another handful out to the right, and then to the left again, and the clump of chickens scattered out after the feed. "There's enough fo' all o'y'all," I assured them. They clucked and pecked the ground frantically like it was their last supper. I scattered the last handfuls and dropped the hem of my dress, dusting it out with the backs of my blistered hands. Then I closed the shed door and latched it, pleased with myself for once that day. *Feeding chickens was one chore I couldn't mess up!*

When I walked into the kitchen a few minutes later, the Graingers and Olivia were already seated at the table eating. My sister's face lit up as it had at lunch time. "Anna!" she squealed. She slid out of Grace's lap and ran to me, arms up; she wiggled all over like a puppy wagging its happy tail.

"Hi, Livie," I smiled. I picked her up with my last bit of strength, and she leaned back immediately.

"Anna, *stinky*," she said, her nose all wrinkled up. I was so tired, but I laughed anyway. Hunger had nearly left me, and I was willing to skip dinner and fall into my pallet – dirt, sweat and all. Grace stood up from the table.

"Let's get y'washed up," she offered. "The firs' day's always the hardes'."

I sat Olivia in her chair and followed Grace to the counter, where she pulled a washrag from a nearby drawer and handed it to me. I wet it in the wash bin and was careful not to rub the new sores on my hands too vigorously. I would show them to Grace *after* Mr. Grainger left the room, knowing she would doctor and bandage them for the night.

I finished washing up my arms, face, and neck, and sat down for dinner... my muscles screaming. I looked at the roasted chicken, boiled potatoes, and green beans in front of me; Grace had already fixed my plate. My mouth watered at the sight of it, and I decided I might eat a *little* before crashing into bed.

Mr. Grainger stood up a moment later, wiped his mouth with his napkin, and excused himself. "I'm gonna go out n'bathe," he mumbled to his wife as he left the room.

I glanced at Grace and forced a quick smile.

"It was a hard firs' day, huh?" she asked quietly.

I took a few bites of chicken and chewed slowly, letting the savory juice dance in my mouth. I honestly couldn't remember anyone's food dancing in my mouth like hers did, not even my Momma's, and I felt guilty about it. I reached for my glass of water to wash the bite down quickly.

"Tell me 'bout y'day," she pressed. I took a second drink and swished the water around in my mouth like Daddy, then swallowed.

"It was fine, ma'am… I got more blisters, though," I said, showing her my hands.

"Oh, Anna. I'm so sorry! I forgot t'wrap y'other hand after lunch… we'll fix it up good 'fore bed, okay?"

I nodded and continued to eat, figuring now that I had started, I better finish my plate. I could hear water splashing through the open window and remembered seeing the large tub around the back of the house. I hoped Mr. Grainger stayed out there for a *long* time; it was much nicer inside when it was just Grace, Olivia and me. "Can I ask y'somethin'?" I said softly.

"Sure, anythin'," Grace nodded.

"How many sacks o'corn could y'fill in a day?"

She smiled sympathetically. "How many did *you* fill?"

"One this mornin', n'one-n'a-half this afternoon. I tried t'finish the second, but I jus' didn't have time." I neared the end of my green beans, and Grace put another scoop on my plate. I decided I better eat those, too. Momma and Daddy wouldn't want me to be rude after all.

"When I was *really* good at pickin', I could fill seven or eight sacks a day." Grace shrugged her shoulders and leaned back in her chair. "But then I got pregnant, n'I jus' got *so* exhausted. Carryin' a baby on the inside n'workin' on the outside was harder on m'body than mos', I guess. I know lots o'women do it, n'I kept tryin' t'work... Jack needed me, but I ended up losin' the baby 'cause of it. I haven't been out in the fields since we put 'im in the ground... it was a baby boy."

"Why couldn't y'keep 'im in?" I asked between forkfuls. The words slipped out of my mouth before I realized how awful they sounded. I swallowed quickly. "I'm so sorry, ma'am," I apologized frantically. "I don't mean... Momma'd be *sick* if she knew I asked such a thin'!"

Grace waved the thought away, got up from the table, and started to clear the dishes. "It's okay, Anna, really. Don't worry a thin' 'bout it," she said. "I imagine I worked too hard, or m'body jus' wasn't strong enough... it still hurts t'think of it is all. I've always wanted children, n'I jus' don't know if it's part o'God's plan fo' me." She began to soap up the dishes and wash them quietly.

I finished eating in silence, still berating myself for unwittingly drudging up her pain.

Mr. Grainger came back inside in a fresh set of clothes and thrust his dirty ones at his wife. He glanced over at me. "We'll be startin' early again t'morrow. Be out by sun-up this time," he said. Then he pushed past Grace and walked into the next room, shutting the bedroom door behind him.

Grace came over and placed her hand on my shoulder. "This mornin' was *my* fault, Anna, not yours," she whispered. "I'll wake y'up earlier t'morrow, n'it'll go better now y'know what's expected." I nodded and got up to help her dry the dishes, putting them away in the cabinets by myself this time. When we finished, she cleaned my hands and put fresh bandages on them. "You'll get use t'the hard work. You'll get faster at it, then y'won't be *so* tired come nightfall."

I wanted to believe her, but I was barely processing her words by that point. My exhausted mind was shifting to Momma. Grace was nice, but she was not my *mother*. If I didn't hear from my parents in a week's time, I determined to write them a letter and leave it at the Corrigans' mercantile. Whether I would tell them how mean Mr. Grainger was, I hadn't decided. I didn't want to make them feel more guilty when I *did* understand this plan was in the best interest of the whole family, my preferences aside.

"Go on n'get some sleep now," Grace said. "I see Olivia's already got a head start." I glanced at the pallet next to the stove. Olivia was snuggled into the pillow, snoring softly. The cornhusk doll pressed against her cheek, leaving little checkered indentions that made me smile.

"She must've had a long day, too," I said.

Grace and I said good night, and she blew the candle on the table out. There I was – left alone in the shifting darkness again. I was too tired to feel scared, though. With a yawn I managed to change into the silk night-gown, which was folded neatly at the end of the pallet, and then I collapsed next to my sister.

I rolled Livie onto my chest and wrapped my arms around her like a stuffed teddy bear. Her weight and rhythmic breathing relaxed me quickly, and my eyes fluttered shut. *Tomorrow, I will fill six sacks*, I thought, *and the day after that, seven!* I promised myself I'd have a better attitude and do as much as humanly possible for the Graingers.

My breathing slowed and deepened, and Momma and Daddy's faces swam before me right before I melted into sleep. I could see them in the wagon, bumping down the road toward a giant oak tree. The sun was barely up; we would stop and eat breakfast soon. I was at the meal barrel, sifting for those little, round, fat worms and beetles. An assorted handful squirmed in my palm, naked and vulnerable, as I let the meal slip between my fingers like powdered sugar through a sifter. I held the bugs up to my face for a closer look. They were so small and helpless, writhing to be left alone. *They just want to eat, like us.* I thought sadly in their defense. Momma called something back to me from the front bench and I startled.

"I'll see y'all later," I whispered to the bugs, then threw them out the wagon hatch. They bounced off the road in all directions, disappearing into the dust the wagon wheels kicked up. Suddenly, an immense wave of regret washed over me. I had *liked* those bugs, and somehow, I knew I would never see them again. Tears filled my eyes. Those were *my* bugs. I had failed to appreciate them when I had them in my hand and to fight harder on their behalf before I let them go. I woke up frantically in a cold sweat, my face and hair drenched with fresh tears.

# 10

The days that followed stretched into weeks, each of them like the first. I got up and worked in the fields from sun-up until sundown, with a quick lunch in the middle. Sometimes Mr. Grainger opted we pack our lunches and eat them in the rows to save time. Save time it did, but it also made for *really* long, lonely days. Summer was fading into fall, like sand rushing through an hourglass, and I knew he was worrying that harvesting weather was on its way out and we'd not finish in time. Summer crops meant winter food and supplies… I wasn't a farmer's girl, but even I knew it was critical to help them beat the cold weather.

As I mentioned, one silver lining to my temporary new life was that Grace was a talented cook. She had meat and more at every meal and fresh eggs at breakfast. I ate my fill, yet still lost weight! I wasn't so thin that I looked sickly, but I was thin enough for Grace to start leaving food out on the stove so I could sneak morsels every time I passed by. Maybe she was afraid that Momma and Daddy would come back and think they were not treating us well, or maybe she just knew how hard it was to work the fields and that I needed extra sustenance. Either way, I would have told Momma how well fed she kept us because I believed Grace genuinely cared for Livie and me – even if her husband did not.

Another nice thing about Grace was that she bought me some paper and a pencil from the Corrigan mercantile. She didn't tell Mr. Grainger they cost her an extra five cents, however; she said that was our *secret*. After the first week, I did write Momma and Daddy a letter, filled with only the good things I could think of, and I had written two more since. I wrote them at night by candlelight, only about a page at a time to make sure the paper lasted. Then I folded them up under my pillow, and when Mr. Grainger and I were out to the fields, Grace and Olivia would take my letter to the mercantile while running other errands in town. It was a kind arrangement, and I secretly enjoyed doing something Mr. Grainger would disapprove of.

I had been with the Graingers for a month and a half now and was still waiting on a return letter from my parents. Grace told me after the second letter that Mr. Corrigan sent their love through him, and that Momma enjoyed my letters very much. Evidently, they were still searching for Daddy a job but hoped to be back before Christmas as promised. Knowing that they were at least *getting* my letters, and that it brought them joy on their journey, was enough to keep me writing and hoping.

September came and went just as quickly, and it was nearly October – the weather turning cool and breezy. I had gotten much better at popping the corn, and when we had finished the cornfields, we moved on to the potatoes. Mr. Grainger said the fastest way to harvest those with two people would be for him to dig them up, and me gather them in his wake. I wasn't excited for us to work side by side, especially after I had gotten used to working alone, but I *was* thrilled to give those blasted shears a rest.

One evening late September, the dinner bell rang, and I heaved my full sack of taters to the edge of the field. The bags were getting lighter to lift or maybe I was just getting stronger. Mr. Grainger had already started toward the shed; he barely talked to me these days unless it was to order me around. He didn't even fuss about my work much anymore. I worked hard and he knew it, so it was like we had mustered a little respect between us. This was his first harvest without Grace pulling her share in the fields, and I think somewhere deep down he was grateful I showed up when I did, even if he'd never admit it.

Darkness began to fall as I went back and forth from the fields to the shed, putting away my bags of potatoes and tools. I handed Mr. Grainger the last sack, and he heaved it up onto the closest stack. The shed was so full of corn and potatoes that we both couldn't fit inside at the same time anymore.

He cleared his throat and said, "Well, I was partly right. Y'cain't do a *man's* work, but y'do jus' 'bout as good as any woman I saw." My eyebrows raised in surprise as a smile snuck across my face. *That was a compliment in my opinion!*

My chest swelled with pride, and I looked him right in the eyes for the first time in a long time. "Thank ya, sir," I spoke as womanly as I could, like Momma and Martha … or Grace.

I held the shed door open for him to step out. Then I stepped in to get the chicken feed from the trough. Mr. Grainger didn't start toward the house as usual though, instead he stood in the doorway and watched me as I gathered my dress up.

I glanced at him and suddenly felt awkward, standing there with the hem of my dress in my hands. I knew I was being modest about it, but my stomach tightened, and my face flushed hot. I held my hem as low as possible and scooped some corn into my skirt, trying to ignore his stare. When I turned to walk toward the door, he was still blocking my way. I just looked past him at the little patch of grass I could see behind his legs and nodded. "Excuse me, sir," was all I could get out.

He crossed his arms and leaned against the door frame. "Y'try so darn hard t'be pleasin'," he said gruffly. "Why?" His face was half hidden in the shadows, and the sight of it made my heart pound.

"Daddy n'Momma told me t'earn m'keep n'not cause y'any trouble, sir," I said quietly. "He said y'all were doin' us a favor."

Mr. Grainger contemplated my answer, then nodded and stepped aside. "That, I am," he said. "Now finish y'work." He turned and headed toward the house, hitting his hat against his trousers like I had seen my Daddy do when he was frustrated about something and working out a solution in his mind.

I exhaled slowly, rolled my shoulders back and stretched my neck from side to side. The sudden tightness in my stomach began to loosen, and as

I stepped out into the fresh air my heartbeat slowed back to normal. *It's been a long day and I'm starved*, I told myself, calling the chickens to be fed. I tossed out the grain and quickly let my hem fall, dusted out my skirt, and headed for the house myself. *Sitting down a spell and having a bite to eat will do a world of good*, I promised myself.

As I pushed through the kitchen door, Olivia greeted me with her usual squeal of joy. She ran and hugged my legs, then said I stunk... for the hundredth time. She had learned early on that the comment made Grace and me both laugh, and that made her giggle all over like a bowl of jiggly jelly.

"Good evenin'," I nodded to Grace, heading to the wash bin to clean up. I knew their routines quite well by now and could follow them without being told.

The skin on my palms had finally callused, but it still hurt to scrub the dirt out of the tough little ridges that had formed. After scrubbing good, I sat at the table and began to eat the roast beef, corn, and green beans Grace piled on my plate. I thanked her for cooking, as I did every night. Momma would have been proud of me for that.

"The potatoes're in," Mr. Grainger stated to no one in particular.

"Oh, Jack, that's good news!" Grace smiled. "Y'all finished a few days 'head o'schedule." Mr. Grainger nodded and shoveled some beef into his mouth, brushing his oily black hair to the side with his other hand.

"Not nearly enough t'make a diff'rence," he said while chewing. He took a drink and swallowed. "It'll still be a press t'get the beans in on time."

"That's the easies' field, though," she nodded. "It shouldn't take much longer."

"Maybe two weeks," Mr. Grainger said, ripping his cornbread in two. "We should be finished by the middle o'October."

"Wonderful." Grace smiled around the table at us. She looked like she was chewing on more words, but she stood to take her dishes to the wash bin instead of speaking them.

Mr. Grainger knew her well. He put his fork down and impatiently wiped his mouth with his napkin. "What's on y'mind, Grace?" he demanded.

I looked from him to her and then back at my plate. I had been with the Graingers long enough to know an argument was brewing. Whatever she was tiptoeing around had the potential to make him angry. I glanced at Olivia. I always tried to carry her out of earshot when they started in at each other, and I wanted to be ready to grab her and go if I had to.

"Well," Grace said, reaching for Olivia's dishes. "I've been thinkin' 'bout *after* the harves'... in fact, it's quite the coincidence... Geneva Sensley came by fo' a visit while y'all were in the fields t'day. She's that young woman from Illinois; she teaches up at the schoolhouse now," Grace said nonchalantly.

Mr. Grainger's eyes narrowed. He exhaled slowly and nodded, licking his teeth with his tongue. I didn't like the way he stared at his wife any more than how he stared at me, like he was a wolf picking apart a rabbit with his eyes. "I don't like where you're goin' with this, so do y'self a favor n'get t'washin'," he warned.

"Jack, please," Grace pleaded, still walking to the counter obediently. She put the plates in the wash bin and said over her shoulder, "What'd it hurt? She wouldn't have t'go all day. Mrs. Sensley said she can come fo' mornin' lessons n'leave at lunch, if y'still need 'er after the beans that is. She'd have only missed a couple o'weeks. Mrs. Sensley said if she's bright, she'd catch up real quick."

My heart leapt in my chest as I understood the conversation. Grace wanted me to go to school! I had forgotten school had started back up, resigned to the fact he'd never let me go or that I was too old to continue my studies now that I was able-bodied enough to work... but maybe I *could* go to school, just until my parents came back... if Mr. Grainger would only agree!

"We didn't take 'er in t'give 'er a higher education, Grace," he sneered. "'Er father n'me made an arrangement; she works fo' their room n'board, period. Nothin' more, nothin' less. She's *hired* help, not some charity case."

Grace continued to wash dishes, her back to us. I knew she was choosing her words wisely.

"*You* ain't out there slavin' y'self t'the bone ev'ry live long day," Mr. Grainger continued, his voice raising even though she hadn't said a word back. He pushed his chair from the table and stood up. "I s'pose y'want me t'work the farm by m'self again? Y'quit on me, woman. Way I see it you're tryin' t'take the little help I've left." He walked toward the next room but when Grace spoke up, he clinched the door frame until his knuckles turned white.

"I didn't *quit* on ya, Jack."

My heart started pounding. *I have to get us out of the way, and I have to do it now,* I thought as I scooped up my sister. "Excuse us," I said and hurried out the kitchen door. I sat down on the steps with Livie in my lap, and the door slammed shut behind us. I looked up at the darkening sky, taking a deep, calming breath, only shaking slightly this time. The stars were just beginning to light up the heavens, a bunch of little specks coming out one by one. I could still hear the Graingers through the open window and tried to block out their fussing.

"I didn't *quit*," Grace was still insisting. "The doctor told me after losin' the baby… if we ever want t'try n'have another…"

"I *know* what the doctor said!" Mr. Grainger suddenly bellowed.

I covered my ears, then quickly covered my sister's instead and hunched my shoulders up around my own. Footsteps charged across the kitchen behind us. "If *you* want t'stay inside n'res' all day n'think y'can carry one better nex' time – then by all means, leave me out there t'fend fo' our food n'shelter by m'self! A baby ain't all I married y'fo', y'know!"

Olivia, wide-eyed and silent, nuzzled into my chest and slipped her thumb into her mouth. I thought I had heard adult arguments before, but Momma and Daddy's spats didn't hold a candle to a fight in the Graingers' household.

"Jack," Grace pressed on, her voice quivering slightly. "Y'said the beans would only take another couple o'weeks; that's finishin' the whole harves' earlier than even las' year when I *was* workin'." She paused for just a second, like she was catching her breath. "Anna has worked really hard fo' ya. Y'*know* she has. She's done more than any other young girl could've.

She ain't our *slave*, Jack. She's jus' a child, our ward fo' the time bein'. She needs more than jus' a place t'sleep n'eat… if we can let 'er further 'er education, even jus' in the mornin's, I think we should give 'er that opportunity. I bet she'll work even harder in the afternoons on whatever chores y'find fo' 'er."

There was a loud thump on the wall behind us, and I jumped, startling Olivia, who grabbed my shirt with a vice-like grip. I imagined Mr. Grainger had hit the wall with his hand. I had seen him smack the wall on a few occasions now. Grace obviously did not stand up to her husband for many things, and for the life of me I couldn't puzzle out why she was doing it now for *me*, over something like school.

"Y'*think* we should let 'er go," Mr. Grainger growled. "Y'*think*. Since *when* in y'life have y'*ever* had a worthwhile thought."

I hugged Olivia to me and started rocking us both, back and forth, back and forth. *Please don't come outside*, I prayed, hoping God up in Heaven was listening. Thankfully, Mr. Grainger's voice moved away from the window as he must have walked back toward the sitting room.

"If I even consider it, the girl has t'come straight home n'finish 'er chores. *Only* after the beans're in, mind ya, n'*only* 'til spring plantin' b'gins… if those deadbeat parents o'theirs ain't come back fo' 'em by then," Jack spit his words at her like he spit tobacco juice, a foulness he no longer wanted to taste in his mouth.

"I think that's fair," Grace said quietly. She sounded like she was backed up against the paper-thin wall behind me. "You're a good man, Jack. Thank ya…"

"N'from now on," he interrupted her, "y'mind y'own business; don't ask me fo' nothin' else. Y'understand me? I do *ev'rythin'* fo' ya… took y'off y'Momma's hands or y'all would've been out in the cold like y'poor, dead *Daddy*. I think I'm bein' mighty generous t'*these* orphans as well." He waited for what felt like forever. "Y'hear me, woman?"

"Yes, sir," Grace said, her voice barely above a whisper.

Mr. Grainger's footsteps faded into the back of the house, and my muscles slowly started to relax. I took a deep breath and loosened my grip on

Olivia, who pointed at a firefly lighting up the night. "Look, Anna," she whispered, too.

I nodded it was okay now and let her slide out of my lap to go chase it. I could hear Grace clattering the dishes, washing and putting them away for the night, but I didn't dare go back in yet. After a few minutes the screen door squeaked open and she came out. I looked up at her, wrapping my arms around my knees. Grace shut the screen slowly, leaning back against it. She took a deep breath herself and her tense face softened, a smile forming around the edges of her mouth.

"I'm sure y'heard more than y'ought've," she said quietly, "but did y'hear the good part?"

My face broke into a similar grin. "He's gonna let me go t'school?"

She lowered herself onto the steps beside me and wrapped her arm around my shoulders. "*You're* goin' t'school, young lady!" she said with a little triumphant laugh.

Before I thought about it, I wrapped my arms around her waist. "Thank y'fo' thinkin' of it, ma'am. I hope I didn't get y'in trouble with y'husband." Grace patted my back, and I suddenly felt self-conscious about hugging another woman besides Momma. I let go of her and wrapped my arms back around my knees.

"Honey, y'don't mind a thin' y'heard," she said, resting her arms in her own lap. "He's *always* focused on the harves' n'plantin'. He cain't see any good in much else – not church, school – anythin'."

"I'll work *really* hard, I promise," I said. "Anythin' he wants me t'do. I'll do it."

"I know y'will. It's in y'blood t'do right by people." Grace said. We looked out over the yard; Olivia was wandering back toward us, her hands gently cupped around a flashing bug. "I want t'tell y'a secret, Anna Beth Atwood," Grace continued quietly. Our eyes met and she winked kindly at me, just like Daddy used to when he wanted to make me feel the most special.

"I was in a very sad place when I met y'fam'ly, *very* sad... n'bitter – t'wards ev'ryone n'ev'rythin'. But since y'all've been stayin' with us, I've begun t'feel better." Grace leaned down and plucked up a blade of grass, feeling it between her fingers. "Y'know, after I los' our son, the doctor told me I couldn't work *and* grow a child. He said m'body jus' cain't take the work on the inside n'outside, all at the same time. He said if we hoped t'have a fam'ly one day, I would have t'get a lot o'res'. He advised me not t'go back in the fields fo' m'own health, n'that made Jack *very* upset. It's a lot o'farm t'work alone."

I bit my lip. "Why cain't y'work n'carry a child, though – if y'don't mind me askin'?" I wondered. I had heard of pregnant women working a farm clear up to time, delivering the baby in the fields and all, then going right back to work! I thought that's how it was for all women.

"Well, I don't really understand m'condition that well," she shrugged, throwing the blade of grass aside with a sigh. "I do know I had a bad miscarriage... I los' a lot o'blood, n'by the time Jack realized I wasn't foolin' n'got the doctor t'our house, I had nearly died. Whether m'body is kind o'broken now, or it was from the start – I don't know why child bearin's so difficult fo' me, but 'tis."

I swallowed hard and thought about a woman's body being broken on the inside. "I'm mighty sorry it's like that fo' ya, Grace. I can tell you're good with kids n'all," I offered.

Olivia came into reach, and Grace pulled my sister into her lap, kissing her curly head. Livie opened her hand with eyes of wonder, then her face fell when the firefly flitted away – here a second and gone the next, like Grace's baby boy.

"Ev'ryone has their troubles, Anna. I jus' want y't'know that you n'Miss Olivia here've been good fo' m'soul." She glanced over her shoulder at the darkened house. Mr. Grainger must have gone to bed. "M'husband's a difficult man t'live with sometimes. But I want y't'know he's a *good* man, Anna; gruff, but good. He took me in n'still takes care o'me, n'I know he'll do right by you n'Olivia 'til y'parents come back. Y'can trus' me on that."

I nodded, not really understanding how someone who yelled and hit walls could also be called caring. I really wanted to ask why he had called us *orphans*, but I held the thought inside... turning it over in my mind and feeling the roughness, like a person unconsciously fingering a sharp rock in their pocket hoping their touch will eventually smooth the edges.

Grace stood up with Olivia. "I know it's gettin' late, n'you'll be up early in the mornin'. Will y'be writing a letter t'y'parents t'night?" she asked. "I'm plannin' t'take Olivia into town t'morrow while y'all start the bean field. I'll also stop by the schoolhouse n'let Mrs. Sensley know you'll be joinin' 'em soon enough." That brought a smile back to my face.

"I'll write one n'leave it under m'pillow t'night, if y'don't mind. I'll tell 'er 'bout school. I'm sure she'll want t'thank y'when she can!" I said.

Grace smiled. "She'll be so happy fo' ya. Ev'ry momma wants 'er children t'have a good education, I think."

She held open the screen door for me, and Livie reached for me when I passed. I took my birthday sister in my arms, kissed her goodnight, and settled her into the covers of our pallet with the little cornhusk doll, which she wrapped in a hug. She was asleep within minutes. Grace gave me a piece of paper and the pencil from the drawer next to the wash bin, where she had hidden them under the dish towels. She said good night, kissing the top of my head, and I sat myself down at the table, careful not to scratch the chair against the floor and make any noise that would wake Mr. Grainger.

I stared at the long pencil, its lead beginning to dull from use, and wondered why Mr. Grainger would get angry if he knew about the writing materials. *Was it that he didn't want Grace to spend the money on such things? Was he afraid I'd tell my parents about him, and they would come back before we finished the harvest and he'd lose the help?* I sighed and turned my thoughts to my letter, dating the top of the paper proper-like, which I had learned in school at Leadwood.

I addressed my greeting to Momma and Daddy both, first telling them about Grace and how we were making her happy, then just a little about Mr. Grainger; how he was pleased that we finished harvesting the corn and potatoes in record time and only had the beans left. I focused the rest of the letter on how I would start school after the harvest. I assured them when they came back for us, I would stay home and help Momma as planned. At the end of the letter I asked about Janie and Emily. I still hadn't heard if they had been taken in by anyone or not. I had asked the Graingers at dinner not long ago if we could ask around town and visit them, in case they were taken in, but Mr. Grainger let me know right away that I was here to work and not play. I stared down at my letter; it was nice to see their names on the paper at least. I finally closed it with "much love" and signed my name in my best cursive. I read the letter a couple of times for spelling and grammar mistakes, then folded it into thirds. After giving it a quick kiss, I wrote Mr. & Mrs. Atwood on the front and tucked it under my pillow for safe keeping.

After changing into my nightgown, the soft, warm silk no longer feeling strange against my skin but comforting and familiar, I blew out the candle. Then I snuggled under the blanket next to my sister. With a yawn I closed my eyes; it felt like I had been holding them open for so long. *But what a day it had turned out to be!* Tomorrow we would start harvesting the bean fields, but tonight I would dream about starting eighth grade in Harlan.

*11*

Grace had been right. It didn't take long to finish the bean harvest at all, or maybe it just felt quick because I had something good to look forward to. Mr. Grainger did start allowing me to attend school and occasionally church, and as work eased up around the farm, he even allowed a leisurely trip to town or two! Time away from the fields was rejuvenating; I didn't miss my family *so* badly during the day when I could distract myself with meeting all kinds of new people... but I still thought about my parents and sisters most nights. I also relished the respite from Mr. Grainger and his back-breaking chores, for he never wanted to accompany us anywhere if he could help it – he just told us what time we better be home.

Church in Harlan *was* the same kind of worship my family did back in Leadwood. The old-time singing, preaching, praying, shouting... it made my heart happy when I was missing my family something sore. If I closed my eyes I could sometimes *feel* home. The building and people were different, but the sound was the same... it was like smelling Olivia's honeysuckle hair at night, the two of us curled under the Graingers' little kitchen window I pretended was our window in our two-room log cabin back home. It always worked until I had to open my eyes again.

School was another kind of wonderful. There were twenty-five of us in one room, all different grades, and Mrs. Sensley taught us everything we needed to know with kindness to spare. She wore her curly, chestnut brown hair pulled half-up with a pretty golden clip that I thought exquisite. I wanted to be *just* like her when I grew up. I started trying to style my hair like hers a few times, but of course I didn't have a clip nor curls. Unfortunately, I wasn't very good at doing anything but a French braid... so the grown-up hairstyle would have to wait.

I looked for Janie and Emily in class on the first day, for we had finally got word that the Pracketts and Carters had taken them in. When I didn't see them, however, I fretted myself sick. We learned through Mrs. Sensley, who had heard from Mrs. Corrigan, that Janie had run away, and Emily's temporary family had moved a few towns over. They left word at the store for Momma and Daddy as to their whereabouts. As sad as I was not to see my sisters in school, I was thankful there were other girls close to my age – even though I was the oldest. One of the girls, Carrie Michaels, and I had even become bosom friends!

Carrie was a grade under me, and she was quiet and shy like Emily. She wore her long, red hair in two pig-tail braids, and the boys, from youngest to oldest, yanked them every chance they could, which made my blood boil. They also made fun of her face full of freckles. We got to be friends because there was this one gang of brothers in particular, the Durrett Boys, whose goal was to make Carrie cry daily. They not only bullied her about her braids and freckles, but they routinely knocked her books out of her hands when she was walking home. The bratty little brothers would spit at her or kick dirt all over her shiny shoes while the meaner big brothers just laughed and egged them on. Chancey, Johnny, Tommy, Timmy, and Chester were their names, and *no one* liked them.

One day, when we were all walking down the hill from school toward the farms, and they were picking on Carrie as usual, I just had enough. I could hear Daddy's words ringing in my ears... *all it takes for evil to triumph is for good people to stand around and do nothing*. So, I hollered at those Durrett Boys to pick on each other instead, scooped up a handful of mud, and slung it at Tommy, Timmy, and Chester. Then I took off chasing Johnny and Chancey. I don't think they would have run from me if I wasn't also waving a good-sized rock in my hand! They left Carrie alone after that, and she had been my best friend ever since. The Good Lord knew I needed a friend.

"What're you thinking about, Anna Beth?" Carrie asked, dragging a stick along the road on our way home from school one day. The little groove in the dirt reminded me of a curvy, dried-up riverbed. It was late November, and the chill in the air made Carrie drop her stick and pull her yellow wool sweater tighter around her body. The yellow complimented her red hair and freckles.

"You're always thinking about something and forgetting to talk," she added. She talked real proper, like our teacher, Mrs. Sensley. I think it was because her parents came from money and owned that two-story hotel in town – she had real good raising. That's why her shoes were always shiny, too.

I reached up and fiddled with the buttons on my new-to-me brown sweater. Grace insisted I *had* to have something for the cooler weather and had found it at the secondhand store in town. It was my new favorite piece of clothing, even thought it was Plain Jane brown; it was the only thing I owned besides my day clothes and the one Sunday dress I came with. Mr. Grainger also didn't get *as* mad about the sweater as when she asked to send me to school, so I wondered if maybe he was starting to like me just a little.

"Oh, I was jus' 'memberin' when I chased Chancey n'Johnny with that rock," I said, a grin sneaking across my face. I could still see those boys scurrying up the road like rats, covering their heads with their arms in case I let loose that rock. Carrie and I were nearing the bend where Johnny had tripped over a fallen branch, and Chancey pulled him up by his overalls as he ran past. It ripped the seat of Johnny's britches right out, and we heard the next day that they *both* got a whipping for it when they got home! Johnny came to school with his overalls all patched and sewed back together, for everyone knew the Durretts didn't have two nickels to rub together, and everyone busted a gut laughing at his stitched behind.

A contagious laugh burst out of Carrie, and then she did my favorite thing ever. She snorted and quickly covered her mouth and nose, causing both of us to laugh all the harder. It felt good to laugh freely, the cool breeze rustling the hair that had escaped my braid backward. I couldn't be so loose and free at the farm, not around Mr. Grainger's critical eye.

I nuzzled into the top of my sweater and smelled Grace, bringing my thoughts to the farm. I had started out doing school in the morning and coming back to work after lunch, but that only lasted a week or two. There just weren't enough chores to keep us all busy. So, Mr. Grainger allowed me to stay full days at school if I could finish the chores before dinner. I *always* got the work done, and I was a happier worker after soaking up all the learning and laughter during school. I think some part of him liked watching me work with a smile because he hadn't been nearly as surly with me, either... so it was a win-win for all of us.

"The looks on those boys' faces were priceless," Carrie said, her laughter slowing to a chuckle. "No one *ever* stood up to the Durrett Boys before *you* came to Harlan," she grinned proudly.

We watched some leaves from a nearby tree break loose and drift to the ground in a rhythmic zig-zag pattern. I didn't like to admit it because it felt wrong to feel joy without my family here to share it, but Harlan's autumns were simply gorgeous. I averted my eyes from the fall display and chided myself not to enjoy such things until my family was back together.

Carrie and I stopped at the fork in the road to say goodbye; this is where we parted ways every day. The right road led down further into the valley to the big farmhouses like the Graingers', and the left led up another hill to a couple of fancy homes like Carrie's on the way to the next town.

"Well, those Durrett Boys got what was comin' to 'em," I smiled. "They needn't be pickin' on girls anyways. See y't'morrow?"

"You can count on it," she answered. Then we hugged and split ways.

I hadn't walked very far alone, kicking a little rock down the hill with every step, when I heard the rattling of pots and pans lumbering down the road behind me. A smile burst across my face when I remembered – *it's Thursday!* I spun around and saw Mr. Jingle, a big grin on his face, headed my way. He honked his horn that gave a worn-out *toot-toot!* and waved at me. He slowed his truck with the big sign on the side reading *Jingle's Goods* in bold red letters.

"Well, good afternoon!" he called. "Would y'fancy a ride, m'dear?"

I met Joseph Jingle soon after I started school, and even though we had known each other for only two months we were quick friends. He was an old preacher man turned bartering peddler. He traveled all over the surrounding counties and slept in the back of his truck at night. Once he told me that God made him a drifter, and he was happy living the transient life. I wasn't sure what that meant, except he was free and liked it that way. I wanted to be free like him, like I wanted to have Mrs. Sensley's half-up hairdo. On Thursdays he would pass through Harlan, and if we happened to be traveling the same road, he always offered me a ride home.

"Afternoon, Mr. Jingle!" I exclaimed, taking his outstretched hand and climbing up into the truck. I sat beside him, my schoolbooks in my lap. Getting to ride in a vehicle was a real treat – he was one of the few people who had one in these parts. His truck looked like a motorized covered wagon to me, except with a real roof, not a canvas top. The front was open all the way around, too, but the back boxed in on the sides with a wagon hatch. It was one of the neatest things I had ever seen!

Mr. Jingle put the truck in gear and off we rumbled. His pots, pans and other assorted goods swung on the sides and in the back of the truck, clattering together and making all sorts of lovely racket. "N'jus how're y't'day, Miss Dignity?" he said with a grin.

Mr. Jingle had taken to calling me *Dignity* from day one, even though he knew very well that my name was Anna Beth Atwood. I had to ask him what the word meant, and he said *having dignity* means having respect for yourself and being an honest person. He said he could tell I was just that – *dignified*. It made me feel ten feet tall and proud to the point of bursting to know he thought so highly of me. I thought highly of him, too... next to Carrie and Grace, he was my closest friend in Harlan.

"I'm doin' well, thank ya, sir, n'you?" I answered, in my most dignified, ladylike way. I even crossed my hands in my lap and my legs at the ankles, like I saw women at church do. He laughed a big belly laugh and thumbed his nose at me.

"*You*'re certainly the definition o'dignity, m'girl."

As we trundled down the dirt road, his tires following in the deep wagon ruts that nearly drove us on their own, our conversation went from school to work on the Graingers' farm. When that topic ran out, he asked if I had heard news from my parents yet.

"No," I was sad to say. My shoulders slumped, and I uncrossed my hands and ankles.

I had received a letter from them the beginning of October, but that was it. Momma had written that they were fine and said Daddy was still trying to find a mining job. There wasn't any work in Harlan, just like that young couple we met on the road had predicted. So, they were widening their search and checking nearby towns. She reiterated the promise that as soon as they found work and got a place to live, she and Daddy would be back for us girls and we'd all be together again. I don't think she knew about Janie running away yet, or Emily moving to another town. If she did, she didn't mention it. December fifth would mark two months since that letter, and I wondered every day where they were and if they had had any luck by now.

"I imagine they're havin' t'travel further out than they expected – lookin' fo' work n'housin' n'all – n'they cain't get back here t'leave a letter with the Corrigans again," Mr. Jingle read my mind and tried to comfort me.

"Why don't they jus' mail a letter from wherever they are t'the Harlan pos' office?" I wondered aloud. It was a question that drifted through my thoughts several times a day.

"Maybe they don't have two nickels t'rub t'gether yet, n'they cain't afford the postage," he said thoughtfully.

I thought about them not having two nickels to rub together… like the Durretts. If that were the case, what would they find to eat, and how would they buy anything they needed with just one nickel… or none? At least the Durretts had their own small farm and could trade for things they needed at the mercantile.

"Aw, now… don't y'go on worryin', y'hear? Keep y'chin up. It'll be Christmas 'fore long!"

That would have cheered most kids, but this year's Christmas meant much more than an apple and peppermint stick in a stocking to me… I was beginning to doubt Daddy could keep his promise, and I hated myself for it, even though I wasn't supposed to hate.

I glanced at Mr. Jingle, remembering his story was sadder than mine. He used to be happily married, a country boy, God-called preacher mind you, with a wife and daughter of his own. He told me how he had been out praying in the barn, like he did a couple times a day, when something happened in the house to catch it on fire. The townsfolk speculated that maybe his wife left something unattended on the stove, or that his daughter knocked over a candle… but no one knows for sure how it happened. Mr. Jingle tried to run into the roaring hot blaze and save his family, but the smoke was too thick to even see his hand in front of him, and then a ceiling beam fell on his leg and crushed it. Neighbors managed to pull him out since he hadn't made it that far in, but they couldn't find the others. The whole house and everything in it burnt to the ground. Mr. Jingle confided that I reminded him of the daughter he lost, that she would have been about my age if she had lived. That was probably why he took such a shine to me.

"Mr. Jingle, can I ask y'a question 'bout *your* fam'ly?" I asked, ready to change the subject. He sat quiet for a minute, then nodded.

"Sure, Dignity. What d'ya want t'know, m'girl?" he said, reaching down to rub his left thigh out of habit. That was the leg injured in the fire, and now he used a cane to walk.

"Is y'wife n'daughter the reasons y'don't go t'church now, n'why y'stopped preachin'?" I had been thinking about that a lot lately, and I put my thoughts right out there in the middle of us. "'Cause they died in the fire n'you're mad at God or somethin'? I mean, y'were a *preacher*. Wouldn't church be the mos' comfortin' place t'be after such a tragedy?"

I looked out the window at the trees passing by. "It's comfortin' t'me, n'I've not got los' yet. Momma said God will tell me when I'm los' with a feelin' I've never felt 'fore, n'that's the only time I can get saved. 'Til then, I jus' have t'wait fo' the feelin'.'"

Mr. Jingle didn't say anything for a little bit, then he nodded and cleared his throat. "Yes, child, they're tellin' y'right. God saved me when I was a fifteen-year-old boy. The good Lord convicted m'soul with such heaviness, n'then He drew me t'an altar o'prayer. When I repented n'met his conditions, he rolled that burden away from m'heart n'joy unspeakable came in. It *was* a feelin' I had never felt 'fore." His eyes filled with tears as he spoke of it. "N'ya know what? It's still there, deep inside, the feelin' 'tis. Even though I don't go into a church house t'worship no more. Once Jesus's blood is applied t'the door posts o'y'heart, it's there fo'ever."

Mr. Jingle smiled and patted my leg. "One day, Anna Beth, the Lord o'all creation *will* speak t'*your* heart n'you'll've y'own experience t'tell. God reveals 'imself t'ev'ryone at some point in their lives, n'if y'b'lieve n'follow that still, small voice inside, He'll lead y'out o'the darkness n'into the light. We're all jus' sinners saved by grace, n'none o'us deserve it – but God made a perfect way o'salvation fo' those who *want* it, 'cause he loved us. Humblin' thought, ain't it?"

"But why did y'leave church then?" I pressed. "Ain't hard times s'posed t'draw y'closer t'God, not drive y'away?" Carrie had told me how his tragic story spread in the newspapers like a wildfire of its own after it happened. I might not have wanted everyone looking at me while I was grieving, either, come to think of it. It had been years ago, and Carrie said he still hadn't come back to church.

"Well, in mos' cases troubles do bring y'close t'God," Mr. Jingle said, downshifting the truck's rumbling engine as the big hill bottomed out and we neared the Graingers' farm. "I guess in m'case, though, it was easier t'find God outside in his great creation. M'case is jus' diff'rent, I reckon. Maybe God wanted me t'be a wanderer... people can worship 'im any-where if they'll jus' humble their hearts, Dignity." He slowed the truck to a stop in front of the white picket fence.

Olivia was out in the front yard jumping in a pile of leaves and laugh-ing. Her blonde curls grazed her shoulders now, the longer hair making her look more like a little girl and less like a baby in a seemingly short period of time. "Hi, Mr. Gee-Gee!" she sang, jumping into the leaves and sending them flying in all directions. Mr. Jingle smiled, waved hello, and gave his horn a *toot-toot!* which made her laugh.

"Well, I'm glad y'b'came a peddler, Mr. Jingle, even if y'don't go t'church anymore. Daddy says gettin' saved is the mos' important part anyways. B'sides, if y'didn't wander the countryside, y'mightn't've met me!" I said, giving him a quick hug and jumping down from the truck. He leaned over and pushed my books toward the edge of the seat so I could grab them.

"You've got that *exactly* right, Miss Dignity! Now y'take care o'y'self n'maybe I'll see y'nex' week." He pointed his finger at me. "Okay?"

"Yes, sir," I said, giving him a soldier's salute. I backed up from the truck as he put it in gear, and it lurched forward. "Bye!" I waved. "Thanks fo' the ride!" I waited for the dust to settle as he drove off and then walked across the road, pushing through the gate.

Grace walked out on the front porch, wiping her hands on a towel, and the screen door slammed shut behind her. Livie was busy covering her legs with leaves, so I walked up the porch steps and gave Grace a hug instead.

"Nice o'Mr. Jingle t'give y'a ride home again," she smiled, taking my schoolbooks out of my hands.

"Yes, he's wonderful. I never knew m'grandparents, but that's how I imagine they'd be if I had," I said. "Is Mr. Grainger 'round back?"

"Yes, I'll take these in fo' y'so y'can get right t'work," she winked. I thanked her and jumped off the porch feeling happy and full of energy.

I found Mr. Grainger chopping wood behind the house by the old cast iron tub and greeted him politely, awaiting my afternoon orders. He spit his tobacco juice, stooped and grabbed the log quarters, and threw them into the untidy pile a few feet away. Then he stood up straight, stretched his back out a bit, and wiped his hair from his glistening forehead. His arm muscles were taut, and when he lifted his arms you could see the yellow sweat circles in full. I had gotten used to Mr. Grainger and his expectations, but I doubted I'd ever get comfortable with him like I was Grace and Mr. Jingle.

"Y'can start by stackin' this wood," he directed. "I want it stacked agains' the house, near the kitchen door. We're gonna need it. Winter is comin' on fas' now." I nodded and unbuttoned my sweater, not wanting to get it dirty with chores. After laying it on the side steps, I returned to make trips stacking the wood, two quarters at a time.

Mr. Grainger stood and watched me, leaning his elbow on his axe handle. I stacked quickly and neatly, giving him no reason to think me too tired from the school day to do a decent job. When his breathing deepened, that prickly feeling from the chicken coop needled me again. He made me feel that way occasionally, especially when he just stood and watched me work. His eyes following me from the wood pile to the stacks, back and forth. I glanced at him once or twice, and finally he picked up his axe and spat more tobacco in the grass.

"When y'finish stackin', do the res' o'y'chores. Make sure you're done by dinner, mind ya," he warned, shouldering the axe and heading to the shed.

I watched him go, my shoulders relaxing instantly, and drew in a deep breath of fresh air. I was always holding my breath around Mr. Grainger, even when I consciously reminded myself to breathe. He was just a man, like Daddy, Jonathan, or Mr. Jingle... but not half as good-hearted. Maybe that's what troubled me about him.

I shook him from my mind and threw myself into my chores, thinking about how Olivia and I had settled into the Graingers' home, learned their routines and expectations, and now I was finally sleeping through the night. Grace and Olivia got along marvelously, and while I was a tad jealous that Olivia preferred Grace over me these days, I understood it was because I had been gone a lot between work and school, and Grace was her new constant. It bothered me a bit more that they both had blonde curls and could pass as mother and daughter. I didn't want Grace getting any ideas, nor did I want Livie forgetting her real family. At the end of the day, though, my birthday sister still cuddled up to *me*, and I continued to bury my face in her hair and smell the sweet honeysuckle from home... a place I desperately clung to in my memory like an old cat stuck to a screen door by its claws with gravity pulling it down and its muscles getting sore.

However, there were days, I am ashamed to admit, when I *didn't* think about Missouri, Martha or Jonathan, or all that was left behind. Some days I didn't even think about Janie and Emily. I did admire Janie for having the grit to run away and sincerely hoped she made it somewhere safe, though. I thought about Momma and Daddy a bit more; they and the dreams of our new life together were always skirting the edges of my consciousness.

Most of the days my thoughts wandered to Carrie and the mean Durrett Boys... or Mr. Jingle and his merry truck that jingled down the road. I knew most everybody's name in town now... and life with the Graingers in Harlan was growing ever more familiar while Missouri slipped away bit by bit. *Where were Momma and Daddy? Had they found work and a place for us to call home? When would they be back to reunite us and our lives begin anew as promised?* The questions cropped up even on happy days and irritated me like a pebble in my shoe. I had written Martha a few letters, but she hadn't heard a word from Momma, either.

The dinner bell rang, and I realized dusk had fallen around me. I had moved through my chore list effortlessly, my mind a million miles away. I finished feeding the chickens, shut the shed door, and grabbed my sweater from the side porch on my way in.

Grace had fixed chicken, mashed potatoes, and broccoli. It was delicious as usual. The four of us ate dinner quietly, with just a little talk of the school day and prep work needed for winter. When everyone finished and the dishes had been washed and put away, I tucked Olivia into our little pallet by the stove and sat down to write Momma and Daddy a new letter.

I told them about my studies, how Mrs. Sensley said I was the best at arithmetic, and I added a whole section about how big Olivia had grown in just the four short months that seemed like forever. I also asked when they would be back for us, as I did in every letter, and reminded them it was getting awfully close to Christmas in case they had gotten busy and forgotten. I sealed it with a kiss and stuck it under my pillow, knowing Grace would check our secret post box when I left for school the next morning.

I had written longer than usual, and by the time I changed into my silk gown and snuggled down between the covers with Olivia, it was very late. She was snoring softly and let out a long yawn before rolling over. Grace had given us extra blankets as fall weather crept in at the window and door and had said if we were still here in the heart of winter, she would burn a log in the oven overnight to keep us warm. I worried about the burning log catching the house on fire and us all burning up like Mr. Jingle's family... but I pushed the thought far from my mind and squeezed my eyes shut. After a few minutes of stillness, I was just about to drift off when I heard voices from the bedroom stirring me back awake.

The Graingers were arguing softly, about what I could not hear. Grace had a hurried and frustrated tone, though; it made me feel uncomfortable and nervous. Mr. Grainger was being persistent about something, and she was seemingly resisting. *It shouldn't be about the harvest... Mr. Grainger sold plenty of crop, and Grace said we were set for winter. It shouldn't be about school... I was getting all my chores done. Maybe it was about Christmas, and how we may still be here through the holidays....* A thump and scratch of furniture against the floor jarred me from my hurried assumptions.

Grace was whimpering now. Then there was a loud cracking noise, and my mind flashed back to a time Jonathan got in a fight with another boy over Martha. He had hit him with his fist – clear across the jaw – and it had made that same sickening crack. *Mr. Grainger was mean and ornery, but he wouldn't hit his wife, would he? Husbands didn't do such things...* I heard another crack, followed by a thump, and Grace fell silent.

I sat up quickly, wondering if I should check on Grace or stay put, and I hit my head on the corner of the table. The wood creaked as the table legs moved an inch or two across the floor. I gasped, partly in pain and partly in fear, and covered my mouth with one hand while holding the top of my head with the other. The bedroom door creaked open, and I held my breath, shutting my eyes tight and praying not to be discovered awake. Thankfully, there were no footsteps, just a silence that choked me in the darkness. The door creaked shut again, and I heard the handle lock. I breathed out ever so slowly, trying to still my racing heart.

I laid back down and faced the wall, quietly pulling the blankets up to my chin. I stared at my birthday sister, both born on February 26, ten years a part. Her delicate curls fell around her milky-white face and rosy cheeks, a little angel that knew no evil. Worries tumbled in my mind one after another. *Mr. Grainger would never actually hit Grace, would he? Even though he yelled and hit walls? He wouldn't hurt a person, especially his wife whom he was supposed to love as his own flesh – would he? He was a good man. Grace said so.* I reminded myself of that conversation over and over.

I closed my eyes and tried to force sleep to come, but it took a very long time for my muscles to relax. My ears kept straining, listening through the darkness like a mouse listens for the cat, but I never heard another noise or whisper. Eventually, I drifted off, but sleep was not at all restful. Right as I had been adjusting to this temporary life and feeling a bit of happiness, the nightmares started up again.

*12*

Grace was moving slower than usual the next morning. I kept sneaking peeks at her during breakfast, but she never met my eyes. Mr. Grainger chewed his bacon like nothing had happened, and Olivia babbled about her plans to play in the leaves again.

As everyone finished, I washed the dishes and put them away. Then I washed and dressed myself for school. As I was walking back in from the tub, Mr. Grainger pushed past me and stalked to the shed. Grace was standing at the kitchen counter holding the rim of it, her back to me. I walked up to her side and gently laid my head on her shoulder.

"Are y'okay, Grace?" I whispered. She pressed her cheek against the top of my head and nodded.

"Yes, sweetheart. I'm fine," she said quietly. She turned around and leaned back against the counter. I took a good look at her face and arms. I didn't *see* any marks… she looked like she did every day, just sad again.

"I heard y'all arguin' las' night," I confessed sheepishly.

She glanced at me out the corner of her eyes, then walked to our pallet, picked up a blanket and snapped it. "I'm sorry y'heard that," she said, folding it neatly. "Married people fight sometimes, Anna, but it's okay. That's jus' the way of it."

I nodded and walked over to help her. "I don't mean t'be nosey, but was it 'bout us possibly stayin' through Christmas?" I asked nervously. I reached to help her smooth the second blanket, but she just pushed it into my hands to finish while she busied herself pushing the chairs in around the table.

"It wasn't 'bout y'all at all," she said distractedly. "I wouldn't do as I was told, that's all. I give in so much that when I refuse 'im, he gets very angry with me." She paused, her hands gripping the back of a chair. "Truth is, I don't *care* if he took me off m'mother's hands n'kept me from freezin' in the snow like m'father." She looked up, her cheeks flushed red with embarrassment. "He cain't *always* get his way, even if he *is* the provider... other people have feelin's, too."

"Yes, ma'am," I answered quickly, afraid my questions were upsetting her more after the night she had.

"It's not fo' y't'worry 'bout, Anna. It's b'tween me n'im, okay?" she nodded, walking toward the sitting room and grabbing my schoolbooks from the side table.

"Yes, ma'am," I said again, taking the books from her as she opened the screen door and ushered me out onto the front porch with a forced smile. I knew what one of those looked like because I had faked a smile with her for weeks after Momma and Daddy left us on their doorstep.

"Ev'rythin'll be fine," Grace said, patting my back. "Jack gets in these spells where he's really demandin' fo' a while, but he comes out of 'em jus' as quick. He's a good man, Anna – jus' difficult sometimes. All men are, I think."

I remembered when Mr. Grainger asked Grace *when in her life had she ever had a worthwhile thought* and bit my lip. She said not to worry, but *still...* what if he wasn't as good as she thought he was?

Olivia was sitting on the edge of the porch with her cornhusk doll, her legs swinging back and forth. She hummed a lullaby Grace had taught her and was making the doll dance in her lap. Grace gently pushed me toward the steps.

"Get on t'school now, Anna Beth, n'have a good day. Tell Mrs. Sensley hello from me," she prompted. I nodded, knowing while I had started the conversation, Grace had just finished it.

I said goodbye to Livie, walked through the gate and down the road like it was any other school day. It felt all wrong, though, like an ankle out of joint. I hoped I could trust Grace – that when she said all is well and everything would be fine it really would be. I also tried my best to go to bed on time from that day on, so I wouldn't be privy to any other spats of that nature.

Life around the farm *did* go back to normal pretty quickly, thankfully. Olivia kept growing like a weed, and I continued going to school and working through the late afternoons. Grace rebounded into her contented, gentle self and Mr. Grainger was back to his usual level of hatefulness. I was quite relieved, truth be told, I guess because familiarity brings comfort even when the normal is uncomfortable at best. With the passage of time, I started believing the argument in the bedroom was a figment of my over-active, nervous imagination.

Winter blew in and frigidly took hold of Harlan not long after that. Grace found me a heavy coat at an affordable price and a little one for Livie. She also took to wrapping my feet with thick strips of cloth and added cardboard to the inside of a worn-out pair of boots. The shoes were really too big for me, but the cardboard took up enough space to make them usable and covered the holes… so at least I was able to walk to school and do my chores without my toes getting frostbit.

Mrs. Sensley held class clear up to Christmas, then we got two weeks off for the holidays. All my classmates were ecstatic to stay home with their families for two weeks, but I dreaded it. School had afforded me so much freedom, and I loved learning with a passion. I was happy to spend more time with Olivia, don't get me wrong, but being at the farm all day every day with the Graingers only reminded me that we weren't at home with our parents.

To add insult to injury and much to my despair, Christmas came and went with no word from Momma and Daddy. I stood by the window all Christmas Eve and Day, waiting to see their wagon come around the bend, and was thoroughly disappointed when Mr. Grainger laughed that mean cackle of his. He called me stupid and foolish and said I might as well sit down – they weren't coming. Hiding my broken heart was impossible.

Grace tried to give us a good holiday despite my sullen mood fraught with tears. She remembered how I had said Momma would make us new dresses as our present each year, so she had bought the best fabric she could afford and had sewn Olivia and me matching smocks. I don't think Mr. Grainger knew how much money she had spent on the project because Grace said she paid for them by selling some of her handiwork. I was grateful for the new garment and the sentiment behind it, but it made me miss Momma and Daddy even more. It was like my very bones were aching deep inside where no one could see. I was homesick for my *real* family, and I couldn't even talk about it. Mr. Grainger would have just made fun of me, and taking the chance of hurting Grace's feelings when she was being so kind was the last thing I wanted to do. I did feel better after Christmas had passed and some semblance of routine started back up with school, church, and chores, however. I was getting good at compartmentalizing the different parts of my life, especially the fact that Daddy hadn't been able to keep his promise. I just told myself they'd be back real soon and tried to ignore how time cruelly marched on in Harlan without them.

My spirits lifted higher when Grace remembered our February birthdays with a double birthday cake and chocolate frosting. I guess I was far enough away from Christmas that this celebration didn't sting as badly. She even gave me and Olivia a nickel each and let us spend it at the mercantile, but I don't think Mr. Grainger knew about that part. Livie got five pieces of licorice with her nickel while I got more paper and another pencil for writing letters with mine.

Carrie and I continued to grow close as well. Her friendship filled that pesky place in my heart that Janie and Emily left behind. We were thrilled when Mr. Grainger allowed me to study at her house once a week while her parents worked in the hotel. I had to do double chores on Saturdays to earn the privilege, but it was well worth it! We did more laughing than studying but kept our grades up, so no one was the wiser.

Mr. Jingle was another friend I could relax around. Our bond was something real special, and riding along talking in his truck was as close to feeling at home as I could find. I felt like we had always known each other, like there was no beginning or end to us. When springtime came and the world was busting open with new life and hope, he also took up the challenge of helping me find my parents. I hadn't heard from them except for that one single letter back in the fall. More concerning than that, they had stopped picking up *my* letters from the mercantile. The Corrigans hadn't heard from them in months.

I was missing school to help at the farm during the planting season and couldn't see Mr. Jingle on Thursdays, but every week he faithfully drove by the Graingers' house to tell me news or no news. He went pretty far out peddling his goods and asked people from all over if any new folks had settled in the area with the name Atwood. When we hadn't heard hide nor hair of them by summer harvest, when Olivia and I had been at the Graingers for just shy of a year, I stopped writing except to Martha. My parents' stack of letters was gathering dust at the mercantile and adding to the pile only wasted precious paper and lead. My heart worried something fierce about what could have happened to keep them away so long, but Grace, Mr. Jingle, and Carrie encouraged me to keep my chin up and just wait it out.

Grace told Mr. Grainger it was time for Olivia and me to have a proper place to sleep, too, and that made my parents' absence really sink in. Mr. Grainger refused for a while, but Grace thought her words out carefully and said when she was able to bear another child, their child could use the bed after we had gone. He finally told her she best get to childbearing, built a little twin bed frame that fit perfectly next to the table and stove, and made sure to tell us we were only borrowing it.

It was hard to believe I was now thirteen and would soon be in the ninth grade, if Mr. Grainger allowed me to go back to school again come fall. No one in the Atwood family had been educated past grade eight, and my heart swelled with pride to even *think* I'd be the first. A year older and grade higher was just a smidgen of my growing up, too. I had gotten a bath in the tub out back once a week since we had arrived at the Graingers, but one day Grace told me I was getting too big to change clothes out in the open. I didn't really understand her concern... there was a little half fence built along the back of the house to change behind and nothing was out there to see me except the cornfields. She just shrugged and said a girl growing into a woman's body needed more privacy. She suggested I wrap up in a towel and change in their bedroom, for it was the warmest room of the house and had a locking door, and I just did as I was told.

I did love the looking glass on her dresser anyway. I hadn't seen my reflection in quite a while and was shocked... the baby fat around my middle and thighs had thinned out, replaced by lean muscle from the hard farm work, while the top part of me had filled out. I became preoccupied with the roundness of my bosom and tried to wrap cloth around my chest to flatten them down. I was happy inwardly to look more like Martha, but outwardly I didn't want to make myself a target for the Durrett Boys' teasing! Grace tried to explain what my body was going through, especially when I got my monthlies, one night when we were sitting alone together on the porch. It was an awkward conversation and made me heartsick for my Momma for weeks afterward. I knew she could have explained this *becoming a woman* stuff in a more matter-of-fact way, and it wouldn't have felt so embarrassing.

By the end of our second harvest, school had been back in session for two weeks, and I was working as hard as I could to help Mr. Grainger finish the fields. I had grown mighty good at popping corn, and Grace said I had filled more bags than she ever could. I also got faster at gathering the potatoes as Mr. Grainger popped them from the earth. Sometimes I would gather faster than he could pop them, and he'd just stop and look at me, wiping sweat from his brow. I knew better than to smile about working faster than him, so I just kept my head down and worked all the harder when he resumed. We moved on to the bean fields, and that too would soon be harvested in full, in record time. If he wasn't such a hard man to get along with, I would have said we made a good team!

"I reckon y'want t'go back t'school when we finish here," Mr. Grainger said one day out of the blue. It was more of a statement than a question, so I didn't answer. We were out in the bean fields, and he adjusted the strap on the bag hanging around his neck and lifted his hat to wipe his sweaty forehead with the back of his sleeve. "Is that right?" He spit tobacco in the grass, looking me over. "That's what y'want?"

"Yes, sir," I answered quickly, then added for good measure, "That is, if y'don't mind me to. I'll come home right after lunch n'work the chores if that's what y'want."

He grunted and we started picking beans again. "If that's what *I* want," he echoed under his breath. "Y'don't know nothin' 'bout what *I* want." He said very little to me the rest of our time in the field, and what he did say was about work, not school.

Grace rang the dinner bell as dusk was beginning to fall, and Mr. Grainger and I made our way to the shed with our haul. He stacked the bags of beans against the corn and potatoes he had yet to sell, while I gathered my hem up and filled my makeshift pocket with corn for the chickens. I had determined not to be self-conscious about it; I was being completely decent, and the chore had to be done whether he was around or not.

"Anna," Mr. Grainger said. I was surprised he used my first name instead of "girl" and turned to face him. His eyes flitted back up toward my face, and I consciously held my hem lower so there was no way I was even showing the lace on my slip.

"Yes, sir?" I asked. He just stared at me and that warm, anxious feeling tingled in my chest and out my arms again. I had grown to *hate* that feeling since living here. My stomach twisted uncomfortably, and I asked again, "Sir?"

"Nothin'," he finally grumbled, tossing the last bag of beans against the wall and hitting the doorframe on his way out. "I was gonna give y'another chore, but it can wait. Feed the chickens n'get y'self in the house."

"Yes, sir," I nodded, racking my brains as to what chore had been left undone. Feeding the chickens was the last of it in a day's work. I shook my head and stepped down from the shed, the chickens running toward me expectantly.

I threw the corn out and called each of them by name. I knew Janie and Emily would have liked that I named them. I had picked out the bossiest chicken and named her Sassy Pants in honor of Sassafras back home. When I finished, I dusted out my skirt and shut the shed up tightly. The smell of Grace's dinner wafted through the air, and I happily made my way to the kitchen, stretching my tired muscles as I went.

Mr. Grainger allowed me to go back to school that very next week – full days to boot! I hurried to get my chores done as soon as I came home and figured it must have pleased him because he was going a bit easier on me these days. That was good, too, because ninth grade was proving quite the challenge. Mrs. Sensley pushed me to do better in every subject, and I was studying every night after dinner. It felt good to be the first in my family that went further than the eighth grade, but if my parents would just come back, I would give it all up in an instant.

Carrie and I met at the fork in the road and walked the big hill to and from school together every day. We ate lunch together at recess and started sitting together in church, too. Carrie had a beautiful voice, and when she sang up front in the choir it was like an angel singing. Sometimes during service, I would hear the foyer doors open late and look back hoping to see Mr. Jingle coming back to the pulpit. It was never him, though. Instead, an angry Mrs. Durrett would come through the doors thumping the back of her boys' heads all the way to their seat for making her late once again. Seeing her scold those mean boys always tickled me, but then I would have to pray for forgiveness for giggling in the Lord's house instead of paying attention.

My favorite part of church was not the singing or Mrs. Durrett, though. It was Grace. Her shoulders would relax down, her breathing deepen, and she'd just look at *peace*. She tried to act comfortable at home, but this was the type of peace a person couldn't fake. Sometimes, during altar call after the congregation had all gone around shaking hands and fellowshipping one another, Grace would testify of the hope she had in her heart – a feeling that let her know, beyond a shadow of a doubt, that she had a home in Heaven because God had saved her when she was a twelve-year-old girl. I watched tears slide down her cheeks, but I knew they were *happy* tears... full of faith, kindness, and love. The difference in people when the Holy Spirit started blessing their souls was nothing short of amazing.

Once she got so happy testifying about how she was just a pilgrim wandering through a weary land, headed to her long home, that she even shouted in praise. I loved her sentiment about a wandering pilgrim, too. I guess because that's how I felt – like I was just passing through Harlan waiting for my parents to come back so we could start our real lives. Her shout was the prettiest sound I had ever heard, like a fountain overflowing or a bell jingling in Heaven.

I sat through most services looking up at the rafters, wondering when God would save my soul and I could feel what His people felt. I knew Momma and Daddy had the same hope Grace was talking about, too, because their testimonies had the same sound about them. I often thought that if I never saw them again down here on earth, I wanted to at least meet them in Heaven... but then the thought of never seeing them again here would make me so sad that I would push it far from my mind. I'd go back to listening to Carrie sing like an angel and not think of anything else but the soothing sound.

After a Sunday morning service much like that one, Grace, Olivia, and I walked out of the church house and into the blinding afternoon sun. It was a warm September day, and the pastor had preached a fiery sermon about how the world would soon end and burn with a fervent heat, and we best find the Lord before it was too late. It had scared me enough that I didn't even want to look at that old man of God who was waiting to shake everyone's hands as we exited the church. I stood behind Grace as she shook his hand, Olivia in a pretty blue dress on her hip, and then followed her out into the yard where everyone was standing around talking. Carrie ran up and hugged me, a smile on her face.

"You should come sing with me some time," she said encouragingly. Her red braids were tied with light green ribbons to match her green and white smocked dress, and her freckles sparkled in the sun.

"I've told ya, Carrie – I cain't sing," I laughed. "They'd run me out o'Harlan if I tried." She shrugged her shoulders, then we both turned at the sound of tinkling pots and pans coming down the road. I could hardly believe my eyes, Mr. Jingle was *never* in town on Sundays!

Carrie and I ran down the little hill to greet him as he slowed his truck to a stop in front of the church yard and waved. "Mr. Jingle! What're y'doin' here?" I asked.

He smiled and thumbed his nose at Carrie and me. "Not sellin' goods on the Lord's day, I can tell y'that!" he said. He glanced over our heads and his smile faltered a bit. We looked behind us and noticed several church members whispering behind their hands with disapproving looks. The circumstances didn't matter to some people... Mr. Jingle had his time to grieve, and they thought he should have come back to the church years ago.

"Never y'mind, Mr. Jingle," Carrie rolled her eyes. "I think nex' month's sermon should be 'bout *gossipin'*. That'd show 'em." Mr. Jingle and I both laughed at her trying to talk country like us, then Carrie's mother called her away to head home. "Aw, shucks," she frowned. "Well, see you tomorrow, Anna Beth – bye, Mr. Jingle!" she said with a wave.

I looked back to my old friend. "So, what brought y'back t'town so soon, Mr. Jingle? Ain't y'usually in another town on the weekends?" I asked.

"Well, Dignity, as a matter a fact I came t'tell y'I heard a bit o'news," he said. I jumped up and down with a squeal that escaped me before I could catch it.

Grace had been chatting with Mrs. Corrigan and Mrs. Sensley, but when she heard my excitement, she excused herself and hurried over with Olivia.

"Now, don't get y'self all in a tizzy, girl. It's not *exactly* 'bout y'parents, mind ya. Jus' news from other parts that hasn't reached Harlan yet," he cautioned. I nodded and composed myself, clasping my hands behind my back with my fingers crossed tightly.

"I've been travelin' all over, y'know, n'wherever I go, I ask after the Atwoods. I can tell y'no one knows the name. I did, however, hear 'bout some mining accidents about thirty miles from these parts. Several mine tunnels collapsed in the same mountain, n'many men were injured or killed," he said. My shoulders slumped and I uncrossed my fingers, letting my arms hang limp at my sides. "Now, now, I don't think y'Daddy was one o'them – 'cause like I said, no one's heard o'any Atwoods in them parts.

"The other bit o'news I heard was that there're more job openin's in towns a week or two's journey from Harlan," he continued. "I don't travel that far out with m'truck, but I was thinkin' maybe y'parents headed farther out again t'find work, n'that's why we cain't pick up their trail." My head dropped and Grace put her arm around me.

"That's a convincin' idea, Anna, don't y'think? If y'Daddy was in the mines that collapsed, surely, they would've had a registry o'workers n'someone would have recognized his name. I agree with Mr. Jingle. I imagine they keep travelin' further out t'look fo' work." If that was the case, I still wondered why they didn't just send a letter and say so.

I stood there, both of them watching me, but I could barely raise my chin. "I 'preciate it, Mr. Jingle, that y'made a special trip t'tell me what you've heard. Really, I thank y'fo' keepin' tryin'." Grace gave my shoulders a squeeze and leaned over to kiss the top of my head.

"*Dignified* young ladies like you cain't give up hope. Y'have t'keep on dreamin' n'waitin' fo' it all t'come true, y'hear? We'll get word one o'these days n'can y'imagine what a story they'll have t'tell ya? Not only y'parents, but y'sisters, too!"

I nodded, feeling a bit better knowing Mr. Jingle and Grace still had hope. My family *would* have really great stories to tell each other once reunited and for generations to come. I'd tell them about church, school, Carrie, Mr. Jingle, the Durrett Boys… and maybe a little about working in the fields with Mr. Grainger and how he wasn't the nicest man to work for or live with. I knew my Daddy would be proud that I was brave and stuck it out this long.

"I do thank ya, Mr. Jingle," I said more sincerely. Grace smiled and thanked him also, and after tipping his hat to us, Mr. Jingle rumbled off down the hill and out of sight.

"Let's go home," Grace said softly, bumping me gently with her hip. She put Olivia down and we both took one of her hands.

As we walked down the road, we swung Olivia by the arms every few steps. She would laugh and beg for more, completely oblivious to the muted moods around her. *Did Livie even remember Daddy and Momma? Did she know she had three other sisters besides me? Would she recognize any of them when they came back into our lives?* She was barely two years old when we came to the Graingers. *Did she think Grace was her Momma, now? Do old mothers just fade away and new ones take root?*

I'd swing and think, swing and think, my thoughts going round and round like a watermill. By the time the wheel dipped down, picked up water and got back upright again, the slippery thoughts had run off it in every direction. Olivia's giggles seemed far away as I'd swing and think, swing and think. Somewhere, deep inside me, the sliver of fear that my parents were *never* coming back for us was growing sharp... cutting into me with every step forward. I was trying to hold onto hope, like Mr. Jingle said dignified ladies do, but the doubts and questions were pressing in on me. *Something must have happened.* I knew it. *Something terrible must have happened.* My parents never would have stayed gone so long if something hadn't happened to keep them from us. They would have at least kept writing letters... but there was just *nothing*.

Grace had said *let's go home. Was the Graingers' farm our home now? Did I have to accept Mr. Grainger and Grace as my parents, like Olivia had already done?* Tears spilled down my cheeks, and I let them run and drip off my chin, a few of them sliding along the groove to my lips, the saltiness sneaking onto my tongue. If Grace noticed, she didn't draw attention to my pain... she just let me have the moment. *Surely this was not how life was going to be from now on. Momma and Daddy had not forgotten us!*

## 13

I couldn't remember Martha and Jonathan's exact address to send her a letter, but Grace had showed me how to address it in care of the post office in Leadwood, Missouri, and assured me it would get to her. I checked the post office in Harlan every time we came in town, and about six weeks after I sent mine, I received hers in return. I was so overjoyed I read the letter over and over for a week.

"Who's Martha?" Olivia asked curiously, peering over my shoulder as I read it on the porch for the hundredth time.

"She's y'oldes' sister," I answered absentmindedly, my eyes devouring the written words like I had never seen them before. "Back in Missouri."

Livie wandered over to Grace in the rocking chair and climbed into her lap. "What's Missouri?" she whispered to Grace.

"That's where y'all came from with y'fam'ly, Livie – 'fore y'came t'me," Grace said, rocking her gently. Livie gathered a handful of Grace's dress and rested her head on her shoulder.

"Janie's with Martha," I shook my head, still in disbelief. I turned to look at Grace. "She said she was half-starved n'skinny as a rail, but she made it all the way home!"

I had told Grace that several times now, but she still answered like it was the first time she heard the news. "Amazin' fo' a child so young t'journey so far on her own. Thank the good Lord in Heaven she made it safely!"

I wrote to Martha often after that and to Janie as well. It was so nice to hear their words in my head and see their handwriting; just knowing their hands had touched the same paper was comforting. Many a night I wished I had taken Olivia and run away back home in the beginning, too, but then I chided myself knowing Momma and Daddy would have disapproved. They were trying to give us a better life in Harlan, and it would have been a slap in the face for us to go backward again. Janie was the one of us that didn't mind to slap back a little, though… she had been slapped plenty in her young life.

One late November day, when Grace, Olivia, and I had come to town so she could pick out some fabric at the mercantile, I walked into the post office to check the mail. Mr. Murphy smiled from behind the counter and handed me a small envelope with my name on it and the Graingers' address underneath. "Here y'go, child! An early Christmas present fo' ya, I imagine!" he said.

I forced a smile. The fact that we would soon be spending our *second* Christmas in Harlan hadn't escaped me, and neither did Mr. Murphy *assuming* we would still be here by then. Everyone had pretty much determined we were here to stay… the abandoned orphans taken in by the charitable Graingers. It made my heart ache and my stomach sick, but there wasn't one thing I could do about it. I fingered the envelope that had traveled all the way from Missouri, thanked Mr. Murphy, and took my leave.

Grace and Olivia were still shopping, so I sat down on the mercantile's porch steps and carefully slid my finger under the flap of the envelope. I gently unfolded the piece of paper inside and smiled at Martha's pretty handwriting. Her cursive was loopier than mine, a *woman's* handwriting now. She had grown up a lot, too. I read silently, holding every word in my heart to contemplate a hundred times over.

*Dear Anna Beth,*

*While I don't have news of Momma and Daddy's whereabouts to share, I do have something exciting to tell you. I imagine by the time you receive this letter it will almost be December, and I will then be seven months with child! Can you believe it? I'm going to be a mother. I didn't tell you sooner cause I wanted to be sure things would be okay. Jonathan is over the moon about it. He says the baby will be a son and we will name it Benjamin, after Daddy.*

*I wish you all were still here in Leadwood to meet the baby, but as I told you before, we know Momma and Daddy did what they thought best when they moved the family to Kentucky. I'm praying we hear word from them soon. Maybe they had to find work in a different state and didn't want to uproot you all a second time, and they're about settled and will be back any day to fetch you. One day, maybe you'll even be able to come back to Missouri for a visit!*

*Take care of yourself and Olivia and pray for Emily, wherever she is – that everyone will be back together soon. We and Janie are doing fine.*

*Much love,*
*Martha*

I stared at the letter a few more minutes, then neatly folded it and put it back in the envelope. A baby – how exciting! Martha was eighteen years old now, plenty old enough to have a baby. I had actually wondered why it took them this long. Most married couples start having babies right away, and I had hoped her body wasn't broken like Grace's. I closed my eyes and said a little prayer for a safe delivery.

I sat deep in thought, cradling my chin in my hands with my eyes closed and pictured Missouri. I could still see Jonathan and Martha's house,

I guess because I had seared it into my memory. I tried to imagine Janie on the front porch… then something hit my shoulder, jolting pain through my whole body, and my eyes flew open as I grabbed my arm with a gasp. A ball was bouncing back toward the street to its nasty owners, and I realized what had happened. The Durrett Boys were standing in the middle of the road pointing my way, laughing hysterically.

"Oh, *sorry*, Anna Beth – we didn't see y'there!" sneered Chancey, the oldest.

"Yeah! If we'd've seen ya, we would've hit y'in the head!" jeered Johnny.

I stood up, hands on hips, and narrowed my eyes at the bunch of them.

"You're lucky I don't have a rock handy!" I fired back. I was so focused on the oldest two, I didn't notice Tommy, Timmy, and Chester coming up behind me – like wolves closing in on their prey. Chester, the littlest and fastest, whipped around and snatched Martha's letter right from my hand.

"Hey! Give that back!" I shouted as he jumped off the porch and ran to his big brothers victoriously. The other boys jumped off the porch, making faces at me as they also joined their rat pack in the street.

"I got it, Chancey!" Chester squealed with delight, waving the envelope in his dirty little hand.

I protested loudly, but Chancey ripped the envelope open and started reading aloud. I ran down the steps and tried to grab it back, but the brothers ganged around Chancey, keeping me at arm's length. I hollered and struggled against them, but Johnny pushed me so hard I tripped and fell backward in the dirt.

"*Aw*, look guys – 'er sister's gonna have a baby! I wonder if they'll *orphan* it like 'er parents did 'er!" Chancey guffawed.

Anger bubbled up inside me and I came up, fists swinging wildly. My right one connected with Timmy's face, and the eight-year-old crumbled to the ground wailing. His brothers broke ranks to pull him back to his feet. His nose was gushing blood onto his shirt.

Chancey pushed through them and charged toward me like an angry bull. I started backing up quickly, all the way to the alley between the mercantile and doctor's office. When I hit the side wall of the mercantile, I knew I had opened a bigger can or worms than I could deal with this time. Chancey was on top of me in a second, and at nearly a foot taller he towered over me.

"Jus' *who* d'ya think ya're, hittin' a little boy like that?" he growled.

I squeezed my eyes shut, sure he'd take a swing at me. Instead, he hit the wall right by my head with his fist. My eyes flew open. I gritted my teeth and forced myself to look him right in the eyes, refusing to show fear. He brought his face so close to mine that our noses nearly touched, and I could smell his foul breath.

He lowered his voice. "Y'think you're all brave standin' up fo' Carrie, but I've news fo' ya. You're a *nobody*. Y'own parents didn't even want y'n'y'stupid sisters."

"That's not true," I hissed. "They'll be back fo' us!"

He laughed and spit in my face. "Y'got a head full o'rocks, y'do. Let me spell it out fo' ya. *They left you*," he spoke slowly, punching every word. "They'll *never* be back fo' ya, y'sorry mutt. They must've hated y'all somethin' fierce, they did – parents who *love* their kids don't leave 'em with strangers fo' nearly two years... y'half-wit."

I wiped the spit from my cheek and was trying to think of a retort when Grace and Mrs. Corrigan came around the corner of the alley. Grace's eyes grew big as saucers, and Mrs. Corrigan covered a gasp with her hand. Chancey saw them out of the corner of his eye, and his whole demeanor changed. He smiled at me, vengeance twinkling in his eyes, then leaned in and *kissed* me! His mouth was hot, sweaty, and wet, nothing at all how I imagined a first kiss. I couldn't breathe. I desperately wanted to shove him away, but my arms felt frozen at my sides. He finally pulled back and winked at me.

"See y'later, *sweetheart*," he said loud enough for Grace and Mrs. Corrigan to hear. Then he waltzed past them and nodded in greeting. "Ladies," he said politely.

They slowly turned and watched him walk back to his brothers in the street. Then they turned back to me. I was shivering with anger and fear, still frozen against the wall.

"*Anna Beth Atwood get over here right now*," Grace said in a strict tone I had never heard before.

I pushed myself off the wall, feeling weak and shaky. Olivia was staring at me, half hid behind Grace's dress, her thumb stuck deep in her mouth. I started toward them.

"*What… what were…*" Grace stuttered. She sounded upset at *me*.

"Bes' get 'er home, dear," Mrs. Corrigan whispered, patting Grace sympathetically on the shoulder and looking all around. "Y'all can sort this out; I'm sure it'll be jus' *fine*." Grace nodded but didn't look at her. Mrs. Corrigan glanced once more at me, shaking her head in disapproval, then she walked around the building and back up the porch steps. I heard the little bell ring when she slipped inside the mercantile door.

I stood at the edge of the alley, staring at Grace. She looked beside herself. "Grace, I…" I started to explain about the letter and fight.

"Let's get home," she cut in with a shake of her head. She reached out and put her arm around me, steering me into the street, looking left and then right. No one was around; even the Durrett Boys had run off.

We walked down the big hill in silence, except for Olivia pointing out obvious things – the schoolhouse, an orange striped cat, the church, a robin. I waited for Grace to speak first, like I waited for Mr. Grainger to ask me a question so I could answer. I wanted to tell her how the Durrett Boys took my letter and made fun of me, what awful things Chancey said about my parents in the alley. I might have left out the bit about me accidentally hitting Timmy… but Grace just kept walking, staring straight ahead, with only the occasional call to Olivia to stay close.

When we reached the farm, it was nearing dinner time. Mr. Grainger was still out trying to sell more crops before the winter snows; it had been a good year for farmers and the excess goods made this season a buyers' market – which was bad news for the sellers. I had heard Mr. Grainger yelling about it to Grace late at night a few times.

Grace got Olivia settled into a corner of the sitting room, then ushered me back out to sit on the porch steps with her. She took a deep breath and finally spoke.

"Anna, d'ya know why I felt upset when Mrs. Corrigan n'I caught you n'Chancey in the alley?" she asked quietly. She crossed her arms over her chest.

"No, ma'am," I answered honestly. I hadn't called her *ma'am* in a long time, and the word felt foreign in my mouth.

"It was very *inappropriate*, Anna, what y'all were doin'," she whispered the words like they were shameful.

"How's fightin' inappropriate?" I asked, really confused now. My parents didn't condone us girls getting into fights, but they didn't act like it was shameful to stand up for yourself neither.

"*Fightin'*? That's not what it looked like t'me, nor t'anyone else young lady," Grace said, her back stiffening. "Y'two were *sportin'* with one another, n'y'all're much too young fo' such thin's at barely fourteen. Y'Momma n'Daddy wouldn't've approved, n'neither do I."

"*Sportin'*?!" I exclaimed. Momma had talked about Jonathan sporting with Martha when they were engaged to be married. It meant teasing each other in a sweet, funny way – because you couldn't wait to be husband and wife. I was dumbfounded how Grace could arrive at such a notion about me and that awful Chancey Durrett. "I was *not* sportin' with Chancey – I was…"

"I'm not interested in what y'*were* or were *not* doin'," Grace interrupted. "What matters is what people *think*, Anna, n'I can tell y'right now, Mrs. Corrigan thought the *wors'* – n'the whole town'll hear of it… they'll doubt y'integrity as a proper young lady! Scandals like that cause trouble y'whole life," she shook her head.

"But that's not what happened!" I cried, standing up. Grace implying I was sporting with Chancey Durrett was one thing, but her refusing to even hear the truth was what really hurt.

"Lower y'voice n'sit back down, Anna Beth. You'll *not* take that tone with me," she ordered. I was so angry and upset I laughed and walked off the porch into the yard. Who did she think she was?

"*You're not my Momma,*" I said slowly, making every word sting. I figured it would hurt her feelings the most, and I was right. Her face contorted and she stood up, starting toward me.

"Now y'see here, young lady..." she started. Then we both heard Mr. Grainger coming down the road. The wagon bounced in and out of the dirt ruts as he jerked the horse's reins; the back still full of crops and a nasty grimace on his face. Grace stopped in her tracks; her whole demeanor changing in an instant. She quickly smoothed back her loose curls from her face and reached out a shaking hand to me.

"Anna, come here please," she said in a much softer tone. I could hear the fear shake her voice and ran right into her arms without thinking twice. She took me by the shoulders and pulled me up the porch steps and inside the door. "Let's not talk 'bout this anymore right now..."

"But, *Grace,*" I insisted. I desperately wanted to tell her the truth about Chancey. I'd even tell her the bit about Timmy if she'd let me.

"Anna, not another word," she warned.

"*But...*"

Grace stopped by the kitchen and spoke quickly, glancing at the open window. Mr. Grainger had pulled the wagon up to the shed and was throwing the crops inside as hard as he could heave them. "Anna, Jack's already terribly short-tempered from worryin' over the bills. If he hears 'bout this, he'll *discipline* ya. D'ya know what that means?" Her eyes pleaded with me to understand.

My mind flashed back to the night I heard them arguing in their bedroom when I was so sure he had hit Grace. The night I convinced myself was merely a dream. I swallowed hard and nodded quickly.

"Good, now get in the kitchen n'help me start dinner. Okay? Pretend this whole thin' *never* happened," she said.

I hurried to get the pots and pans out of the cabinets as the front door banged open. Grace greeted her husband, and the door slammed shut again. He grunted a hello, gathered a towel from the bedroom, and traipsed through the kitchen, mumbling how he was going to wash up in the tub. Grace joined me at the stove and sighed in relief. Her whole body was shaking.

Side by side we worked quietly and efficiently to get food on the table. Then, after a little small talk over dinner, I helped her wash dishes and we all went to bed. She never brought up the incident in the alley again... and as much as it ate at my insides, neither did I.

*14*

Grace and I may have kept quiet about what happened in the alley, but as she predicted, Mrs. Corrigan did not. Carrie was right – the preacher needed to deliver a good sermon on the sin of gossiping! The rumors about me and Chancey courting in secret spread like wildfire through the women's circles. Chancey was also bragging to his friends that I let him steal a kiss, but that was just to kids. Maybe the men in town were none the wiser, and I prayed every day that Mr. Grainger didn't hear any of the talk. If it wasn't for Carrie and Mr. Jingle, who believed my side of the story and supported me with kind words of *this too shall pass*, I don't know how I would have survived the speculation and ridicule.

It was now February – and very cold. Blankets of snow had been dumped on Harlan that winter, and it had barely melted. Grace celebrated my fourteenth and Livie's fourth birthdays with another big cake and nickel each, but the feeling wasn't the same as the year before. My insides still burned with the injustice of her disbelief as I'm sure hers did of my proposed wantonness. It had been two and a half months since the incident, and we still hadn't sorted out the details.

School was my refuge, for the most part. At home I was always caught between a rock and a hard place with both Graingers, and at church everyone looked at me disapprovingly through the whole service. At school, though, the most I had to shoulder was snickers and one-line insults behind Mrs. Sensley's back.

Mrs. Sensley let us eat our lunches inside during winter so we could all stay warm. Carrie and I often huddled in the front left corner of the room, near the old pot-bellied stove that glowed with heat, and other little groups of friends were sprinkled throughout the desks and in the back of the room. They would chat and laugh with one another, still talking about the good Christmas they had. Someone would end up asking Chancey how it was going with me and the conversation would take a nasty turn.

One day I was staring at them with all the hatred I could muster, taking slow bites of the turkey sandwich Grace had packed me. Carrie held out her apple and cleared her throat.

"I'll trade you my apple for your orange," she offered, breaking me out of my trance. I handed her my fruit and took hers in return. "Anna, the talk about you and Chancey will die down any day now. Harlan is such a sleepy little town; something else will happen, and then everyone will be talking about that." I shrugged my shoulders. I didn't really want to talk about it even though it monopolized my thoughts. "Have you seen Mr. Jingle lately? Any news of your parents?" she asked, changing the subject.

I shook my head with a sigh. "No, I don't think he can get his truck down the roads in this kind o'snow, though. I ain't seen 'im in a couple o'weeks, so I imagine he's snowed in somewhere."

Carrie sighed, too. "I sure do miss him." I nodded in heartfelt agreement that time. Right at that moment we heard a kissing noise and looked up to see Chancey kissing his hand passionately and all his brothers and friends laughing. I turned away, disgusted.

"He makes me sick," I said, putting my half-eaten sandwich and Carrie's apple back in the bag.

"He's just a big bully. Don't even look at him," my friend said. I smiled a bit at her and really took in her appearance for the first time in a long time.

Carrie had taken to leaving her hair down; instead of braids she gathered it half up and fastened it with a pretty clip like Mrs. Sensley's. Her red hair shimmered in the light of the window, and I envied that clip. It made her look older – she was now thirteen. I remembered all the changes *my* mind and body went through the year before and wondered if she had the same thoughts and feelings. If she did, she dealt with them privately, as I had.

After school, Carrie and I bundled up in our heavy coats and scarves alongside the other kids and headed out into the cold for the long walk home. The bitter wind lashed at our faces and bit our hands through our gloves. None of the kids wanted to play snowball fight or make snow angels, not even the little ones. Everyone was intent on getting home to their fireplaces. Carrie and I couldn't even talk because our teeth were chattering and our lips too frozen! Finally, we reached the fork in the road and just waved bye to one another. Carrie's cheeks and nose were bright red, making her hair that stuck out beneath the hat look like it was ablaze.

As I trudged on down the hill toward the Graingers' farm, my mind turned to Momma and Daddy for the millionth time. The continual questions of where they were, what had happened, why they weren't getting my letters – or sending me any – swirled in my head like an angry snowstorm. Not the mesmerizing kind that you stand at the window and watch, but the destructive kind that kills a person if they're caught out in it for too long. There were no answers to calm the raging, either. I just let myself dwell in it a bit… then packed it back inside me like ice that wouldn't melt.

I forced my thoughts to Olivia, who was now four years old. She never mentioned Momma or Daddy, Janie or Emily, Martha or Jonathan… they were people *I* knew, not her… she only knew the Graingers and me. Since it caused her confusion, I didn't mention them often, either. I also didn't want to upset Grace with too much talk of our family any more than I already had with the Chancey incident. She had really taken to Olivia, and I didn't want her to think I was ungrateful for their hospitality in letting us stay long past our welcome… or forever, for that matter. *There I am, back to my parents again.* I thought bitterly, and I shook my head hard.

When I reached the Graingers' farm, I was so cold I could barely move. I jammed the gate into a snowdrift and squeezed myself through. Mr. Grainger, who was in the side yard chopping wood, hollered for me to come stack it. I was exhausted from fighting my way home in all that heavy clothing, and I couldn't even feel my hands, but I obediently went and stacked the log quarters as best I could. Then I rushed through the rest of my chores to finish before dark which closed in around us much faster in the winter months. When I was finally inside, I went straight to the fireplace to warm up. My boots, soaked through despite the cardboard and extra wrappings, were set on the hearth to dry out next to me.

"Did y'have a good day at school, Anna?" Grace asked from her rocking chair. She was cross-stitching a winter scene of a deer standing in front of snowy woods to sell at the mercantile.

"It was okay," I lied, rubbing my hands together in front of the fireplace to get some feeling back in my fingers. She knew I didn't have a good day. I hadn't had a good day since the gossip about Chancey started.

"Spring n'warmer weather're comin'. I bet they bring better days with 'em," Grace offered, her eyes on her handiwork while she rocked. I rolled my eyes.

"I'm goin' t'school with ya, Anna Beth!" Olivia said from the corner, grinning from ear to ear. Her blonde curls reached her waist now, and Grace had taken to pulling the sides up in blue barrettes that matched her pretty eyes. Olivia held up her cornhusk doll, all worn out and well-loved, and the matching cornhusk boy doll Grace had made her as a Christmas present. She wiggled the dolls, pretending they were talking back and forth.

"Yes, Livie, nex' year when you're five y'can go t'school with me," I told her.

Grace laid her work aside and stretched. "Well, it's 'bout time fo' dinner. Jack'll be in from the cold soon n'he'll expect a hot meal on the table t'warm 'im up."

I got up and followed her to the kitchen. We fixed roast beef, mashed potatoes, and corn… and the delicious smell took my mind off all my worries and heartaches. The heat rose from the meat in little tendrils, and I let a forkful hover in front of my mouth, feeling the warmth on my lips before slipping it in and feeling it melt on my tongue.

After dinner, Olivia and I helped Grace clean up. I washed the dishes, handed the silverware to Olivia to dry and put away, and gave the breakables to Grace. Mr. Grainger usually excused himself right after eating and retired to the bedroom, but for some reason he sat at the table and watched us work. When we finished the last dish, he was still just sitting there. The shadows from the moonlight streaming in through the window hid half his face, making him look even more temperamental than usual.

"Jack? Is ev'rythin' ok?" Grace asked, surprised when she turned around and saw her husband. She wiped her hands on a towel and eyed him warily.

"Mind y'own business, woman," he said gruffly. "Go on 'bout y'night."

Grace glanced at me, put her towel on the counter, and took Olivia by the hand. They had started reading a storybook together in the rocking chair before bed these days, and it was one of Olivia's favorite things to do now. She usually fell asleep before the story was finished, and Grace tucked her into bed with an extra kiss. They walked into the next room, and Mr. Grainger looked back out the window into the dark night.

"Y'forgot t'feed the chickens," he said.

"Sir?" I asked, thinking back on my chores. I was so cold and hurrying through them – I thought I had got them all done before I came in. Chores have a way of running together in your mind when you do the same drudgery day after day, year after year.

"Y'hard o'hearin', girl? I said *go* feed the chickens," he ordered, his eyes settling on me. There was an unusual coldness in them... he also hadn't called me *girl* in a long time.

"Yes, sir," I answered quickly, walking to the kitchen door and taking my heavy coat down from the peg. I bundled up, wrapping my scarf around my neck.

Grace had put my dried boots by the door, so I wrapped extra cloth around my feet and slid them back into the oversized shoes. I stole one last glance at Mr. Grainger, who was looking out the window again, then pushed out the door into the darkness.

The cold air hit my face like a knife. I readjusted my scarf to cover my ears, mouth, and nose and made my way through the heavy snow to the shed. It was *so* dark I could barely see the outline of things; the shed seemed a mysterious shadow in the distance that kept shifting in the sliver of moonlight. The chickens heard me coming and poked their heads out of the coop, looking at me curiously, their heads cocking to one side and then the other.

"Sorry, girls," I mumbled, "but I don't think y'all would've starved in one night."

I unlatched the shed door and yanked it open, continuing to grumble. Mr. Grainger just liked to be in *control*. He took pleasure in ordering us around and watching us obey him like a king. He had probably been waiting for me to forget a chore so he could rub my face in it.

I walked to the trough, feeling my way along the wall in the dark, and gathered the hem of my dress to make a pocket for the grain. It was much more cumbersome with the heavy coat and gloved hands. My eyes slowly adjusted to the dark, though, and I was grateful for the bits of persistent moonlight squeezing through the cracks in the walls. I filled my pocket with corn kernels and was just about ready to go out when I heard the shed door creak open behind me. I startled and jerked around quickly, pulling my hands up to my thumping chest in fright. I could barely make out Mr. Grainger's figure in the doorway, the shadowy edges of him twisting out into the darkness behind him.

"Mr. Grainger, y'frightened me!" I gasped. Then I remembered not to show my slip and lowered my hands, still holding the hem of my dress with the pocket of corn. I tried to slow my breathing and regain my composure. *What was he doing out here? I came to do what I was told.*

Mr. Grainger stepped into the shed and pulled the door firmly shut behind him. He looked strange, and it scared me. I couldn't decide if he was angry, upset, or something else entirely.

"I'm feedin' the chickens like y'asked," I said quickly.

He took a step toward me, and I instinctively took a step back. "This ain't 'bout no chickens," he said. "I'm sick n'tired of not gettin' paid what I'm owed – and I've not nearly got my worth outta ya."

"I can do anythin' y'want, sir," I nodded. "Help anyway I can…"

He took another step toward me, and I backed into the wall, the memory of Chancey in the alley consuming my thoughts. My mind started racing. He was angry at me like Chancey was, and he was going to hit me like he had Grace. I thought about screaming for Grace, but she probably couldn't hear me – and oh, would that make Mr. Grainger angrier!

"Don't think 'bout screamin', girl," Mr. Grainger said, reading my mind. He was *so* close to me now I could smell his sweat, and it turned my stomach. *How could he be hot in the cold night's air?*

"Didn't y'Daddy tell y't'earn y'keep n'not cause any trouble? He said y'would do us a favor, n'the way I see it, I've done a lot more fo' y'all than you've fo' me. Keepin' y'fed n'housed ev'ry single day since they left y'all on m'doorstep... come summer it'll be two years. *Two years*, girl." The last words came out of his throat like a low growl. "I mightn't not b'able t'get m'fair pay outta them crops, but I sure can get m'pay outta you."

I swallowed hard and looked for a way out. The shed was too tight to get past him. I searched for something to say instead. All I could think about, however, was not spilling the grain in my dress and making matters worse. *What was he upset with me for anyway?*

"I don't know o'any other parents that leave their children with strangers fo' two long years n'not even write, d'ya?" he asked with a sneer.

"No, sir," I tried to speak bravely, "but I know they'll..."

His sneer twisted into a nasty smile, and I cowered against the wall with tears welling up in my eyes. "They ain't comin' back, girl, n'y'know what that means? *You're mine.*"

Mr. Grainger grabbed my arms and squeezed them so hard I cried out. I begged him to let go, but he pushed me to the floor and grain scattered everywhere. I screamed, my heart pounding in my throat, but he easily pinned my body under his knee and covered my mouth with his sweaty hand. I was sure he was going to beat me, and after the fact, I *wished* he had. I pictured Grace in the house, sitting in the rocking chair while she read a sweet story to Olivia...

I cried hysterically and thrashed against him, but he was too big and strong. Eventually, I stopped struggling, my muscles exhausted under all those winter clothes and his weight. I had felt pain before, but nothing like this. It was like repeatedly using the shears in my blistered hands the first time I worked the fields – open, close, open, close. By the time he finished with me I felt blood soaking my undergarments. He stood up with a grunt, adjusted his clothing and swaggered back to the door saying *I was well worth the wait.*

"Happy birthday," he laughed. "I made a woman out o'ya." His voice sounded far off, like hearing something through a waterfall. My ears were ringing, I was sick to my stomach and dizzy, and the little bits of moonlight I had been so thankful for were swimming in and out my vision as I desperately clung to consciousness.

Mr. Grainger paused with his hand on the door and spoke quietly. "If y'think I don't listen t'the town's gossip n'didn't know 'bout y'*seducin'* that Durrett boy, you're denser than I thought. I've been watchin' y'fo' a *long* time. I *knew* what kind a girl y'were when y'Daddy gave y't'me. I imagine that's why they wanted t'get rid o'ya in the firs' place… *y'think men don't see y'sinful wiles?* Y'got what was comin' t'ya – n'it's y'own shameful fault." The shed door creaked open and a gush of cold stirred my senses. I gasped for air, feeling smothered in all the winter clothes, like his body was still on me.

"N'another thin' – y'tell *anyone* 'bout me givin' y'what y'clearly asked fo', they won't *b'lieve* ya. You're already known as a little liar n'hussy. If y'try n'tell anyways, jus' 'member you're mine now, n'I can make y'wish y'were dead." He walked out of the shed and looked back at me. "Now finish feedin' the chickens like I told y'to."

I laid as a heap in the floor, listening to the snow crunch under his boots as he stalked back to the house. It hurt to even *move*. I felt rubbed raw from the inside out. After great deliberation, I managed to roll onto my stomach and pull my knees under me, but I just sat there, drawn into a tight ball, my forehead pressed against the dirty wooden planks of the shed floor. A fresh wave of hot tears stung my eyes. When I sat up, everything started spinning and I felt more nauseous, so I just laid still, breathing in and out between sobs that shook my whole body.

Eventually the nausea subsided, and I gripped the edge of the trough. I heaved my aching body into a standing position though my legs wobbled beneath me, and held onto the trough with both hands to balance. I slowly made a pocket with my dress and filled it with new grain, the old crunching beneath my boots. I carefully stepped down from the shed into the snow and just dropped my hem, letting the corn fall in a big heap at my feet, then I doubled over and threw up off to the side. My throat burned and tears streamed down my cheeks as I looked up at the Graingers' darkened house. *I'm truly alone in the world, and there's no way back home now.*

*15*

It's an odd thing, how life goes on after something terrible happens. It's as if since the world can't see your pain, it doesn't *really* exist. Martha once told us about a carnival Jonathan took her to when it came through Leadwood. She said the carousel ride had moving horses going up and down, while the whole thing spun round and round, and music filled the air. It sounded like a fun dream when I was just a girl, but now the thought was a dizzying nightmare. I could see myself standing alone in a field, watching the carousel of life moving up and down, round and round, music blaring... yet *I* wasn't able to move forward or backward myself. I was stuck, watching and wishing I could run far away from Harlan, but not knowing who would even want me anymore – and I could never leave Olivia here alone.

My body might have healed after the attack, but I remembered every word Mr. Grainger spoke to me that dreadful night. He seared the bad into me the same way I had tried to sear in the good. *Your Daddy said you would do us a favor. What parents leave their children with strangers? They're not coming back.* His words about my family burned bad enough, but the town gossip was red hot. *You seduced that Durrett boy. I knew what kind of girl you were. Men see your sinful wiles. It's your own shameful fault.* He warned me not to tell anyone, and I hadn't dared. I was ashamed of what had happened and tried to understand how I had asked for such an awful thing. All I could figure was that Chancey's vengeful kiss *had* smeared my good name as Grace said it would, and now everyone thought I had loose morals. If I told the truth, if I tried to make them listen, they'd call me a liar. Mr. Grainger said they would.

"Anna Beth!" Mrs. Sensley hit my desk with a ruler, and I jerked out of a fitful dream.

I rubbed my eyes, struggling to pull myself out of a foggy remembrance of carousel horses staring at me with large unblinking eyes. The rest of the class snickered behind their hands and whispered to one another.

"Young lady, you've gotten terribly off track with your studies the last couple of months! You're failing your math tests, turning in chicken scratch of writing assignments, *if* you turn them in at all… and now you're *sleeping* through your lessons… is the history of this great country *boring* you that much?" Mrs. Sensley asked, smacking her ruler against her open hand.

"I'm sorry, ma'am," I apologized, glancing around at my classmates. Carrie was the only one who sat quietly, her eyes cast downward. I saw what book she had on her desk and hastily switched my science book out for *History of America*.

"You know what I think," Mrs. Sensley said, "you best pack up your things and go on home."

I looked up at her with wide eyes, not sure I heard right. "Ma'am?"

"Pack up your things and leave my classroom. Take the rest of the week off, in fact. Let's see if you can come back next week with the work ethic I'm accustomed to."

She stood in front of my desk, watching me slowly slip my book back into the strap with the others, gather my lunch and sweater, and walk toward the door. The whole class turned in their seats to watch. I glanced back at Carrie. She had tears in her eyes. I pushed open the schoolroom door, walked down the steps, and began my slow journey to the dirt road in utter dismay.

*What would I tell the Graingers?* I worried as I walked to the farm. Grace would be upset… but it would leave me more time to help with spring planting which would please Mr. Grainger. I couldn't quit helping him; Olivia and I'd be out on the street. It was April, and I knew school would only be in session for another month or so before summer break. I feared my failing grades and sleeping spells would warrant expulsion. The thought of being kicked out of school made me feel more abashed. That would be yet another dark mark on my good name.

I heard the familiar sound of pots and pans jangling behind me and knew it was Mr. Jingle without looking. He slowed down beside me and saluted like always. "Well, if it ain't Miss Dignity! Out a school early t'day?" he asked.

I shrugged my shoulders and kept walking, my eyes on my shoes. He let his truck creep along next to me.

"Huh," he said. "Seems t'me you've been pretty down since winter. The world's perkin' up 'round ya, child, comin' back t'life n'warmin' up now. What's got y'so down-trodden?" He stopped the truck and I stopped, too. "How 'bout a ride?" After a moment of hesitation, I climbed up beside him and he patted my leg.

"Is it y'parents?" he fished, putting the truck back in gear.

"I don't think they're comin' back," I said quietly. "If that's what y'mean."

The truth tasted bitter, so I didn't chew on it very long. Then the truck bounced over a dip in the road and my stomach jolted. It felt like wind blowing through my belly, like a tickle, and my hand flew to my middle. I breathed deeply, staving off a wave of nausea.

Mr. Jingle glanced at me and rubbed his nose. "Y'got a stomachache?"

"Not really," I said, rubbing my stomach tenderly.

"Y'sure're a lady o'few words these days."

We drove down the big hill to the farms mostly in silence, him asking a question here and there and me giving a few words in answer. When we arrived in front of the Graingers' house, Grace came out and stood on the porch. Olivia was sitting on the steps playing with her cornhusk dolls, and she and Grace both waved. Mr. Jingle waved back, then turned to me, his eyebrows knitted together with concern. "Dignity, is ev'rythin' okay?" he asked quietly.

Our eyes met, and for a brief moment I considered telling him everything. I wanted someone to hug me and assure me things would be alright
again. Most of all, I wanted to hear him call me *Dignity*, even after he knew
I was tarnished. Mr. Grainger's words rang in my ears, though. *You're a liar
and a hussy. No one would believe you, so don't even try.* My head dropped. Mr.
Jingle would never call me Dignity again if he knew the truth. I climbed
down out of his truck and hugged my books to my chest.

"I'm fine, Mr. Jingle – thanks fo' the ride," I said quietly. I bit my lip
until I tasted blood. It was a pain I could understand, a pain I could control,
unlike the other wrestling inside me.

My old friend nodded. "Alright, Dignity. I'll see y'soon, then. Y'take
care o'y'self." His truck rumbled off and I watched him go, his tires creating little dust clouds that swirled in the road. *If I couldn't tell Mr. Jingle then
who in this world could I trust?*

Grace walked to the gate and opened it for me. "Anna Beth, why're
y'home early? Are y'sick?" Sick sounded like a pretty good excuse to me…
at least I wouldn't have to tell her the truth about school and Mrs. Sensley
right away. She felt my forehead for fever.

"I can still do m'chores," I told her, pulling back so her hand dropped
from my forehead.

"Well, y'don't have any fever. I imagine if y'feel up t'it y'can get 'em
done. Then come on inside t'res'… don't overdo it, okay?" Grace went
to wrap her arm around my shoulders, but I shoved my books at her and
walked toward the side yard.

"Yes, *ma'am.* I'll be right in," I said over my shoulder as I headed for
the woodpile and chickens.

I was so angry with Grace these days that I had just stopped trying to
make up with her. I didn't want her to talk to me, touch me, nothing. She
had never asked my side of the Chancey story, and now there was another
secret between us, an *awful* secret about her *good* man of a husband. The
ugliness of it consumed my thoughts. *How do I even begin to talk about such
things?* I wondered. Then just as quick, his words flooded my mind. *No one
would believe you, so don't even try.*

I cycled through my outside chores and helped make dinner. Grace told Mr. Grainger I hadn't felt well, and that's why I came home from school early... and I didn't correct her. Olivia finished drying and putting away the silverware and asked to be excused to play with her dolls before bed. Grace watched her go in the other room, her golden child, and a soft smile turned up the corners of her mouth. From the table, Mr. Grainger was watching me tiptoe as I reached to put the last clean dish in the cabinet.

"Why did y'leave school t'day?" he demanded, a frown creeping across his pockmarked and ruddy face.

Grace glanced from her husband to me, confused. "Jack, I told y'Anna Beth didn't feel well," she said. Mr. Grainger narrowed his eyes at his wife, and she fell silent.

"I asked *you* a question, girl," he said in a threatening voice.

My head started spinning, and I suddenly struggled to grasp a thought. It was like someone opened a trap door in my brain and all the words fell into my stomach. "I – I haven't been fe – feelin' well lately, sir." I stuttered, pulling each word out with great effort. I stared at the floor like Grace did when he started in on her about something.

"Look at me, girl," Mr. Grainger growled from the table. I jerked my head up. When our eyes met, my stomach flipped. "I'm not buyin' *sick*," he said. "I heard in town that Chancey Durrett also skipped school t'day. You've been meetin' up with 'im, ain't ya?"

Grace looked at me with an audible gasp. "Anna Beth, *tell* me this ain't true! Y'were t'have nothin' else t'do with that boy!"

I was feeling dizzier by the second, my vision narrowing in and out of focus. "No..." I mumbled, closing my eyes and shaking my head. My mouth flooded with hot saliva. "I wasn't with Chancey... I – I *hate* 'im! I jus' ain't fe – felt well..."

"Y'*liar*," Mr. Grainger growled. He stood up and started toward me – *you're a liar and a hussy, a liar and a hussy* – and the world spun out of control.

I could hear hot blood pulsating in my temples, yet my arms and legs felt cold. A hot wave of nausea hit me like a slap in the face. I doubled over and threw up all over the kitchen floor, then fell to my knees. I felt like I was drowning, not knowing which way was up, as another wave broke over me. Mr. Grainger jumped back in disgust, but Grace ran to me and held my shoulders. I couldn't sit up. I couldn't lay down… then suddenly I just collapsed in my own vomit, the cool floor feeling good and solid against my cheek.

"*Oh, m'goodness! Anna!*" Grace cried. She ran to the sink and pulled several dishrags from the drawer. She wet one and wrapped it around my neck, then started mopping up the vomit with the others. "I told y'she was sick!" she screamed at her husband.

Mr. Grainger cursed at us and stormed to his bedroom, slamming the door shut. Grace helped me sit in one of the chairs and told me to put my head between my knees. She cleaned the floor up, and then went to wiping me off. With several deep breaths and my eyes closed, I started to regain control of my senses and the world uprighted itself. My field of vision widened, and the spinning slowly came to a stop.

I lifted my head and watched her, this woman who *seemed* to care about me, yet simultaneously thought the worst of me. She still thought I was sporting with Chancey Durrett, even skipping school to see him. A surge of emotion welled up within in me, and tears came with great, shaking sobs. This terrible secret was eating me from the inside out like acid – I needed to talk to someone… anyone, but *no one* would ever believe me!

Grace, dismayed by my uncontrollable outburst, quickly finished cleaning and got a fresh rag to wipe away my tears. She patted my shoulder, saying I couldn't help being sick and I'd feel better in the morning. I just cried all the harder. I *knew* I wouldn't feel better in the morning. *I would never feel okay again!*

Olivia stood quiet as a mouse in the doorway, sucking her fingers. "Is Anna okay?" she whispered to Grace. She was on the verge of tears, too. Grace motioned for her to come over. Livie drew close, and Grace lifted her in my lap.

"*There, there, Anna* – don't worry a thin' 'bout it! Ev'rythin's okay now. Jus' calm down. You'll feel better after a good night's res', I *promise*," Grace said. My parents had promised me things, too. I no longer had faith in them, and I certainly wasn't going to put my faith in Grace.

Olivia wrapped her arms around me and squeezed. The pressure felt good. I wrapped my arms around her and cried until my tears ran out. I missed my parents and my other sisters... I missed Leadwood and my old life that was whole and unbroken by time, circumstance, and others' hateful selfishness. I buried my head in Olivia's long curls and smelled that sweet honeysuckle hair. It was amazing that she smelled the same after all this time. My heartbeat eventually slowed, my stomach settled, and suddenly I felt completely exhausted. My muscles were heavy, my eyelids sagging. I could have fallen asleep right there in the kitchen chair. Grace helped us change into our gowns and get into our little bed. She blew out the candle on the table and gave me one last pat on my shoulder.

I tried to stay awake to figure out what to do next. I could *not* keep living like this... what Mr. Grainger had done was going to rip me wide open. Secrets have a life of their own; they scratch from the inside, clawing their way to the light. Right before I slipped into darkness, a picture of Carrie swam into view. I could see her glimmering red hair, pulled half up in a clip, her smiling face full of freckles. *I can trust Carrie.* I dreamt I was trying to find her – searching her house, the hotel, school, church. By the time the sun rose my dream had melted into the shadows, but it was like a spark of hope caught fire inside me. I would find my best friend and let my story out before it killed me.

*16*

Mr. Grainger tried to make me continue my chores as normal but quickly tired of me throwing up in the yard. I didn't think I was really sick; I was just terribly nervous around him. He finally told Grace to have me sleep the "illness" off, and Grace kept me home for a couple of weeks, nursing me back to health with chicken and dumplings and lots of rest. I was truly grateful for her tender care, even though I was still sore with her for all the other.

When I was sleeping, finding Carrie filled my dreams. When I was conscious, I'd lay there in our little bed by the stove, staring at the striped wall and planning what to tell her when the chance presented itself. I worried she wouldn't believe me, but my heart stirred with cautious hope when I thought of letting my secret break free. When Grace proclaimed me well enough to go back to school, it was late May. There were two more weeks of classes before summer break and then the harvest would begin.

The morning I was to go back to school I got dressed and headed out early, waiting for Carrie halfway up the hill at the fork in the road. I watched the sun stretch over the green trees, bathing the dirt road in golden light, and then there she was, coming down and around the bend. She was dragging a stick behind her making miniature dried-up riverbeds like always, and my heart burst with affection for my best friend.

"Carrie!" I called excitedly. When she looked up and saw me, her face lit up in a smile. She dropped the stick and ran to wrap her arms around me. The warmth and closeness were refreshing; I didn't want to let go.

"Oh, Anna Beth! I'm so happy you're better!" she squealed breathlessly, pulling back and looking me up and down. "Mrs. Sensley felt *awful* about how she treated you that day in class." I smiled, figuring our teacher attributed my recent shortcomings to the onset of my "illness." She hadn't even told Grace about my falling grades and sleeping in class, much to my relief!

Carrie and I turned and started walking up the last of the hill toward school. I bit my lip. I had rehearsed this moment so many times… but now that I was *with* Carrie, I struggled to find the right words to get myself started.

"You're awfully quiet… are you sure you're back to your old self?" Carrie asked in her soft voice. I glanced at her and drew a deep breath. *It's now or never.*

"Carrie, I… I don't think I'll *ever* be back t'm'old self. I'm not sure who I even am anymore."

Carrie's face crinkled in confusion. "What do you mean?" I stopped walking and she stopped with me, adjusting the book strap that hung over her shoulder.

"I… I need t'tell y'bout somethin' that happened t'me, somethin' that changed me," I said. "Somethin' that's jus' made me *sick* inside."

Carrie nodded. "You can tell me *anything*," she said sincerely.

The unsavory story spilled out, raw and unkempt, leaving my friend's mouth gaping open by the end of it. I told her how Mr. Grainger had hurt me in the shed, the horrible words he said, and how I had *asked* for it because I had been caught sporting with Chancey Durrett. "But y'know me, Carrie!" I suddenly started crying. "I *wasn't* sportin' with Chancey… he'd stolen m'letter from Martha, n'I accidentally hit Timmy…" my voice trailed off.

Carrie's cheeks were burning bright red with embarrassment, and she covered her face with her hands for a few seconds. Her hands slid slowly down her face, her eyes brimming with tears, and she crossed her arms tightly over her chest. "Anna, I am so, *so sorry*. What an awful… he's *vile*… there's no way on earth you asked for such a thing." Carrie took hold of my

hand with trembling fingers. "He took advantage of you, and your situation – living away from your parents and all. It just makes me sick to think
about – and angry!"

"Y'b'lieve me?" I asked. "Y'*really* b'lieve me? Mr. Grainger said no
one'd b'lieve me, 'cause I was a liar n'a hussy." My friend's eyes grew wide
and her cheeks flushed again.

"You are *not*! And of course, I believe you... you're my best friend!"
Carrie said. "Mr. Grainger is not who we all thought he was... saying and
doing such unspeakable things to a girl. *He's* the liar!"

We started walking slowly in the direction of school, still holding
hands. We were both at a loss for words, me completely drained at last and
her still in shock. I felt relief that someone else in the world knew the truth
besides me, Chancey, and Mr. Grainger, yet I still felt burdened down. I
was constantly chewing on the whole memory that wouldn't grind up to
be swallowed.

"What are you going to do?" Carrie asked softly.

"I don't think anythin' *can* be done," I shrugged my shoulders. "I have
no parents. If the Graingers kick me out, I've nowheres t'go. I'd lose m'las'
sister, too." I kicked a rock and let go of my friend's hand with a sigh. "I
didn't even know who else t'tell, Carrie. I don't think grownups'll b'lieve
me."

Carrie stared up the road ahead. "What about Mrs. Sensley," she
suggested.

"I don't know..." I worried about telling anyone else. Mr. Grainger
had made it quite clear that if I told, he would make life miserable for me.

"I'll go with you if you want. We can tell her after school today," Carrie
pressed on. "She's a *teacher*, Anna – she'll know what to do."

I thought about that and decided that she was probably right. Teachers
dedicated themselves to the welfare of their students. Mrs. Sensley was
always telling us if we needed anything to just ask. "Okay," I finally agreed.
"I guess it's worth a shot."

The school day went better than expected. Gossip of me and Chancey
had died down. Now everyone was talking about how old Mr. Rickert

died, and Johnny supposedly saw his ghost in the church's graveyard. It was the biggest bit of nonsense I had ever heard, but I was thankful for the distraction, nonetheless. When Mrs. Sensley rang the bell for us to go home, Carrie and I looked at each other. The classroom emptied quickly, all the kids itching to get outdoors and enjoy the late spring sunshine. I swallowed hard, and my stomach twisted itself into another one of its famous knots.

Carrie walked over to my desk and held her hand out. I stared at it only for a moment, then slipped my hand in hers and stood up. We approached our teacher's desk together and waited for Mrs. Sensley to finish erasing the black board. When she noticed us, she smiled in surprise, put the eraser down, and dusted her hands off.

"Hello, girls – how can I help you?" she asked, sitting in her chair.

My lunch crept into my throat like a backhanded reminder from Mr. Grainger not to talk. I swallowed hard and glanced at Carrie, unable to speak.

"Anna Beth has something important to tell you, ma'am," Carrie spoke for me, squeezing my hand in support. "It's... it's about Mr. Grainger."

Mrs. Sensley looked curiously from Carrie to me. "Okay. What is it, Anna?"

My heart was pounding. I had come too far to back out now. "Well, ma'am... Mr.... Mr. Grainger made advances t'ward me, an'... an'," I stuttered.

Mrs. Sensley furrowed her eyebrows and leaned forward, elbows on her desk. "Advances?" she questioned.

I nodded, searching for a different word. "Like *sportin'*, ma'am... except he..." I paused and tried to figure out how to respectfully describe it to an adult. "He did what a husband does with his wife."

Our teacher stood up abruptly from her desk, and I let go of Carrie's hand, backing up several feet. My breath caught in my throat. *What have I done? She isn't going to believe me!* My worry turned into frantic fear. *Mr. Grainger will find out and he'll hurt me again... he could kill me and bury me in the field. No one would ever find me!* I didn't put anything past Mr. Grainger;

the monster had the whole town eating out of his hands. I bet no one knew he hit Grace behind closed doors, neither.

"That is a *very* serious accusation, Anna Beth. Are you sure you understand what you're saying he did?" Mrs. Sensley asked sternly.

"Come on, Anna," Carrie pleaded softly, reaching for my hand again. "Tell her what you told me. Tell her the truth." I remembered Daddy telling me to be brave, and I stirred up a bit of my Momma's grit. With a deep breath I steadied my voice.

"Yes, ma'am – he treated me like 'is wife… n'if that's how a husband treats a wife, then I'm not sure I ever want t'be married."

"That's quite *enough*, young lady!" Mrs. Sensley gasped, her neck and cheeks flushing red like Carrie's had. She tugged at her tight, buttoned-up collar and began to pace behind her desk, hands on her hips. She paused and glanced at us. "Have you told Grace?" she asked me.

"No, ma'am… I didn't think she'd b'lieve me," I said quietly.

"And why wouldn't she?"

"Well, ma'am, she saw Chancey kiss me in the alley by the mercantile… but what she didn't understand was that we were actually fightin'. He was jus' puttin' on a show t'get me in trouble." I glanced at Carrie who nodded encouragingly.

"Is *that* what happened…" Mrs. Sensley crossed her arms and nodded. "I see. Well, let's keep this all between us three for now. You understand? This is not something you go telling until we get a handle on the matter and know how to move forward."

"I told Anna Beth it was alright to tell you because you're our teacher," Carrie said hopefully. "Teachers always know what to do."

"Yes, we do," Mrs. Sensley agreed with just a slight hesitation. Her eyes were cast downward, her thoughts far from us. "You all go on home now," she dismissed us with a forced smile. "Thank you for talking to me, Anna Beth – I'm sure we can clear all of this up in time."

Carrie and I thanked her, then gathered our things and quietly walked out. I knew my secret had come as a terrible shock to her, but I prayed Mrs. Sensley would know what to do next. Carrie and I walked home mostly in silence, although she occasionally reaffirmed why she thought every-thing would be okay now. When we paused to say goodbye at the fork, she hugged me tighter than ever.

"Don't worry," she said sincerely. "Adults *can* help." I prayed she was right.

Spring gave way to summer, and school let out. Mrs. Sensley busied herself through class and after school, and the opportunity to talk about Mr. Grainger didn't present itself again. I tried to have faith, telling myself she was still thinking about it all, but I decided it was just better to forget about it as best I could and move on somehow by myself.

Once summer chores started around the farm, staying distracted was easier. I didn't quite have the strength and stamina of the two previous harvests and attributed it to everything that had happened and the extra stress on my body from being nervous all the time. It was like some days I would be working just fine, then suddenly I would feel winded and need a break. Other days I would get incredibly thirsty and steal drinks of cool water from the pump when Mr. Grainger wasn't looking. As long as I still pulled my weight, he didn't say a thing to me – and for that I was grateful.

One hot day in June, after stacking the firewood, I sat to rest on the side steps to the kitchen. My stomach pressed against my thighs and I rubbed it gently; it felt swollen and tender to the touch. My bowels had never got back quite right since I had gotten so sick in the kitchen that night when Mr. Grainger had accused me of skipping school with Chancey. I also hadn't been eating much, but I was seemingly gaining weight. Martha told me once that when you starve yourself your body holds on to every morsel and packs it on as fat to use later. I looked down at myself for the first time in a long time and with a sigh decided worrying about my girlish figure was vanity. Looking attractive was the last thing on my mind – I couldn't stomach thinking about boys in a romantic way anymore, and it would suit me fine never to have a husband. With that resolute thought I drug myself back to work.

About a month later, I was weeding the flower gardens around the front porch when Grace came out and suggested we go into town. "I only have a few supplies t'pick up, n'we'll be back in time t'fix dinner," she smiled. "Why don't y'take a break n'walk up with us? Y'can finish y'chores after we eat, okay?"

I pulled my gloves off and nodded, thankful for the chance to leave the farm. Mr. Grainger had been working me hard and had barely allowed me to even go to church. He was out of town on business that week, trying to get the next town over to make a contract to buy his produce, so Grace was taking advantage of the more relaxed schedule.

"We can check fo' letters at the pos' office n'mercantile, n'then maybe get some penny candy," she added as we started out the gate.

"Candy!" Olivia squealed, clapping her hands. "Oh, thank ya, Grace!" she said politely. She hopped and skipped up the road in front of us, singing her alphabet song, and chasing a butterfly as it flitted across our path.

We walked quietly past the school and up the hill further to the church house; once the ground leveled a bit we were in town. I went to the post office while they headed to the mercantile. I walked up the steps and pushed the door open, my eyes adjusting to the dim indoor light. I didn't expect a letter from my parents, but Martha was bound to have had her baby, and I figured I'd hear news soon.

Mr. Murphy heard the door open and came around the corner from the back office. He looked surprised to see me waiting at the counter. I smiled, but he took a step back and looked around, like he didn't know what he was supposed to be doing.

"Good day, Mr. Murphy," I said, wondering why he was acting strange. "Is there any mail fo' me t'day?" He nervously stroked his mustache, then thumbed through a stack of nearby envelopes. That's when it hit me, and my heart started racing. *He had heard word from my parents, and it was bad news.*

"Nope, not t'day, Anna Beth," Mr. Murphy said without looking up. I took a deep breath and let it out slowly. *No news is good news.* I told myself.

"Hey, d'y'happen t'know where Mr. Jingle's been?" I remembered to ask him. Between me being home sick a spell and Mr. Jingle traveling around, I hadn't seen him in quite some time and was getting worried.

"Not lately. Las' I heard he was 'bout a week or two journey over in Clear Water. What he's doin' that far out I don't know," he said.

*I* knew what Mr. Jingle was doing that far out – he still hadn't given up looking for my parents. I waited for Mr. Murphy to make more polite conversation, but when he busied himself dividing the stack of mail into the wall cubbies, I said goodbye and took my leave.

I paused on the steps outside and shook my head. Mr. Murphy was generally a jovial fellow, and we got on quite well together, but perhaps he just wasn't feeling top notch. I shrugged my shoulders and made my way across the street to the mercantile. I walked up the steps and pulled the door open but stopped just inside – there were hushed voices talking quickly, and I had heard my name. I peeked around the corner. Mrs. Sensley, Grace, and Olivia were standing at the back counter talking to Mrs. Corrigan.

"I just thought you should know *that* is what she's saying, Grace," Mrs. Sensley was whispering.

"What a shame, too – t'*accuse* y'fine husband o'such viciousness!" Mrs. Corrigan chimed in, a little louder so other people in the store could hear no doubt. "We all know Jack would *never* do such a terrible thin'!"

"I'm certain it was the Durrett boy," Mrs. Sensley spoke quickly. "I've seen the way he looks at Anna Beth, and there were days that they were *both* absent from school at the same time."

"An illegitimate pregnancy would certainly account fo' 'er bein' so tired n'sick the las' few months, too," Mrs. Corrigan surmised. "We've *all* noticed 'er swelling middle at church, dear."

"Such a shame you all were the ones to take in the likes of her," Mrs. Sensley sighed. "Taking in strangers' children… you never really know what you're getting into."

I stood there frozen in shock, my hands drifting down to my stomach. *Pregnant?* I looked down at my slightly swollen belly. *Like Martha? Was that why I've been so sick and tired, why my stomach fluttered from time to time?* The ugly truth slammed into me and took my breath away. *I was pregnant with Mr. Grainger's child… the child Grace was too broken to bear.*

The mercantile door opened and in walked Carrie with her mother. They looked as surprised to see me standing there as I was to see them. I hadn't seen Carrie since school ended two months before.

"Come, Carrie," Mrs. Michaels said quickly, gripping her daughter's shoulder and steering her away from me. Her eyes traveled down to my stomach and back up. "We do not *associate* with girls like *her*." Carrie glanced over her shoulder at me, her eyes welling up with tears. She mouthed the word *sorry*.

The women at the counter must have heard Carrie's mother and realized I was there. They fell silent, except Grace, who excused herself and brought Olivia back around the corner. She grabbed me by the hand and pulled me out the door with Olivia clinging to her skirt, the little bell above the door ringing our hasty departure.

She yanked me all the way down the street, looking left and right like a deer trying to duck out of the hunter's sight. I tried to speak, not really knowing what to say, but she adamantly shook her head no.

"Is Anna Beth sick again?" Olivia asked, still gripping Grace's skirt. She had to jog to keep up with us.

"Ev'rythin's fine, Olivia," Grace told her. "Come along."

We made it down to the farm in record time and saw Mr. Grainger's wagon parked in the yard. He had arrived home a day early. Grace stopped in her tracks, completely panicked.

"Olivia, go play in the yard, honey," she said, ushering my sister through the gate. Livie bounded around the side of the house to the little place she liked to dig for worms.

Mr. Grainger walked out from behind the house and looked our way. Grace forced a smile and waved. He was swinging the axe at his side and whistling as he walked. When he disappeared inside the shed, Grace looked down at her hands. She was gripping the gate in front of her so tightly her knuckles had turned white.

"Grace... I..." I started, my voice quivering. I dared to hope that this was the moment she would willingly hear the truth. If she would just listen, she could help us to safety so Mr. Grainger wouldn't hurt either of us again.

"*Not a word, Anna*," Grace said through gritted teeth. Her voice was calm, but her body was shaking. "Not a *single* word." She dropped her hands from the gate and crossed her arms as she turned around to face me. Then she covered her face with her hands and let them slide down to cover just her mouth, which was hanging open in disbelief.

"Alright," she said with a nod, going back to gripping the gate with her back to me. "This is what we're gonna do. *I'm* gonna let out y'skirts n'blouses, *n'you're* t'wear extra garments – like an apron – that can help hide y'shame fo' as long as possible. We're gonna speak nothin', n'I mean *nothin'*, 'bout this. You'll stay home n'*not* go t'town or school 'til it's born... then we'll give it away in another town."

Grace closed her eyes and spoke sincerely. "I *pray* t'the good Lord in Heaven that Mr. Grainger never hears the gossip – n'the *stories* you've been tellin' on 'im! I honestly don't know what y'were thinkin'. When he finds out, *if* he finds out..." She paused and turned to look me right in the eyes. "I hope y'know what you've done, young lady. Y'jus' brought the *whole* world down on y'head."

I stared at Grace, utterly speechless. Then my eyes filled with tears and everything swam out of focus. *How could Mrs. Sensley have betrayed me like this? She acted like she believed me to my face and then spread the truth as a rumor behind my back! Now I was in a bigger mess than before*, I thought bitterly.

I clenched my jaw tight and closed my eyes. Hot tears spilled out the corners and burned my cheeks, like the acid that had been eating me inwardly was now free to destroy me outwardly. What hurt most was that *Mr. Grainger had been right*. No one that mattered would believe me. I was destined to suffer this alone. My parents sure had given me a good life when they brought me to Harlan... and I hated them for it as much as I hated Grace, who let it happen.

*17*

Grace did what she said she would, and I let her without argument. When Mr. Grainger retired to the bedroom after dinner, she got out a needle and thread and let out every piece of clothing I owned an inch or two. She also gave me an apron I could tie loosely around my waist to help hide the growing bulge. I understood about marriage and babies, but this wasn't how it was supposed to be. I was carrying a bit of that man *inside* me, and I cried myself to sleep because of it and a million other reasons. *How would I live down the shame of an unwed pregnancy at fourteen? How could I put the pieces of my life back together after this?* I had even lost Carrie, my one best friend, who was forbidden to speak to me because my shame might rub off on her.

I continued working the harvest as we kept the pregnancy a secret from Mr. Grainger, and I welcomed the time in the fields. Being in the house with Grace was suffocating... I despised pretending that nothing was wrong when everything was falling apart at the seams. I also despised being under the same roof with the man who did this to me. When I was lost in the corn, I didn't have to look at *either* of them.

Grief, hatred, envy and strife were consuming my every thought. Some days I contemplated running away, and other days I contemplated taking my own life. I knew that was a sin, that God is the giver and taker of life – but wouldn't a big enough reason like this justify ending the pain? What future did I really have? The only thing that held the urge at bay was

Olivia, my birthday sister who needed me – her real big sister – even when she thought Grace was her Momma and would always take care of her. Grace hadn't taken care of me, not the way I needed.

One late August day, while working the cornfields far from the house, I was weighing peace through death and Olivia's needs in the balance of my mind once again. I was way out at the edge of the stalks where the field met the road that arches up and into town. It had to be nearing dinner time, for the sun was drooping in the sky like the will to live in my heart. I was bent over low, picking the bottom ears, when I heard the jangling pots and pans of Mr. Jingle's truck. I jerked up and ran to the edge of the row to watch for him. I hadn't seen my old preacher turned peddler friend in *so* long, and I had no idea what he had heard about me. *Would he still love me like the daughter he lost after this?*

I dropped my tools and sack and ran out of the corn toward the road. I had to know. When Mr. Jingle came into view and saw me there, he honked his feeble horn and pulled over. Then he slowly climbed down from the front bench, leaning heavily on his cane, and once steadied, *he opened his arm to me.* Tears flooded my eyes as I sobbed from deep within, running toward his warm embrace. He stumbled backward slightly, but I wrapped my arms around his waist, and we steadied one another, anguish gushing out of me like a shook-up bottle with the cork removed.

"*There, there, Miss Dignity,*" he soothed softly, stroking my hair. "Come on now, let me have a good look at ya." He held me at arm's length, then smiled.

"How can y'still call me *that*?!" I cried. I crossed my arms over my bulging stomach and couldn't look him in the eye. "You're bound to've heard what they're sayin' 'bout me in town!"

"Yes, Dignity, I have… *n'I don't b'lieve a word o'those nasty tales,*" he said, shaking my shoulder slightly with one hand while balancing himself against the cane with the other. "I jus' got back in town n'came t'hear *your* story, m'child. Y'tell me what really happened now."

Bits of truth mixed with raw feelings gushed out of me that were jumbled, messy and hard to grip. I told him everything – starting with Chancey that day in the alley, then about Mr. Grainger in the shed and how Grace didn't believe any of it, but Carrie did… how we told Mrs. Sensley, just for her to go and tell the whole town it was Chancey who put me to shame. I even told him all the hateful things Mr. Grainger said to me that night, and that Grace refused to talk about it, but that she promised to help deliver the baby at home and give it away in another town. I even told him how I was scared if Mr. Grainger found out, he'd kill me and bury me in the fields, and no one would be the wiser. When I got out the frantic regurgitation of facts that had sat on my stomach and spoiled for so long, my shoulders slumped forward, my face wet with tears and sweat.

Mr. Jingle straightened up, adjusting his cane under his weight. Then he closed his eyes for a moment, thinking deeply. When he opened them again, he reached out and rested his strong hand on my shoulder. If I didn't know better, it could have been my Daddy's strong hand. I slowly reached up and laid my hand on top of his, tears still streaming down my cheeks.

"Now y'see here, Miss Dignity," he said sternly. "Y'did *not* ask fo' such a thin' t'happen t'ya n'it's in *no* way y'fault that it did happen. This sin n'shame're 'is, *not yours*. D'ya hear me? You're as *dignified* as y'were the first day I met ya, even more so now that you've shouldered such a burden. He *cannot* take that away from ya. No one can, m'child, but y'self." I looked up at him, shocked by his words.

He leaned on his cane and held my chin up with his free hand. "I tell y'the truth, child. Y'can trus' me… n'more than anythin', y'can trus' the good Lord. He's been walkin' 'side y'through this storm. Keep y'chin up n'show people what real dignity looks like. Walk 'round town, go t'church, be you – *beau'ful, kind-hearted, gentle you*. This'll all be 'hind y'eventually. There *is* life after this. One day, you'll move on from here t'a place no one knows y'story… n'it'll be y'choice what y'tell 'em. If you're true t'y'heart, it'll never lead y'wrong."

His words were like sweet, glistening honey dripping from a comb. I had longed for someone to listen to me and tell me it was not my fault – that things would be okay someday… but something was still nagging at me.

"Mr. Jingle, y'want *me* t'go on bein' m'self n'not let what happened ruin *my* life... but *you* never went back t'church after y'wife n'child died. Y'story seems as much a tragedy as mine," I said quietly.

Mr. Jingle's head dropped slightly, and he nodded. "Well, you've got me there, child. It would be better t'practice what I preach, wouldn't it? I told ya, though, m'case was diff'rent..."

A marvelous thought burst in my mind. "Then *my* case is diff'rent, too," I said suddenly. I grabbed his hand and squeezed hard. "I don't need anyone, neither... I don't need church. I don't even need God – I jus' need you! Take me away with ya, Mr. Jingle, *please!* We'll wander t'gether – we can go where no one knows us, n'I'll be y'daughter fo' real! I'll even steal Olivia away n'I can take care of 'er...." My thoughts were racing a mile a minute; I barely had time to make sense of them all.

"Now, m'child – calm y'self down," Mr. Jingle said, patting my back. "Don't ever say y'don't need the Lord! We *all* need the Lord. He hung this world in its frame, n'He has complete control. If he sees each sparrow fall, he certainly sees our pain, too. I'm sure of it." He paused to wipe his brow with his handkerchief. "I cain't take y'with me, Dignity – y'parents may come back fo' y'all, n'who could tell 'em where you've gone?"

"They're *not* comin' back!" I screamed, jerking away from his firm hand. It was like a beautiful gift I handed him slipped through his fingers and shattered on the ground. "They left us here n'they're *never* comin' back! You've even traveled weeks out lookin', n'there's no trace of 'em – is there?!" I heard a rustling sound behind me and glanced back to the fields.

My eyes grew wide with fear, and I began to shake as Mr. Grainger emerged from the cornstalks, stalking toward us. I could see his anger boiling just beneath the surface, potently dangerous. I started crying uncontrollably, and my bladder let loose – I wet myself all the way down to my shoes. I backed up against Mr. Jingle, his firm arm wrapped around me, but Mr. Grainger just reached out, grabbed me by the arm, and twisted it into the air as he yanked me away. I yelled with a gasp of pain.

"Jack!" Mr. Jingle pleaded. "Let 'er *go!* She's jus' a child!"

Mr. Grainger spat at Mr. Jingle, and with a nasty sneer, he raised my arm higher. Something popped and I screamed. Pain flooded my arm and swirled into my stomach and eyes. Nausea started churning, and my vision narrowed with black dots bursting at the edges like a firework.

"See here, y'meddlin' old man," Mr. Grainger threatened. "She's *mine*, t'do with as I please! 'Er parents left 'er on *my* doorstep, n'we haven't seen hide nor hair of 'em in two long years – so y'get back up in y'little truck n'go on y'way – *now*. Don't let me catch y'round these parts again, neither!"

Mr. Jingle took a step toward me, his hand outstretched, but Mr. Grainger kicked his cane out from under him and my friend tumbled to the ground. He groaned and tried to get up, but he needed his cane. He felt around the ground for it, trying to lift his head, which was bleeding at the temple from where it hit the edge of the truck on the way down. Mr. Grainger kicked the cane away and laughed.

"Stop it!" I screamed, "Don't hurt 'im!" Then I doubled over and threw up. Mr. Grainger cursed and turned me toward home with a jerk of my hurt arm.

Fresh pain spread through my neck and back like wildfire. I howled, trying to keep my feet under me, as he dragged me toward the farmhouse. It was a long way in from the field, him mumbling and cursing as we went, his eyes fixed straight ahead. Grace heard my wailing and came running out the kitchen door and down the side steps. When she saw the state of us, she ran across the yard, her hands held up in front of her like she was cautioning a dog baring his teeth, ready to attack.

"What happened, Jack? Is she hurt?" she called, reaching for me.

"She's sure gonna be," he growled, throwing me down at his wife's feet.

I hit the ground hard, the yard spinning in and out of focus. She stooped and tried to help me stand up, but I screamed every time she touched my shoulder and arm. She looked up at her raging husband. I had never seen anyone look so terrified.

"Y'two think you're *so* clever... like I don't know what you've been doin'!" he yelled at her while unlatching and taking off his belt. He snapped it and Grace stood up, holding her hands back out in front of her.

"Jack…" she said timidly. "Please calm down n'we'll talk 'bout it…"

"I know *exactly* what y'all've been doin' – y'think I'm *stupid*, Grace?" he snarled. He swung the belt at her, and I heard it wrap around her like a whip. I covered my ears as he swung it again and she screamed. "I'll show y'how stupid I am!"

Grace cowered, trying to protect her head with her arms. "Jack, please!" she cried.

He slung the belt at me, and it slapped my thigh. I started crying harder, trying to think of a way to escape but the world was still spinning.

"This *hussy* brought shame t'our fam'ly, n'*you* let 'er do it! I told y'when we took those brats in that y'were the one t'watch 'em – but here she went messin' 'round with that Durrett boy n'bringin' sin down on us all!" Mr. Grainger yelled. He reached over and grabbed Grace by the hair, pulling her head back and talking right in her face. "Y'don't think I hear what they say in town? Huh? N'here *you* are, tryin' t'help 'er cover it up!" He dropped the belt and struck Grace with his hand, knocking her to her knees.

I slowly pulled myself up on my good elbow, cradling my injured arm. Mr. Jingle's faith in me had renewed my courage just enough that whether I lived or died, the truth was going to come out. "Chancey did *not* bring sin n'shame down on me," I said through gritted teeth. "*You did!*" I screamed at him. "Y'did this t'me, n'it was *not* m'fault! I did nothin' t'ask fo' it… it's y'shame t'bear n'God in Heaven knows it!"

Mr. Grainger flew at me and grabbed a fistful of my hair, jerking me off balance and throwing me back to the ground. He hit me across the face and my nose crunched. Warm blood ran everywhere like I was laying under a faucet, choking in its flow. He hit me again, and the world narrowed to a pinprick of light. Then he stood up and kicked the breath out of me. He kicked me a second time, my ribs feeling sticky as I gasped for air.

Grace was screaming at him to stop; I could see glimpses of her reaching for me, but Mr. Grainger twisted his fingers into her hair and held her at arm's length. He kicked me all the harder, forcing her to watch while she begged and pleaded with him to have mercy. Then he turned on Grace, hitting her so hard she tumbled backward and rolled a few feet. She was struggling to get back up when Olivia wandered out on the front porch and froze.

Livie took one look at Grace and me laying in the yard, bloody and crying, and Mr. Grainger standing in the middle panting, his oily hair out of place and a wild look in his eyes. She started shrieking and shaking all over as a sickening smile crept across Mr. Grainger's face. He stepped over Grace and stalked toward the house. Grace tried to grab his pant leg, pleading with him to stop, but he yanked loose from her grasp and headed for my sister. Olivia tripped over the rocking chair as she backed up but scrambled to her feet like a jack rabbit and ran back into the house, slamming the screen door shut behind her.

Grace heaved herself up from the ground and was torn. There were two of us, and only one of her. She looked at me, sprawled in the grass moaning, then toward the house, where somewhere inside sweet, little Olivia was cowering in a corner. I knew in that moment, seeing the impossible choice play out in her tear-filled eyes, that Grace *did* love me, and always had, and my heart ached for her. She loved us both as only a mother could love her children. It didn't matter that we weren't blood – we were all heart. I groaned for her to go save Livie, not able to bear the thought of him putting his hands on her, too.

She pointed at me, tears streaming down her cheeks, and cried, "I'll be back fo' ya, Anna Beth! I'll be back!" Then she limped as fast as she could toward the house.

Dusk was falling around me, and I began to panic out there alone, barely able to breathe. *I can't stay here out in the open.* Mr. Grainger could come back for me as easily as Grace could. I started crawling to the road, first by pulling myself forward with my good arm, then getting my knees under me some. When I reached the fence, I pulled myself up. Letting it support my weight, I moved toward the gate one picket at a time. Once through the gate, I shoved off the fence, hobbling into a jog while cradling my throbbing arm. I was moving slow and it hurt with every jarring step, but at least I was moving.

I looked for Mr. Jingle's truck when I passed the edge of the cornfield, but he was long gone, and I didn't have time to think where to. Getting up the big hill to town and finding help for Grace and Olivia consumed my thoughts. Surely someone would believe me now, when I showed up broken and bruised by Mr. Grainger's hand. Past that, the only persistent thought that propelled me forward, and that which I repeated to myself with every step, was *I had finally broken free, and I would never go back to where I've been.*

*Part 3*

## Going *Where* I've Never Been

*18*

I limped as far as the church house before stopping to catch my ragged breath. I knew I wouldn't make it up the next hill and into town if I didn't stop and rest a bit; someone would soon find me passed out in the road. I stared at the quaint building, sitting still and quiet on the ridge. Its cross on the steeple shimmered in the moonlight. *I doubt Mr. Grainger would come looking for me in the church...* to my knowledge he had never set foot inside one. An urgency to get safely within its doors seized my heart. I pulled myself up the steps, holding tight to the railing with the arm that still worked and pushed inside.

It was dark, and the moonlight streaming through the windows cast long shadows on the floor. For the first time since Mr. Grainger came charging out of that cornfield, I felt my chest begin to loosen and my breath slow. Holding onto the ends of the benches down the center aisle, I made my way to the piano in the front corner. The matches were kept in the piano bench, and with them I lit a few candles. A soft dancing light filled the room, but I dared not light too many in fear someone would notice the glow through the window.

My body was exhausted and melting into a puddle on the floor. With great effort I limped back to the front pew and lowered myself down to rest. My whole body ached as I cradled my arm, careful not to jar my shoulder. I rubbed my nose gingerly and pulled back a hand crusted with dried blood. *What would Momma and Daddy say if they could see what had become of their brave daughter?*

My eyes drifted to the altar up front. There was a plain, wooden bench stretched out in front of the preacher's stand. Folks called it the *Mourner's Bench*, and it was reserved for broken hearts in search of God. Mourning was exactly what I felt like doing. I thought of my parents and sisters... *why couldn't we have just stayed in Missouri?* I thought of Olivia and tears stung my eyes. I prayed Grace got to her in time. She was so small and innocent in all this, so precious... my honey-haired birthday sister, the only remnant of a home and life I had all but forgotten. Then I thought of my abused and battered self. Here I sat, with not one friend in the world to come to my aid... no home or family to call my own... *I truly am an orphan.* The ugly truth I had tried to ignore for so long broke over me in a fresh wave of despair. I sobbed out loud, not able to hold it in any longer. *What am I going to do? Where can I turn? How am I ever going to find my way again?*

The church door creaked open, and scared out of my mind, I jerked around to see who had discovered my hiding spot. A searing pain shot through my shoulder with the sudden movement, and I grabbed it with a sob. My eyes, swimming with blurry tears, fought to focus. The figure at the door was slightly bent and leaning, not upright and big like Mr. Grainger. As he slowly moved toward me, I heard the familiar thumping of a cane, and my eyes grew wide in surprise.

"*Mr. Jingle?*" I whispered. He made his way down the aisle and stopped next to my pew. I cried harder and leaned my head against his side. He rested his palm on the side of it for a moment, then gently smoothed the hair from my face. "What're y'doin' here? How'd y'find me?" I sputtered.

He stood quietly for a few moments, still supporting my head in his hand. I looked up at him, but he just stared straight ahead at the preacher's stand. "The Lord told me t'come, child," he spoke quietly.

I wiped tears from my face, wondering how he could *hear* God. Mr. Jingle patted my head and then walked to the preacher's stand, laboring up the little step to the pulpit. Something was different about my old friend, and I watched him closely. He took the Bible that lay there and flipped it to a new page, first reading silently to himself, then looking out at his congregation of one. A fleeting thought occurred to me that maybe my time to find the Lord had finally come, like my parents and Mr. Jingle said it surely would. Bits of my broken heart pulled toward each other like magnets. I dared to hope that something good could come out of all the bad.

"I need t'read y'somethin', m'child, n'I jus' want y't'listen fo' God's still, small voice t'speak right t'*your* heart," Mr. Jingle said, his voice quivering. I sat up a little straighter, and he looked back down at the Bible, cleared his throat, and read aloud.

"*Fo' we know that if our earthly house o'this tabernacle were dissolved, we have a buildin' o'God, a house not made with hands, eternal in the heavens. Fo' in this we groan, earnestly desirin' t'be clothed upon with our house which is from heaven: If so be that bein' clothed we shall not be found naked. Fo' we that're in this tabernacle do groan, bein' burdened: not fo' that we would be unclothed, but clothed upon, that mortality might be swallowed up o'life. Now he that hath wrought us fo' the selfsame thin' is God, who also hath given unto us the earnes' o'the Spirit.*

"*Therefore we're always confident, knowin' that, whils' we're at home in the body, we're absent from the Lord: (Fo' we walk by faith, not by sight:) We're confident, I say, n'willin' rather t'be absent from the body, n't'be present with the Lord. Wherefore we labour, that, whether present or absent, we may be accepted of 'im. Fo' we mus' all appear 'fore the judgment seat o'Christ; that ev'ry one may receive the thin's done in his body, accordin' t'that he hath done, whether it be good or bad.*

"*Knowin' therefore the terror o'the Lord, we persuade men; but we're made manifes' unto God; n'I trus' also are made manifes' in y'consciences. Fo' we commend not ourselves again unto ya, but give y'occasion t'glory on our b'half, that ye may have somewhat t'answer 'em which glory in appearance, n'not in heart.*

"*Fo' whether we be b'side ourselves, it is t'God: or whether we be sober, it is fo' y'cause. Fo' the love o'Christ constraineth us; 'cause we thus judge, that if one died fo' all, then were all dead: N'that he died fo' all, that they which live should not henceforth live unto themselves, but unto 'im which died fo' them, n'rose again. Wherefore henceforth know we no man after the flesh: yea, though we have known Christ after the flesh, yet now henceforth know we 'im no more. Therefore if any man be in Christ, he is a new creature: old thin's're passed away; behold, all thin's're b'come new.*"

Mr. Jingle closed the Bible and looked up, but his eyes weren't focused on me. He was looking far off to something beyond this world. I hadn't understood all the words Mr. Jingle read, but while he spoke them, I *felt* something I had never felt before. My heart started pounding in my chest, like a fish thrashing in a net, but it wasn't for fear of Mr. Grainger anymore – it was in fear of the Lord. *The fear of the Lord is the beginning of wisdom*; the verse in Proverbs came back to me. I knew in that moment God was real, not a made-up story, and He was more powerful than any man. He was all powerful, and my life always had been, was, and would be in His hands.

Mr. Jingle cleared his throat and started talking about Jesus, the son of God, and how he died for the sin of all mankind and made a "whosoever will" plan of salvation. It was all things I had heard as a child, but somehow like I had never heard it before. He took a few steps from the preacher's stand, his hand still holding onto the side of it to steady himself, and said how things on this earth, including what happens to us down here, are temporal. All men's experiences, all their knowledge and works, would pass away when Jesus came back to gather his children home to Heaven… and Jesus *was* coming back. When he said it, I knew it to be true for my heart burned more fervently. His voice grew stronger.

"The only thing that matters in this life is finding salvation – the eternal redemption of one's soul!" he preached. "When man reconciles themselves to God, he is *washed in the blood of the Lamb*, which is the blood of Jesus, the perfect sacrifice. He gave his life willingly on the cross for every person everywhere…" Mr. Jingle pushed off from the preacher's stand and left his cane leaning against it. He started moving around the altar like he had never limped in his life!

His voice took on a rhythm that connected perfectly with my pounding heart, and the longer he preached, the heavier my heart grew. I felt an urgency to do *something*, but I didn't know what. Thoughts of my family and the Graingers, all that had happened since I had been in Harlan, slipped from my mind one by one. All I could think about was how badly I, too, wanted to be saved. Deep in my soul I desired what my loved ones had – *to be absent from my body and present with the Lord*, as Mr. Jingle had read. *What a wonderful thought – to let go of the flesh and find perfect peace!*

I had seen sinners bow at the Mourner's Bench all my life, begging the Lord to save their souls and then rejoicing when He did the work. I wondered if it was that easy... just get up and go to God. I closed my eyes, no longer hearing the words Mr. Jingle was preaching. *God, if I'm lost and it's my time to be saved, please just let me know for sure*, I prayed right from my heart.

"Anna Beth," Mr. Jingle said suddenly. My eyes flew open. "The Lord has a satisfyin' portion fo' even *you*, m'child – but you're gonna have t'dig it out fo' y'self!"

My heart thumped within my chest, like it was going to burst if I didn't move, yet there was a stillness about the feeling, too. *Come*, it urged from deep within. *God speaks to the heart with a feeling*, I remembered, and I began to tremble all over. *This is too great for someone like me. I don't deserve to be saved after all that I've done...*

*Come*, the feeling urged again. *Where else could I go? Out the door back to the Graingers? No way.* I took a deep breath, lifted myself from the bench with a yelp of pain, and made my way to the altar. My shoulder still ached, and it hurt to breathe, but I could barely feel my legs under me – it was as if I was floating. If the God of all creation could bring Mr. Jingle back to church and make him walk without a cane... if He could talk right to my heart and let me *feel* his presence, then surely He would redeem my poor soul if I did my part and followed the feeling!

I dropped to my knees, cradling my hurt arm, and let my forehead rest on the edge of the Mourner's Bench. Tears flowed from my eyes as I begged the Lord to save me – I was filled with this yearning to be heard, accepted, and *loved* unconditionally. Mr. Jingle knelt beside me and joined me in prayer. The rhythm of his steady words encouraged me to pray even harder. I told the Lord *everything*, even though He knew it already. The grief, envy, hatred, and strife I had been wallowing in came up before me, and I begged Him to forgive me. I made him promises, too. I promised to live my life for Him, if He would just give me this great gift of salvation.

My prayers became more contrite when I realized there was nothing I could do in myself to obtain His grace. The fate of my soul was completely in my creator's hands. All I kept saying was that I wanted the old to pass away and to start new with Him.

I felt a gentle hand touch my back and realized Grace had found her way to the church, Olivia huddled at her side. Grace was praying as hard as Mr. Jingle, her fingers patting me, spurring me on. I let my head fall below the bench, even to the floor, and with my last bit of strength I whispered, *Lord, please save me – I'm broken but I'm yours, if you'll have me.* In that moment, I didn't care who was around me, or who heard me beg… I wanted to find grace in His sight more than *anything* in this whole world!

As soon as the prayer left my heart, I *felt* to hug Grace. That still, small feeling that had beckoned me to come to the altar was prompting me to *hug Grace.* I wrestled against it at first, thinking of all the reasons I didn't want to. Part of me was still furious with her. As I backed up from that urging in my heart, it lightened and flitted away leaving nothing but awful heaviness. Then I worried hugging Grace had been my only chance to fully reach God and I had refused it… so I begged Him all the more earnestly if He'd only send the feeling back, I would go with it.

That urge breezed back past me – *hug Grace.* I sat up and reached for her with my good arm… and then she and Mr. Jingle started shouting praises to God, one after another. The heaviness and fear that had gripped me so suddenly had just as quickly rolled away, and waves of peace and joy broke over all three of us – connecting us together in God's great love. I loved them more than I had ever loved anyone else! Their faces shone with light like angels. Heaven was *real,* and I had just secured my ticket.

Grace gently wrapped her arms around me, and the glistening, bubbly, light, skipping feeling swelled even more! I felt like a new person, barely noticing my physical pain… and that started me laughing.

"I'm saved!" I shouted. "I feel like I can face anythin', n'it'll be okay!"

"Look at that countenance, Grace," Mr. Jingle cupped my cheek in his hand. "She's jus' a shinin'!"

Olivia came out from behind Grace and nestled into my lap. I wrapped my good arm around her and kissed the top of her curly head. She was perfectly okay – not a scratch or bruise on her. God had watched over her as well. We all sat together in the altar for a long time it seemed; even when the Holy Spirit dissipated, there was still a feeling of contented calm. I was no longer sad but fully satisfied. *Amazing Grace, how sweet the sound, that saved a wretch like me. I once was lost, but now am found, was blind but now I see…*

I looked at Mr. Jingle, realizing God had performed *two* miracles that night. "God saved me, n'He brought *you* back t'preachin'!" I grinned. Mr. Jingle's eyes filled with tears.

"Yes, Dignity, He sure did. God knew exactly how t'draw me back t'*the old paths, wherein is the good way.*" He carefully placed his hand on my back. "N'I want y't'know that even though we'll come down spiritually n'get back in our carnal minds – fo' it's not possible t'be in the Spirit all the time – as soon as we put the thin's o'this world aside n'look t'Jesus again, God'll send that good feelin' back n'reassure y'that you're 'is. No one can take it from ya, neither. It'll be with y'*forever.* It'll lead n'guide ya all the way home. He's y'Heavenly Father now, Dignity, n'He'll take care o'ya all the days o'y'life if y'put 'im firs' in all thin's."

*God is my Father now. I'm not an orphan after all…* I looked up at Grace with sudden mixed feelings. Her smile was bright and beautiful, even though her cheek was bruised and her eye swollen. What was she to me now? What would happen to me and Olivia? She opened her arms and I leaned into her embrace, taking Olivia with me.

"Anna Beth," her voice quivered as she stroked my hair. "I'm *so* sorry I didn't b'lieve ya… 'bout Chancey… 'bout Jack… I didn't even give y'a chance t'explain. I was so busy tryin' t'hold m'own life t'gether…" her voice trailed off with thoughts she couldn't put into words. I nodded, trying to let her know I didn't hold anything against her anymore. *Old things had passed away and all things were new, even between us.*

"I told y'that it only mattered what people think, n'that was wrong o'me, Anna. I was too wrapped up in the natural n'needin' people's approval."

Grace spoke again, gently tilting my chin up so she could look into my eyes. Hers were brimming with tears. "It only matters what *God* thinks, Anna, n'if *He* approves of us. He baptized y'with the fire n'Holy Ghos' t'night, Be thankful fo' it all y'life n'live fo' 'im so y'light shines out n'can help someone else still wanderin' in darkness."

I nodded again and nestled my head back into her chest. It was bittersweet that I felt as at home with her as I ever did with my own mother. "I forgive ya, Grace," I whispered. Her body heaved with a sob, and she kissed the top of my head then leaned down to kiss Livie's.

Mr. Jingle smiled at the three of us. "*Fo' if ye forgive men their trespasses, y'heavenly Father will also forgive you,*" he remarked. "That's what y'got t'night, Anna, forgiveness – n'not 'cause Mr. Grainger's sin was yours n'y'needed forgiveness fo' what *he* did. Y'know that weren't y'fault. But we all need forgiveness fo' the fall o'Adam, whose sin was imputed t'all mankind." He brushed the hair from my face, and I smiled back at him. "I'll tell y'another thin', too, you're never gonna have t'walk through this valley again, Dignity – n'you're not goin' back t'Jack Grainger, either."

He put a hand on Grace's shoulder. "N'neither're *you*, Grace. Y'all're gonna stay with me from now on – n'we'll pull through this as a fam'ly."

A *family*. There was no sweeter word.

We stayed in the church a little longer, talking everything over from Chancey Durrett to Mrs. Sensley and Mrs. Corrigan. Mr. Jingle listened a second time while I told Grace the whole truth. My fingers absentmindedly twirled Livie's curls, her head nestled in my lap where she had fallen asleep between me and Grace on the floor. When I had told her every detail I could remember, Grace filled us in on what happened after she followed Mr. Grainger into the house.

Olivia had wedged herself under the bed, kicking and screaming like a wet cat as Mr. Grainger tried to drag her out by the ankle. Grace fought with him in the house but a shout from outside startled them all – it was the town sheriff at the gate.

"I fetched the sheriff jus' as soon as I could get m'cane n'drive back t'town," Mr. Jingle interjected. "I knew y'all would need more help than an old man could give."

"I'll be forever thankful fo' it, Mr. Jingle... I think he would've killed us if Sheriff Todd hadn't got there in time," Grace said quietly.

Mr. Grainger had grabbed his gun and with the wild eyes of an animal being cornered, he threatened she better not come out of the house or make a sound. When he went out the front door, however, she boldly followed with a wailing Olivia in her arms. She didn't even have to confirm the reported abuse, for Sheriff Todd drew his gun immediately when he glimpsed her bruises and swollen eye for himself. Mr. Grainger started waving his gun, screaming for the sheriff to stay out of his family's business and to get off his property, and that's when Sheriff Todd shot Mr. Grainger in the knee to bring him to the ground. After he got handcuffed and put in the patrol wagon, Grace assured the sheriff she and Olivia were fine, and they came looking for me.

"When I saw Mr. Jingle's truck outside the church house, I knew y'all were in here... I jus' felt it," Grace smiled and shook her head like it was hard to believe now.

"We bes' be gettin' y'two t'Doc Mitchell," Mr. Jingle finally said. Grace nodded and managed to roll Livie into her arms without waking her.

I had been mostly comfortable in the floor, but as I tried to stand the physical pain rushed back into my body like a tidal wave. I nearly fell back to my knees, but Mr. Jingle caught me. Grace shifted Olivia to her shoulder, and with her on one side and Mr. Jingle on the other, we made it out to Mr. Jingle's truck. It was still dark, but the stars were sparkling up in the night sky. My stomach clinched tighter as we drove up the bumpy hill to town, and by the time we stopped in front of the doctor's office, I was crying pitifully again.

Doc Mitchell saw us arrive and had come out to help me out of the truck. He looked at Mr. Jingle and Grace, but no one said a word. Livie had stirred awake and quietly twisted her fingers into the part of Grace's hair that slipped from her bun.

"I'll be back soon as I can," Mr. Jingle finally broke the silence. "I'm jus' goin' over t'talk t'the sheriff n'see where we're with gettin' a judge t'town." He held the doctor's office door open as Grace and Doc Mitchell helped me inside.

"Take the little one," Doc Mitchell said to his nurse. The woman in white hurried around the desk and pulled Olivia from Grace's arms. She started to fuss and reach for Grace, but the nurse showed her some toys in the corner to distract her while the doctor ushered the two of us into the back room.

My stomach was twisting in on itself so violently by then I could barely stand up; it was knife-like cramps, worse than any of my monthlies. He instructed Grace to help me undress, but I pushed her hands away. I was embarrassed to be naked in front of a grown man and wanted no part of whatever was about to happen.

"He jus' needs t'examine ya, Anna Beth," she said soothingly, pulling a curtain between us and the doc. "I'll be with y'the whole time, I promise." She managed to get the dress off me and started pulling my stockings down. When I caught sight of the blood caked all over my undergarments, I fell to pieces. *Could I die from losing that much blood?! Is this what it felt like to die?*

"Grace, no!" I begged, trying to cover myself with the dress again. Grace just kept nodding and saying it was going to be okay, and she corralled me up onto the examination table where I began to kick and scream.

Grace grabbed my face and held it in her hands, forcing me to look her in the eyes, one of which so black and blue it was nearly swollen shut now. "Anna Beth," she said sternly, and my screaming fell to sobs. "You're safe now. I've got ya. I'm not *ever* goin' t'leave ya." The words registered somewhere deep inside me. Grace had been Livie's Momma for a long time, and now she was mine.

"I've got to give her something, Grace, to help her calm down – and for the pain," Doc Mitchell spoke quickly as he pulled open the curtain. Grace nodded and held my good arm down. I struggled against her, scared out of my mind and feeling like my middle was going to tear in two, but when Doc Mitchell sunk a syringe in my arm, I immediately felt relief from the pain, like my body was floating upward all of a sudden.

"What – what's happenin'…" I managed. Grace looked at Doc Mitchell, and he nodded. She swallowed and stroked my hair gently.

"Anna, listen – you're havin' a miscarriage, honey. Do y'know what that is?" she asked. Her face started slipping in and out of focus and I blinked my eyes, trying to see her through the tears. "'Member when I los' m'baby boy? Y'body's losin' the baby inside ya… probably 'cause Mr. Grainger kicked y'in the stomach so many times. You're gonna go t'sleep fo' a while, n'when y'wake up it'll all be over… I'll stay right here, the whole time."

My body was growing heavy; I was fighting to keep my eyes open. Her voice sounded like it was under water – garbled like Janie's when we'd go swimming, duck our heads in the pond, and try to decipher what the other person said. When Grace slipped her hand in mine, I felt safe enough to let go of consciousness and drift into the darkness.

When I woke up a few hours later, Doc Mitchell patted my arm and said I had done well and that the baby had *come away*. That's how he phrased it. "You're going to be alright, Anna Beth," he assured me. "The worst is behind you now." I learned he had also reset my broken arm, and when the swelling went down, he would cast it.

Grace came over to the bed carrying a little hand towel all bundled up. She pulled back a corner to reveal the tiniest baby I had ever seen. I just stared at it. That tiny life was tangled up with mine and then wrenched away. Tears came to my eyes and I wiped them away with the back of my good hand. My heart felt broken again, even though I knew God had fixed it. Grace started crying, too. "I know, I know…" was all she could say – and she *did* know.

I didn't want that baby, but I hated the loss of life all the same. It wasn't the baby's fault neither; none of this was fair. I must have cried myself back to sleep at some point, for when I came back to myself a second time, I was in a new room. Grace was lying in the bed next to me, her head propped up on her arm as she watched me sleep. Olivia was playing with her cornhusk dolls and some blocks quietly on the floor between us. She had built them a small house and chairs to sit on.

"Where are we?" I asked groggily, trying to look around. It hurt to even lift my head.

"Still at Doc Mitchell's," Grace answered. "He said we can stay here in the recov'ry room long as we need to… 'cause that's what we both need t'do now – recover."

"Where's Mr. Jingle?" I asked, suddenly wanting the comfort and safety only he could bring.

"Mr. Jingle's already been in t'check on us twice, n'he told me t'tell y'again not t'worry. We'll *never* have t'go back t'that farmhouse again. We're a fam'ly now. The four o'us. Okay?"

I nodded. "Are *you* okay?" I asked. Parts of her body were bandaged like my own, and she had a salve rubbed on her face that made her skin shiny.

Grace sniffed and rubbed her nose, which was red from crying her own tears while I was asleep. "I *will* be. We *both* will be."

News of what really happened to me – to us – spread through town like wildfire. It caught from one dry gossip tree to another and burned them to the ground with shame. Sheriff Todd came and asked us a bunch of questions and took something called our statements for the court. My good name was finally restored, and everyone felt horrible for how they had treated me. Mr. Murphy from the post office brought me a book of stamps, paper, and a freshly sharpened pencil so I could write Martha and Jonathan any time I wanted. Mrs. Sensley brought me tenth grade level schoolbooks and sincerely apologized for not believing me that day in the classroom… and for contributing to the hateful rumors.

"The student taught the teacher a powerful lesson this time, Anna Beth," she had said with genuine tears in her eyes. "You are the brightest girl in class. You can do *anything* you put your mind to – never forget how strong you are."

Even sheepish Mrs. Corrigan stopped in with a plate full of homemade cookies, which made Olivia's week. I was more thrilled when Carrie and her mother came by, though. They gave me and Olivia two store bought dresses each, and Mrs. Michaels told Grace that we could stay at their hotel, free of charge, if we needed a place to go while getting back on our feet. Carrie held my hand the whole visit, and when her mom offered a hotel room, she leaned over and whispered in my ear that that the hotel just got *electric* lights put in. I grinned to think of it. The Michaels were always a step above the rest, yet that was the first time Carrie ever acknowledged it, and it was for the sole purpose of making me happy.

Mr. Jingle visited daily as well. He, above everyone else, made sure we had everything we needed. After two weeks of healing, when we took the Michaels up on their hotel room offer, he brought us every belonging we requested from the farmhouse. It took a month or so for Grace's face to look normal again, and nearly six weeks for both our bruising – and broken ribs – to heal well enough that it didn't hurt to breathe.

It was early November by then, and the circuit judge and twelve jurors from the county had arrived on the train. The appointed day for Mr. Grainger to answer for his crimes had come. The whole town packed themselves into the county courthouse; the *true* nature of Mr. Jack Grainger, who had the whole community fooled, was the biggest scandal Harlan had witnessed in years – maybe its history. No one was going to miss the conclusion.

Grace, Olivia, and I dressed in our Sunday best, and Doc Mitchell helped fit a sling over my smock to cradle my casted arm. As we made our way to sit on the front bench behind the table set for the prosecutor, right next to Mr. Jingle who was saving us seats, people nodded encouragingly at Grace and neighbors patted on me and Olivia. Mr. Grainger sat on the left with the lawyer who was sent to defend him. Grace pointed out the prosecutor when he walked in and said it was his job to prove Mr. Grainger committed crimes against us. Then she motioned to the jurors sitting on the right-hand side past the prosecutor's table.

"N'it's their job t'decide if he's guilty or innocent," she breathed nervously. I looked up at her face. She was as pale as I've ever seen her, but sweat was gathering on her brow. I swallowed hard, feeling butterflies kick up in my own stomach.

Mr. Grainger turned in his chair, and its legs made a scratching noise against the floor. He stared at us with his cold black eyes, and Grace looked down out of habit. I reminded myself she had suffered at his hands her whole marriage, but I, who had only suffered his abuse for a little more than two years, steeled myself against the feeling and refused to lower my eyes. I stared right at him, my jaw set, until the judge walked in and his eyes cut away first. He had hurt me for the last time, and with God as my witness – I would never give my power over to a man again.

## 20

Sheriff Todd motioned for everyone to stand as the judge walked into the courtroom and said, "All rise, Harlan circuit court's now in session, the honorable Judge Stephen Collins presidin'. All havin' business 'fore this court draw nigh n'y'shall b'heard. May God save the Commonwealth n'this honorable court. Y'may be seated."

I stared at Judge Collins, a short, balding man with a narrow nose and glasses, as he walked up the steps to sit behind his raised bench. As small as he was, he still appeared to tower above us. He cleared his throat and spoke loudly, "Gentlemen of the jury, this case is the Commonwealth versus Jack Grainger. Is the Commonwealth ready?"

The prosecutor, a tall man in a blue suit, rose to his feet and replied, "Ready, your Honor."

"Is the defense ready?" the judge asked, looking toward Mr. Grainger and his lawyer.

"Ready, your Honor," the man next to Mr. Grainger stood slightly and nodded his answer. I didn't think his black suit looked nearly as nice as the prosecutor's blue one, but then again, I was partial to who was going to argue for our justice.

The judge motioned to the prosecutor, "You may give your opening statement."

The prosecutor spoke for a few minutes, telling the jury what the evidence would show and how he would ask them to find Mr. Grainger guilty.

Then it was the defense lawyer's turn. He did his best to contradict everything already said and told them he would ask them to find Mr. Grainger not guilty. I glanced up at Grace again, but she just reached over and intertwined her fingers in mine.

The prosecutor called Grace as his first witness. She took the stand cautiously, her hand visibly shaking as she placed it on the Bible and was sworn in by Sheriff Todd. She had to answer questions about how Mr. Grainger had hit and mistreated her over the last several years. I could tell it was very difficult for her to talk so openly about what had been hidden for so long, especially with Mr. Grainger staring daggers at her the whole time. She admitted she felt she deserved the ill treatment most of the time, that her husband had told her she wasn't a good enough wife and homemaker, and his correction would make her a better help mate. She raised her chin at that point and looked right at Mr. Grainger, who crossed his arms with a sneer.

"But deep down I know no man should treat his wife that way, n'never again will I allow a man t'raise his hand t'me. That may be the only good lesson I ever learned from m'husband." As she finished her testimony, I could see Mr. Grainger's jaw muscles flexing. I imagined he'd like to get a hold of her one more time.

When the prosecutor finished with Grace, the defense attorney stood eagerly. "Mrs. Grainger, you *say* my client has been beating you for years – practically since you first got married. Correct?" He had a smug grin on his face I didn't like.

"Yes, sir," Grace replied.

"Well," he said, turning to look out at the crowd, "why didn't you tell your neighbors? Your friends? Isn't there *anyone* who saw the bruises, anyone who can collaborate your story?" he asked, spinning on his heels to stare at Grace again.

"He... he didn't like me t'have friends, n'we live in the farmin' country down in the valley... so we don't have a lot o'neighbors," she answered nervously, brushing a stray curl from the side of her face and tucking it behind her ear. "He only let me go into town maybe once a week, if that...

n'he usually hit me where m'clothes would cover…" I could tell the question had rattled her, and I closed my eyes and prayed for God to give her strength.

The defense attorney was nodding. "You're not exactly answering my question, Mrs. Grainger," he interjected. "Why didn't you ever *tell* anyone what was happening to you?"

Grace took a deep breath. "'Cause I was scared he'd kill me, sir." Murmurs broke out in the crowd, and Judge Collins banged his gavel to get everyone's attention. He warned the defense attorney to get on with his questioning.

"Your Honor, I just want the court to realize that the story she has told us today, painting my defendant's character in such a negative light, cannot be backed up by one single person except for the one assault that was witnessed by a child, a child who also has a vendetta against my client," the defense attorney said. "There is no credible evidence…"

Judge Collins cut him off with a wave of his hand. "Save it for closing arguments, Counselor." The defense attorney nodded his compliance, sat down, and the Judge released Grace from the stand. When she sat down next to me, I reached over and grabbed her hand, squeezing it tight. We both knew I was next, and I didn't want to go up there in front of everybody.

As the prosecutor called my name, the words Grace and Mr. Jingle helped me prepare got all jumbled up and mismatched in my brain. I shook my head and whispered, "I cain't… I cain't…", but Mr. Jingle patted my back and pushed me forward.

"Y'can do this, child – show 'em why I call y'Dignity," my old friend winked at me. His words stirred a new courage within me, and I stood up, slowly making my way to the stand.

Thankfully, the prosecutor was gentle with me; he spoke with a soft voice and asked me very pointed questions so I could tell my story like Grace had done hers. I recounted to the judge and jury all the mean and threatening things Mr. Grainger said to me throughout my time at their farm and what Mr. Grainger did to me that night in the shed. With a quivering voice I also recalled how he hit and kicked me, how he broke my arm and a few of my ribs the day I ran away.

"The beatin' caused me t'lose the baby, too," I said, my eyes filling with tears. I looked up at the judge. "I didn't want a baby, sir – I know I'm much too young fo' motherin' even though I've taken care o'm'baby sister all m'life. I jus' don't think it was fair fo' the baby t'die is all."

The judge nodded his understanding. When the prosecutor said he had no further questions and turned me over to the defense attorney, I gulped, my throat suddenly dry as a bone. I stole a quick peek at the jurors – I couldn't tell by their expressions if they believed me and Grace or not.

"Miss Atwood," the defense attorney started, jarring me from my racing thoughts. "Is it true your parents moved your family here from Missouri and left you on my defendant's doorstep?"

"Yes, but…" I stammered.

"And is it true that he gave you a roof over your head, food to eat, and even sent you to school?" he cut me off.

"Yes, sir… but I…"

"And don't you *hate* him, deep down, for taking the place of your Daddy who never came back for you? Aren't you just making this whole story up to one, lash out at the person you have misplaced feelings toward and two, cover up your own irresponsible and sinful decisions…" his voice got louder the longer he spoke.

My anger kindled and I stood up suddenly. "No! I hate 'im 'cause he really did those thin's t'me!" The judge banged his gavel several times, and the noise that had swelled with my outburst died down just as quickly.

Judge Collins eyed the defense attorney threateningly. "Counselor, I advise you to be careful as you are questioning a minor," he warned. The defense attorney opened his hands and backed toward his table with a nod, then the judge nodded for me to take my seat again.

I sat down slowly, my smoldering anger still popping; I was on fire from my neck up to the tips of my ears. The defense attorney cut his eyes toward me; the corner of his mouth turned up in a sneer. "Miss Atwood, why didn't you tell anyone about the alleged attack when it first happened?" he asked calmly.

I took a deep, steadying breath to calm my racing heart. I glanced at Grace and Mr. Jingle. He had his arm around her, and Livie was sandwiched in the middle, her arms around Grace's waist. Grace steeled her jaw and nodded for me to answer. I swallowed hard.

"I was afraid, *sir*." The last word soured on my tongue, and I spit it at the defense attorney.

"Afraid?" he questioned, feigning surprise. He turned and pointed at Mr. Grainger. "This man took you in on a temporary bargain and then gave you shelter and food for over two years when your parents abandoned you! Did he not?"

Tears welled up in my eyes and the courtroom went blurry. "Yes, he did."

"Then why were you afraid? A man of good standing in the community, a hard working farmer, an upstanding citizen of this town – why should we believe the story of a girl who was dropped on his doorstep, a girl who, unlike my client, has a tainted reputation?" He ended on a triumphant note and the tension in the room became tangible.

I blinked and the tears ran down my face, but I didn't drop my head. "Y'should b'lieve me cause I've got dignity – n'I'm tellin' the truth." The defense attorney chuckled and waved his hand at the judge.

"I have no further questions, your Honor."

The judge looked at the prosecutor and said, "Any redirect?"

The prosecutor rose to his feet. "Yes, your Honor." He approached me and put his hands on the railing of the witness box; our eyes met, his smile warm and gentle. I felt my muscles relax, and with a quick swipe, I wiped my face dry. "Anna Beth, can you please tell the court why you were afraid to tell anyone about the attack directly after it happened?"

I remembered that we had practiced this question, and the words came flooding back. "Well, fo' one, Olivia n'me didn't have anywhere else t'go, n'I wanted t'keep a roof over her head n' food in her belly. Two, Mr. Grainger said nobody'd b'lieve me, n'if I told, he'd make me wish I was dead." Audible gasps and whispers filled the courtroom, and the judge let the sound dissipate on its own this time.

"I tried t'tell Mrs. Sensley later," I continued, "but he was right – she didn't b'lieve me." My teacher's head dropped and caught my eye. She was sitting next to Mrs. Corrigan who also looked miserable. "She b'lieves me now, though," I added kindly. The prosecutor gave me a quick wink and then told the judge he had no further questions.

"You may sit down, Miss Atwood – thank you for your testimony," Judge Collins said kindly. When I sat back down next to Grace, she patted my leg and Mr. Jingle wrapped his arm around my shaking shoulders. At least my and Grace's parts were done.

Mr. Jingle and Doctor Mitchell were the next witnesses, and the lawyers took turns questioning them in the same fashion. Mr. Jingle told the court how he witnessed Mr. Grainger break my arm and how Mr. Grainger kicked his cane away causing him to fall and get hurt. Doc Mitchell discussed our injuries in more detail – my dislocated shoulder and fractured arm, how internal trauma caused my miscarriage, how both Grace and I suffered broken noses, not to mention the broken ribs and countless cuts and bruises. He also spoke of Mr. Jingle and how he sustained a torn muscle in his leg and a head injury. I hadn't realized my old friend had been injured in the fall, and then I thought how even more amazing it was that he was able to preach me the Gospel!

When Sheriff Todd took the stand, he testified to what he witnessed the night he was called to the Graingers' farm and how Mr. Grainger came out of the house waving a gun. He called the attacks by their legal names – *wanton endangerment, assault... rape.* The last was a nasty word for an unspeakable act, and Mr. Grainger just sat there in his chair with his arms crossed. His eyes looked straight ahead; he was a shell of a person with no feeling inside. It made me sick to look at him, and I prayed the jury could see him for the monster he really was.

The last witness called was Chancey Durrett. My eyes grew wide as the courtroom buzzed with whispers as he walked up front. We didn't know

Chancey would take the stand, and obviously neither did the defense attorney who rose to his feet and objected.

"Your Honor," he addressed the judge, "Mr. Durrett is just a minor whose testimony has no credence in this case." Chancey froze and looked around for someone to tell him what to do, his hand trembling on the witness stand.

"Your Honor," the prosecutor interjected, holding up his hand, "Mr. Durrett is being called as a character witness for Miss Atwood, and his testimony certainly has credence in this case."

Judge Collins, nodding his tolerance, said the defense's objection was overruled and noted for the record. Then he motioned for Chancey to take the stand and the sheriff swore him in.

"Do y'swear t'tell the truth, the whole truth, n'nothin' but the truth, so help y'God?" Sheriff Todd asked. Chancey squirmed like a worm but placed his hand on the Bible and swore. He took his seat, and my body tensed. Grace instinctively wrapped her arm around me.

"Mr. Durrett, the defense implied that a minor, *you*, were the one who had relations with Miss Atwood, and that those relations resulted in a pregnancy," the prosecutor started.

The defense attorney stood and objected more vehemently. "Objection your Honor! The prosecution is leading the witness!"

"Sustained. Counselor, be careful with your line of questioning," Judge Collins advised.

The prosecutor nodded and rephrased. "Mr. Durrett, whether you are the minor targeted by the rumor or not, you can answer this question. Under oath, mind you – have you ever had relations with Miss Anna Beth Atwood?" he asked.

Chancey shook his head quickly, his face flushing red. I glanced at his Momma, who was sitting near the back in a row with his brothers, and it looked like her eyes were going to pop out of her head. I imagined she wanted to drag him out of that chair by his ear and thump his head all the way home for getting himself into such a major mess.

"No, sir – that's a lie," Chancey finally found his voice and told the court. Some of the jurors glanced at each other.

"What was a lie?" the prosecutor pressed.

"That I got... got 'er *with child*. We never... I never..." he stuttered.

The prosecutor continued, "Have you ever been sporting with Miss Atwood in the alley between the mercantile and hotel?"

"Sorta," Chancey hem hawed, chewing on the word to buy himself some time.

The prosecutor spoke slowly and precisely. "Mr. Durrett, did Miss Atwood ever *willingly* kiss you in the alley between the mercantile and hotel?" Chancey looked up at him, shifting his weight uncomfortably. He was sweating buckets, and I almost felt sorry for him.

Chancey glanced at me and my breath caught in my throat. Then he dropped his head. "No, sir, she ain't. I forced one on 'er one time... n'I'm not proud of it."

I exhaled slowly as a smile broke out across my face. The head of the rat pack actually admitted it! I glanced at Carrie, who was seated across the aisle with her mom, and she gave me a thumbs up. Grace gave my shoulders a squeeze, and I faced front again.

"In what month did you do this?" the prosecutor pressed.

"I b'lieve it was late November, sir," Chancey answered. The prosecutor looked triumphant and turned to stare right at Mr. Grainger and his defense attorney, the latter of whom sunk down an inch or two in his chair like a deflating balloon.

"I have no further questions, your Honor," the prosecutor said with a satisfied smirk on his face.

When the defense attorney passed on the chance to cross-examine Chancey, Judge Collins nodded and called for a much-needed recess. Grace picked up Olivia, who had fallen asleep, and carried her outside while Mr. Jingle and I followed. We all stretched our legs and talked quietly, and it felt like no time at all that we were called back into the courtroom.

The judge gave the jury their instructions, then announced it was time to hear closing arguments. "Prosecution may begin," he said, leaning back in his chair to listen himself.

The prosecutor took his time looking out over the crowd, then at Mr. Grainger, and finally his eyes came to rest on me and Grace. "We have assembled here today to find the truth, and nothing but the truth – so help us, God." He turned to the jury and started walking back and forth in front of them, his hands clasped behind his back. "The truth seems pretty simple after the facts that have been presented today. I would like to remind the court of Doctor Mitchell's testimony which stated Anna Beth Atwood was approximately six months pregnant at the time of her miscarriage," he said with an air of confidence that filled the whole room. "Young Mr. Durrett has just confessed that he forced Miss Atwood to kiss him, and *only* kiss him, in November. According to the Doctor, Miss Atwood got pregnant three months after that juvenile incident in *February*, which is the timeline fitting the defendant's alleged rape."

The prosecutor went on to talk about Grace and Mr. Jingle, proving how Mr. Grainger was a repeat abuser and needed to pay for his crimes. He also talked about how Mr. Grainger endangered not only Grace and Olivia's lives but also the life of an officer when he was waving that gun around. When he finished, the judge turned the floor over to Mr. Grainger's defense attorney. There wasn't much left to defend, however, and he kind of floundered like a fish hooked and jerked hard out of the water. Finally, the judge called for a second recess so the jury could deliberate on the facts presented by both sides. Sheriff Todd helped the twelve jurors file into a back room, and we all sat there waiting – no one wanting to even go to the bathroom in fear of missing the verdict.

Grace reached over and took my hand in hers. Her palm was sweaty but firm. Olivia was still asleep, sprawled across our laps now, and I twisted one of her curls around my finger. The jury didn't deliberate long so when they filed back in my heart started to pound. *That was too quick*, I worried. Grace squeezed my hand, sensing my anxiety. We both knew this was the moment of truth... Mr. Grainger would either be held responsible for his crimes and we would be free, or he would go free and we would live with the fearful knowledge that he was out there somewhere no matter how far we ran. I closed my eyes and whispered another prayer to God. I knew for sure now that He not only hears heartfelt prayers but answers them, too. He would be our refuge, our strong tower in times of trouble.

"Who is the foreman of the jury?" Judge Collins asked, and a large fellow in suspenders stood up at the far end of the jury box.

"I am, y'Honor," he said.

"Have you reached a verdict?" the judge asked.

"Yes, y'Honor," the man said, handing a folded piece of paper to Sheriff Todd who walked to the bench and handed it to Judge Collins. He read it quietly, then cleared his throat.

"Will the defendant please rise," the judge said. Mr. Grainger and his lawyer stood up, Mr. Grainger's knuckles turning white as he pressed his fingers down on the table. "In the case of the Commonwealth versus Jack Grainger," Judge Collins began solemnly, "the jury finds the defendant guilty of three counts of assault, one count of rape, and three counts of wanton endangerment." The room exploded in applause, and Judge Collins banged his gavel to restore order.

I blinked several times, letting the verdict sink in. *We won. Mr. Grainger was going to jail. He'd surely be locked up long enough for us to be gone and never seen again.*

Once the room was quiet, Judge Collins nodded toward the defense attorney and continued. "Your client has been found guilty of the charges against him; we will return to this court on November sixteenth for sentencing."

Sheriff Todd turned Mr. Grainger around and handcuffed him, then led him toward the side door. Mr. Grainger tried to look back over his shoulder at us, but the sheriff jerked him front ways again, and I couldn't help but smile. Next to me, Grace exhaled deeply, a smile tugging at the corners of her mouth, too.

"It's *over*," she said quietly, a tear slipping down her cheek. Her smile widened, and she brushed the tear away with a laugh and shake of her head. "It's *really* over…" Mr. Jingle patted her on the shoulder and then reached to shake Doc Mitchell's hand, who was standing in line to offer his sincere congratulations.

Grace looked down at me, her eyes dancing like a tiny bird who had escaped the captor's snare. "We're *free*, Anna Beth – he'll never hurt us again." She hugged me tightly and we both cried for joy. "We're gonna make a new start, n'this time we're gonna be *happy*!"

The following week was a busy one; the hustle and bustle was reminiscent of when Momma and Daddy packed us up to leave Missouri nearly three years before. Now I had a mother and grandfather packing us up, and I was more than excited to help. The only thing that tinged the edges with sadness was that I had to leave behind my best friend, Carrie, like I had once left Martha and Jonathan, Momma and Daddy... Janie and Emily. She wrote down her address, though, and gave it to me all tied up with the green ribbons she so often wore in her hair. We hugged tightly and promised to always stay in touch. I knew she would – loyalty was one of the reasons I loved her like another sister.

Mr. Jingle's truck held a few of our belongings with plenty of room to spare. Grace said it was like our futures – we had what we needed with plenty of room for new memories. Mr. Jingle said we would wander the countryside, going wherever God directed our hearts – that God *always* had the best plans and our job was to trust and obey. I honestly didn't care where we went; I was just ready to start over again, this time on my own terms. Grace said we would know the right place to call home when we saw it, and Olivia's only request was a nice school... and no cornfields to take her big sister away. It made us all grin every time she put her two little cents in, her hopes and dreams as sweet and pure as her honey blonde curls and blue eyes.

Grace told Mr. Murphy to hold our mail, and when we found a new place to call home, we would let him know where to forward it. Of course, I still wondered what happened to my parents and Emily, and I probably always would. The difference was it didn't *consume* me like it once did. Maybe one day I'd learn the truth or maybe not. Either way, I just hoped everyone was safe and happy wherever they were.

The day we left town, I sat on the mercantile steps and wrote one more letter to my parents.

*Dear Momma and Daddy,*

*If you're reading this, then you know by now that Olivia and I left Harlan with Grace Grainger and Mr. Jingle, the town's preacher turned peddler turned preacher again. I imagine you may have heard some of the things that happened to us while you were away. I want you to know I was strong and brave, and everything turned out okay. Whenever we get where we're going, Mr. Jingle said he's going to put down more roots, open a store, and sell his goods. Grace says she'll make sure Olivia and I go to school and get as much education as we can, so we can be anything we want to be when we grow up. She plans to sell her handiwork in Mr. Jingle's store, and maybe even open a cafe. She is a talented cook, although I miss Momma's cornbread fritters. That's one thing Grace can't fix quite the same. Regardless, we trust that God will provide.*

*I'm excited for my new life to finally begin, but I'm sad you all and my other sisters won't be a part of it. I will always wonder what happened to you, and why you didn't come back for us... but I'm trying to move on. I pray the Lord has watched over you on your own travels, and if we ever meet again this side of Heaven, I look forward to hearing your stories and telling you mine.*

*It's important for you to know two more things. Firstly, the Lord saved me on August 29, 1920. So, I will see you again, at least in Heaven! And the second thing is I forgive you. I forgive you for everything. None of what happened to me in Harlan was your fault, just like it wasn't mine. I know you were only trying to do what was best for us kids, and I was just trying to make the best of it, too. Please know I still love you with all my heart.*

> *Your daughter,*
> *Anna Beth Atwood*

"Are y'ready t'go?" Grace placed her hand on my shoulder and startled me from my thoughts. The pencil in my hand was shaking slightly. I was tying up the last bit of my old family and getting ready to strike out fresh with my new one. That wells up some big emotions, but I smiled through my fears. *Parents know best.*

"I'm ready," I nodded, folding the letter and giving it a kiss. I pulled my brown sweater closed, buttoned it, and felt the sleeves inch up my arms. It was just about too small for me now. Grace said we'd buy a new one somewhere on our travels and that it didn't even have to be second-hand.

I stood and took the letter inside to Mrs. Corrigan. She added it to the stack of old letters, letters I doubted would ever be received. She must have sensed my sadness because she gently said, "I'll keep 'em long as it takes, Anna Beth." She pulled out a drawer under the counter and showed me a little key. "I'll lock 'em right up in here and that's where they'll stay 'til I hear word from the Atwoods."

I thanked her, knowing she was trying to make up for the hurt she had caused, and pushed back out the heavy door – the little bell at the top ringing the last time for me. Olivia ran up the steps and took my hand.

"Mr. Jingle says it's time t'go," she breathed. She was bouncing with excitement, her blonde curls bobbing up and down. She didn't remember our first move, so this was all new to her.

I looked at Mr. Jingle, who was standing with his arm propped up on the truck hatch next to Grace. He raised his hand in a wave. I squeezed Olivia's hand in mine, the last piece of my blood family, and together we walked to our new Momma and Grandpa. The four of us were now sewn together like a patchwork quilt, each square with its individual flaws but when pulled together just right no one really sees the blunders anymore.

"It's 'bout time we make a fresh start, don't y'think, Dignity?" Mr. Jingle winked at me. I hugged his waist with a nod, then we all climbed in the cab with me in the middle and Livie in Grace's lap. As we drove out of Harlan, I turned around and looked back out of habit. A person must fully understand where they've been to get to where they're going.

The autumn trees were dropping their colorful red, orange, yellow and brown leaves, and I watched them flutter to the ground. It would soon be winter. The trees would be naked and exposed, reminding me that it's the bare bones of things that matter anyway – family, friendship, love… dignity. When something old and broken has good bones, you can clean it up, fill it out, and make it beautiful again. I turned back around and looked from Mr. Jingle to Grace and to my birthday sister. The pots and pans jangled behind me as they swung from the truck and clinked together. These here were the best bones I could have hoped for.

*And after winter comes spring*, I smiled.

*Q & A with the author*

## WHAT WAS YOUR INSPIRATION FOR *WHEN DIGNITY CAME TO HARLAN?*

This historical fiction novel is based on the story of my great-grand-mother, May Wood Elliott Kerr. Her daughter, my grandmother (Lois Elliott Duvall), told me many stories about the family that came before us, but May's was always the most fascinating to me. It was captivating how she traveled in a covered wagon from Missouri to Kentucky with her parents and sisters – hoping to start a new life – only to be parceled out to strangers and not know what happened to her family until later in life. May, like Anna Beth, grew up in a harsh and unwelcoming foster home and was even listed as the "servant" on local census reports. She somehow overcame these great odds and became a wonderful, God-fearing woman who won people over with faith and kindness – even though she, too, was raped but not privileged to the same justice Anna Beth had.

May's story planted a literary seed within me – a tribute to human grit, the spirit of dignity and perseverance, and above all, redemption. My only regret is that my grandmother who planted the seed didn't live long enough to see it come to full fruition, although I believe she knew in her heart that one day it would.

## IF YOUR NOVEL IS BASED ON A TRUE STORY, WHICH PARTS OF IT ARE TRUTH VERSUS FICTION?

My grandmother sat down with me at the kitchen table and told me everything she remembered about her mother's life. I wrote it all down in a notebook and then acquired more information from a cousin's genealogy work on my great grandfather's family tree (May's first husband).

Here is how truth compares to fiction within *When Dignity Came to Harlan*:

| *Truth* | Fiction |
|---------|---------|
| • Asberry Wood worked in the lead mines in Missouri and heard Kentucky was prosperous. He brought his family to Edmonson County in a covered wagon, and it was such a hard journey that the horses died topping Temple Hill near Mammoth Cave. His wife, Emily, cooked fritters from meal in a barrel over an open fire with an iron frying pan and served them with pones of bread (cornbread). | • Ben Atwood worked in the lead mines in Missouri and heard Kentucky was prosperous. At his wife's urging, he brought his family to Harlan County in a covered wagon, and it was such a hard journey that one of the oxen died. His wife, Laura, cooked fritters from meal in a barrel, and cornbread was mentioned through several meals. |
| • The Family left their 1st born, Betty, in Missouri with her husband, Davis, and had nothing to eat and nowhere to stay once they got to Edmonson County. They took their 4 daughters (Clarcie, 10, Maggie, 8, May, 5, & Cora, 3) to separate residences asking people to take care of their children until they could come back for them. All 4 girls were placed in separate homes, but in the same town. They were left with families of a religious background. | • The family left their 1st born, Martha, in Missouri with her husband, Jonathan, and had nothing to eat and nowhere to stay once they got to Harlan. They took their 4 daughters (Anna Beth, 12, Janie, 9, Emily, 8, and Olivia, 2) to separate residences and asked people to take care of them until they could come back. Anna Beth and Olivia were placed together, and Janie and Emily in separate homes. We know from Mrs. Corrigan all three families were religious. |

| *Truth* | Fiction |
|---|---|
| • The Woods had no money; it was hard to find work because so many people had come with high hopes of a better life. Asberry died, and Emily came back after three years to visit her children. May was 8 years old by then. Emily could not afford to care for her girls, however, so she left them in foster care. She must have kept in touch because after May married and had her own house, her mother came to visit and stayed a week or two. | • The Atwoods had no money; it was hard to find work because so many people had come with high hopes of a better life. We never know what happened to them; Ben could have been killed in a mining accident and Laura not capable of caring for her children alone, even though she doesn't come back to tell them that. Foster care may have been the most loving solution. |
| • Clarcie, who was 10 years old at the move, ran away at 14 and somehow made her way home to Betty, her oldest sister, back in Missouri. Maggie, who was 8 years old at the move, stayed with her family and eventually married. Cora, who was only 3 years old at the move, grew up to marry the son of the couple who took her in, and they had a house full of kids. | • Janie, who was 9 years old at the move, ran away from her foster home shortly after her arrival and made it all the way back to Martha, her oldest sister, in Missouri. Emily, who was 8 years old at the move, moved to another town with her foster family and is not heard from again. Olivia, the baby of the family, is a happy child who grows to school age in the same foster home as Anna Beth. |

| *Truth* | Fiction |
|---|---|
| • May, who was 5 years old at the move, did not exceed the 3<sup>rd</sup> grade. Instead she worked for her new family in-home when she was younger, and in the garden when she was older. She did all the chores on the farm and could plow corn like a man. When they did not need her, they hired her out to neighbors for money. She wore hand-me-down men's shoes with cardboard to cover the holes and wrapped her feet in rags in the winter. Rain and snow would still seep through, and, at some point, she got frostbite. She liked chicken and dumplings when she was sick, and at 12 years old she was saved at Good Springs Baptist Church and professed her faith in Christ. | • Anna Beth was 12 years old at the time of the move and we see her fall short of completing her 9<sup>th</sup> grade year – but we know Grace is going to put her back into school after they settle in a new town. Mr. Grainger worked Anna Beth hard for the four years she stayed with him; she did all the chores he gave her, and at times she could work faster than even him. Grace taught her to wrap strips of cloth around her feet in the winter to keep them from getting frostbite, and when she was sick, Grace nursed her back to health with chicken and dumplings. At 14 years old she got saved at the little church on the hill and professed a great faith in Christ. |
| • The man of the house, who was an upstanding man in the community, raped May in the corn shed. May endured ridicule from the town's people; being pregnant out of wedlock was a great sin. She was permitted to stay with the couple who took her in only because she was a hard | • Mr. Grainger, an upstanding man in the community, raped Anna Beth in the shed. She endured ridicule from the town's people for being pregnant out of wedlock. The town attributed it to Chancey Durrett, but they found out in the end that it was indeed Mr. Grainger's child. |

| *Truth* | Fiction |
|---|---|
| worker. She carried the baby full term, but it died at birth and was buried at Good Springs. No one knew the baby was the foster father's; the wife may not have even known or she may have killed it herself. As May grew up, she lived down the shame through goodness. She made clothes for people and gave them away, and everyone loved her as an adult. She often would go around the house singing *Wayfaring Stranger.* | Anna Beth miscarried after Mr. Grainger beat her, and through the arrest, trial, and conviction of Mr. Grainger, her good name was restored. |
| • May grew up to marry John D. Elliott, a Civil War veteran, and they had three children. (She was 24 years old and he 73 years old at the time of marriage.) When he passed, she married a second time to Lewis Kerr and had three more children. Her greatest joy was in her salvation and serving the Lord. | • Anna Beth leaves town with Mr. Jingle, Grace, and Olivia, and we know she has a brighter future ahead, naturally and spiritually. |

## DID YOU DO ANY RESEARCH FOR YOUR STORY?

I researched Harlan, Kentucky to get an idea of the coal mines and landscape for the setting. Since dating barely overlaps (May Wood Elliott Kerr lived in foster care from around 1900-1919, and Anna Beth lived with the Graingers from 1918-1920), I also researched basic time period details, like when electric lights and indoor plumbing started coming into the homes, when covered wagons and early motorized vehicles could co-exist, and especially the legal system in Kentucky concerning rape and wife-beating – so at least in the *story*, justice could be served.

## HOW LONG DID IT TAKE YOU TO WRITE THIS NOVEL?

Anna Beth's story evolved over a period of about twenty years with me first putting pen to paper as a senior in college. For a creative writing class my final grade was based on a 70-page original work, and I turned in my first several chapters of this novel – Anna Beth's family had made the move, and she had arrived at the Graingers to work the first harvest. My professor shook my hand on graduation day and said five words I'll never forget: *Rebecca, please finish the story.*

Marriage and raising two beautiful children filled my life with other wonderful obligations for several years after that day, but I eventually picked my writing back up to publish an important self-help memoir (containing all the research, intervention strategies and positive attitudes that pulled my family through our son's sensory processing disorder diagnosis). That's when I also cast my eyes and heart back to a little tender-hearted girl, my Anna Beth Atwood appropriately nicknamed Dignity, who was still in Harlan. She had been patiently waiting there for me to come back and tell the rest of her story – and I finished my first novel within weeks.

## BUT WHAT HAPPENED TO ANNA BETH AFTER SHE LEFT HARLAN?

*When Dignity Came to Harlan* is the childhood half of my great-grandparents' amazing story, and Anna Beth Atwood does grow up into a beautiful and dignified woman. Fiction and truth will continue to intermingle as the story unfolds.

## PTER COMPREHENSION QUESTIONS

### Chapter 1

❖ Why do the Atwoods have to leave Missouri?

❖ How do you know Ben and Laura Atwood have a difference of opinion when it comes to moving their family to Kentucky? Support with text evidence.

❖ Which sisters are closest to each other? How can you tell?

### Chapter 2

❖ What evidence from the story supports the idea that Anna Beth and her sisters are nervous about the move?

❖ Why does Anna Beth's father ask her to be strong and keep her spirits up? In what ways does she show she is trying to have courage?

❖ What seems to be the hardest part of leaving Missouri for Anna Beth? What do you think would be the hardest part of leaving where you live?

### Chapter 3

❖ What are some problems the Atwoods encounter on their journey to Kentucky?

❖ How does Janie lighten the mood of her family?

❖ What did Ben and Laura learn from the couple leaving Kentucky? Why did this widen the emotional divide between the parents?

Chapter 4

❖ How do you know that assuming the role of the oldest sister was more difficult than Anna Beth originally thought? What does she struggle with?

❖ Why does Ben leave his wife to tell the children they will be parceled out to foster homes by herself?

❖ Characterize the personalities of Anna Beth, Janie, and Emily. How are they interdependent on each other?

Chapter 5

❖ Why would dressing in their Sunday best make a difference when they got to Harlan?

❖ What caught Anna Beth by surprise when they visit the mercantile?

❖ Discuss how first impressions are important in this chapter; consider the Atwoods, Corrigans, and Graingers when you answer.

Chapter 6

❖ Why does Anna Beth say she understands the saying *Ignorance is bliss* where her younger sisters are concerned?

❖ What were some reasons Ben said it would be good for the kids to stay with strangers while he and Laura looked for a job?

❖ How did Ben and Grace Grainger persuade Jack to take in Anna Beth and Olivia?

Chapter 7

❖ What kind of a person do you think Mr. Grainger is just from witnessing his interactions with his wife and the Atwoods? Support your opinion with text evidence.

❖ What seems to be the point of contention between Jack Grainger and his wife, Grace?

❖ Why is Anna Beth obsessed with Olivia's hair?

Chapter 8

- ❖ Why do
  doesn't
- ❖ In cont
  Anna
- ❖ What
  her?

Chapter 9

- ❖ How
  day?
- ❖ Why does Anna Beth miss Janie and Emily so much when, generally, they always got on her nerves?
- ❖ Dreams can be an odd mix of memories, thoughts and emotions.
  What do you think Anna Beth's dream about the mealworms and
  weevils meant?

Chapter 10

- ❖ Why do you think Mr. Grainger would object to Anna Beth writing letters to her parents?
- ❖ How does Mr. Grainger make Anna Beth nervous in the shed?
- ❖ Why did the idea of sending Anna Beth to school spark such a big
  argument between the Graingers?

Chapter 11

- ❖ What were Anna Beth's favorite places? Why?
- ❖ Do you think having a best friend is important? Why or why not?
  What difference did it make to Anna Beth to have Carrie?
- ❖ Why does Mr. Jingle nickname Anna Beth *Dignity*?

## Chapter 12

❖ What are some ways Mr. Grainger abuses Grace? Think about mental, emotional and physical abuse. In your opinion, why doesn't Grace just leave him?

❖ What made Anna Beth especially homesick at Christmas?

❖ Why did Anna Beth stop writing letters to her parents?

## Chapter 13

❖ How can the Durrett Boys be compared to a pack of wolves? Support your ideas with text evidence.

❖ Why did Chancey kiss Anna Beth in the alley?

❖ What hurt Anna Beth's feelings more than anything after the Chancey incident?

## Chapter 14

❖ What rumor spread around town about Anna Beth?

❖ Why do you think it took Mr. Grainger so long to attack Anna Beth?

❖ Why was Mr. Grainger saying "No one will believe you" the perfect way to silence Anna Beth?

## Chapter 15

❖ What analogy/simile/metaphor does Anna Beth use to describe how she feels in the days after the attack? Why is it an accurate description?

❖ Why does Anna Beth get asked to leave school? Why can't she perform like she used to?

❖ Why do you think Anna Beth got sick and threw up when Mr. Grainger confronted her about leaving school early?

Chapter 16

- ❖ How come Anna Beth feels all alone when she has so many people around her? Who does she finally decide to tell her secret to and why? Do you think this is the best choice?
- ❖ What was Anna Beth and Carrie's mistake, even though they had no way of predicting the outcome?
- ❖ Once the truth came out about Anna Beth's pregnancy, why did so many people chose to believe a lie and spread unconfirmed rumors?

Chapter 17

- ❖ Why did Anna Beth run to see Mr. Jingle? What did she want to know?
- ❖ What did Mr. Jingle say to Anna Beth that helped renew her courage? How can we tell something changed within her after hearing his words?
- ❖ Why do you think Mr. Grainger got so angry with Anna Beth and Grace? Discuss how anger can be a façade for fear.

Chapter 18

- ❖ A theme of spiritual redemption is woven throughout the novel and comes to its peak in this chapter. What does Anna Beth have to do with her natural feelings in order to embrace the spiritual healing she needs in her life?
- ❖ Why do you think hugging Grace was part of Anna Beth's spiritual journey?
- ❖ What are the reasons Grace gave for not believing Anna Beth from the beginning, even though she originally thought she was an honest person?

Chapter 19

❖ How did Mr. Jingle help Anna Beth naturally *and* spiritually?

❖ Explain Anna Beth's conflicting emotions about having a miscarriage.

❖ How did the town's people show their regret for gossiping about Anna Beth and treating her like a pariah?

Chapter 20

❖ What two main arguments, one with Grace and one with Anna Beth, did the defense attorney use to presume Mr. Grainger's innocence?

❖ What was the "hinge pin" for the prosecution that alleged Mr. Grainger's guilt? After hearing Chancey's testimony, do you feel differently toward Chancey?

❖ Life experiences, both positive and negative, have a way of shaping a person's thoughts and behaviors. Pick three characters and discuss how their life experiences shaped them into who we see by the end of the book.

Chapter 21

❖ Part 3 is titled *Going Where I've Never Been*. Why is this an appropriate section title, both physically and spiritually?

❖ Why do you think it was important for Anna Beth to write one more letter to her parents before she moved on with her new family?

❖ Anna Beth talks at the end about "the bare bones of things" being what matter. What are the bare bones of her new life, and how do you know that Mr. Jingle, Grace, Anna Beth and Olivia are going to be happy together?

## THINK DEEPER QUESTIONS

❖ Anna Beth was in Harlan for four years. How did you see her change and grow? What other characters showed growth (personal, emotional, mental, physical)?

❖ Think back to your first impressions of the Corrigans, Graingers, and Mrs. Sensley. How did your opinion of them change as the story unfolded? Do you think they became better people by the end because they knew Anna Beth Atwood?

❖ When you think of people, why is it important to *Never judge a book by its cover*? Give positive and negative examples of people from the story.

❖ At one point, Anna Beth wanted to grow up and be just like Mrs. Sensley. Do you think she will still become a teacher? Why or why not? If so, what may she do the same or different than Mrs. Sensley?

❖ In chapter 7, Grace says, "Sometimes I think a good name is all that matters to folks around here, but then again, I *do* know the Bible says to choose a good name over great riches." Explain the worth of character, a genuine good name versus a façade people may put forth to deceive you.

❖ Think about the events from Grace Grainger's perspective. Do you think she had low or high self-esteem? How did she transform throughout the novel?

❖ The novel is titled *When Dignity Came to Harlan*. You can think of Dignity as both a personification of Anna Beth's morality and perseverance, and as its own definition: the state or quality of being worthy of honor or respect. In what ways did Anna Beth bring dignity to Harlan?

❖ Discuss Mr. Jingle, the humble preacher-turned-peddler-turned-preacher-again. In what ways did you see him redeemed, and in what ways did he facilitate redemption in the other characters?

## ESSAY THEMES

- ❖ Courage
- ❖ Dignity
- ❖ Domestic Abuse
- ❖ Family
- ❖ Freedom
- ❖ Friendship
- ❖ Honesty/Deception
- ❖ Loyalty
- ❖ Morality
- ❖ Narcissism
- ❖ Perseverance
- ❖ Personal Growth
- ❖ Redemption
- ❖ Truth/Perception

# Acknowledgments

*How do I begin to thank the people who have encouraged me to write this novel and helped shape the story over the course of twenty years?*

*My deepest gratitude…*

**To my family and friends** for always believing in me, my writing, and the deep importance of being a story-keeper. I wouldn't be who I am without all of you.

**To Dr. Frederick Smock,** my creative writing professor in college who shook my hand on graduation day and said, *Rebecca, please finish the story.* The confidence you had in my novel's vision stayed tucked in my heart all these years.

**To my excellent Editorial Board members** who not only caught grammatical errors but helped me realize the natural beauty in the story, like a diamond in the rough, and taught me how to make it shine.

**To Reverend Stephen Doyle** who helped me nail the time-period details that made the historical elements authentic. Our hearts are knit together in many ways, with our mutual love for Christian historical fiction just one of them!

**To the team at Emerge Publishing** who took one look at the first few chapters and said, *Yes.* I sincerely appreciate your faith in me and this book, and your hard work to bring it to readers all over the world.

# Keep in Touch

o   Rebecca Duvall Scott
o   Rebecca@RebeccaDuvallScott.com
o   www.RebeccaDuvallScott.com

CPSIA information can be obtained
at www.ICGtesting.com
Printed in the USA
LVHW032115260121
677513LV00002B/89

9 781949 758955